PYRAMID SCHEMES

A tale of Sir Apropos of Nothing

PETER DAVID

CRAZY 8 PRESS

WHEN I AWOKE, THE SUN HAD just descended into its rest. Darkness stretched across my surroundings and the air was somewhat cooler.

A small furred creature was staring at me.

I had no idea what it was, nor I suspected did it have any idea what I was. We exchanged looks and I kept its gaze fixed upon me as my hand stealthily crept toward the knife I had on my hip. In one smooth motion I yanked the knife out, brought it around and slammed it through the creature's chest. It let out a startled yelp, kicked several times more in surprise than anything else, and then died.

I skinned it as quickly and efficiently as I could. Then I made my way back to the bush that had, hours earlier, been aflame. I stared at it for a long moment and then shifted my gaze to the heavens. Stars twinkled down upon me.

"Would you mind?" I asked. "If it wouldn't be too much trouble."

For a brief time there was silence, and then suddenly the bush flared back to life.

"Thank you," I said and proceeded to cook the creature. It only took a few minutes because the fire was quite brisk and the creature was small. Once it was sufficiently roasted I devoured the flesh from its bones. It tasted nothing like chicken, which actually surprised me a bit.

I tossed the bones aside when I was done, wiped my face, and then walked away from the oasis. The bush surrendered its flame and restored itself to a standard, ordinary, not remotely holy piece of vegetation.

PYRAMID
SCHEMES

CHAPTER 1

Bush League

I DON'T DO WELL WITH GODS. I never have, and I likely never will.

I must admit, I've never understood gods in the least. Their obsession with humanity borders on the pathetic, nor do I comprehend their endless desire to be worshipped. Of what use is worship, anyway? Sitting around upon their clouds or mountain peaks or perhaps perched on the shell of an endlessly wandering turtle seems to me to be a somewhat limiting—bordering on abysmal—means of spending the immortal lives that all gods possess. Certainly one would think that, given an infinite amount of time upon which to ponder their lot, the gods would come up with some engagement that is more fulfilling.

I have had my face-to-face encounters with my share of supernatural and unorthodox beings, but it had been many years since I had found myself engaged with an actual god. That streak ended, however, one bright and sunny day in the heart of Rogypt. I should emphasize that every single day in Rogypt is bright and sunny, because the entirety of the country is one large, vast damned desert.

You may be wondering what in the world I was doing in such an undesirable place. For that matter, you may indeed be wondering who I am in the first place. I will endeavor herewith to give you a succinct description so as not to bore the doubtless dozens of readers who are already familiar with me and my previous endeavors. It is important to understand, after all, whence someone has come in order to fully grasp where they are going, and so I will avail myself of this space for a few moments in order to accomplish that.

My name is Apropos. I am also known as Apropos of Nothing and, for a brief time, Sir Apropos of Nothing. Yes, that is correct. I, a lame of leg (albeit quick of wit) trickster and bastard, was temporarily walking beside kings and knights. My life began ignominiously enough when my tavern wench mother was brutally raped by a group of knights. When I finally emerged from her nether regions, those who were present beheld that my right leg was twisted and lame and advocated the notion of abandoning me on a rock somewhere. My mother fought for my continued existence and won, although to be completely factual, I am unsure whether that was a fight worth battling, much less winning. In what I laughingly refer to as my career, literally thousands of people have died due to my various undertakings. It was rarely due to circumstances that I had brought on deliberately. In typical situations, all I was trying to do was survive from one day to the next, and yet I incessantly discovered myself in predicaments in which I set off a chain of circumstances that resulted in people dying. There are knights who dedicate their lives to serving their kings and queens in times of war by becoming slaughtering machines who have not in their lifetimes come close to killing the number of people I've dispatched through accidents, cowardice or incompetence.

Nevertheless, looking back on my life from the advantage of the extreme number of years that I currently am, I cannot help but feel the most regret over the demise that ultimately resulted in my first face to face—or face to whatever—encounter that I ever had with a genuine god undisguised in mortal form.

I had aged, that much was certain. My mop of red hair was still thick and curly, but gray hairs were now strewn through it. At least my hair was starting to match my gray eyes, so that was an advantage of some sort, I imagine. My angular face had become more rounded, so that the manner in which my ear stuck out (I'd lost one; don't ask) was not as obvious, although the rest of my body—lanky and with an excess of elbows—had remained more or less consistent over the years. The muscles on my arms had continued to strengthen thanks to my having to depend on them so much, courtesy of the overall lameness of the lower half of my body.

I had spent many years wandering the length and breadth of the world, drifting further and further away from the small village that had spawned me. I had frankly lost track of how old I was because I had not only ceased paying attention to the passage of days, but also various places that I traveled to reckoned the passage of time in different manners. Many places had their own calendars, a different number of days in a week or weeks in a year. Some did not believe in the passage of time at all and refused to try and keep a track of it, feeling that doing so was somehow presumptuous on their part.

I had to admit that every so often, my mind would wander back to the Princess Entipy. She was the young and demented woman whom I had become engaged to, bedded in one insane night of passion, and then been forced to abandon for reasons I will not go into at the moment. Still, one never forgets lovemaking of that intensity, and every so often my thoughts would return to her. Was she now the queen? Was she ruling the land with the insanity that so pervaded her every waking moment, and likely most of her sleeping ones? I had no idea, but I supposed there was no harm in speculating every now and then.

My wandering path had taken me to the heart of Rogypt. I had naturally had adventures along the way, and perhaps someday I shall describe them to you, but that someday is not this one. Instead my slow, steady progress had brought me to one of the larger cities in Rogypt. It was called Giro. Ostensibly centuries old, its primary export was sandwiches, which I considered to be a rather strange commodity, but go argue with Rogyptians. It was especially annoying because I thought that I had been present at the creation of sandwiches, but it had turned out that the food had originated in Giro centuries earlier. Imagine that.

I had grown up in a heavily forested area and had become

most conversant in navigating such environs. In most of the places that I visited in my life, the majority of them likewise had copious areas of greenery. That was unquestionably not the case with Rogypt. I have referred to it as a desert, yes, but that does not begin to describe just how wide open and arid it was. There were no trees, no bushes anywhere save for an occasional and far between oasis. There were patches of grass here and there that seemed determined to grow even though there was nothing in the environment to encourage their development. For the most part the grass was brown and burned, thanks to the sun. I wondered how it was possible for people to subsist without any manner of greenery around them. I felt bereft, as if old friends of mine had turned away from me and left me on my own.

The only thing that allowed Giro to survive was the vast river along which it was built. The Giro River served multiple functions, ranging from providing drinking water to allowing boats to sail from other cities with various produce and farm equipment. Small tributaries ran off it that the women would make use of to wash their clothes or bathe in. As for Giro itself, it was a vast walled city, brick and mortar surrounding it to provide it protection against whoever they felt might try to attack them. I honestly had no idea if there are an abundance of individuals who might want to attack Rogypt in general or Giro in particular, but if having a wall erected around their city gave them a measure of peace of mind, I truly saw no point in arguing over it.

It was upon that river that I first arrived in Giro, having made my way down from the general outlying desert area. Giro seemed to have a good deal of potential for someone such as myself, who was constantly endeavoring to acquire two coins to rub together so that I could purchase food and clothing and on occasion the company of a woman with whom I could relieve my urges. A few coins had garnered me travel on the ship, which moved slowly down the Giro River and delivered us to our collective destination within a day or so. The sun had beat down upon us relentlessly during the journey, and since it had been a relatively small vessel with a minimum of places for slumber, I had wound up sleeping on the deck, wrapped in my cape while making sure to keep my staff nearby me at all times. This was a degree of reasonable caution considering that, first of all, my staff facilitated my walking around. Secondly, my staff was an occasionally lethal weapon that I had used on any number of occasions in combat, and it had yet to let me down in a fighting situation. We had grown quite close over the years and I had come to think of it not merely as a tool, but as a constant and boon companion. Do not misunderstand: it was not as if I had lengthy conversations with it. But it was always with me whenever I needed it. The entirety of my life, no one else had ever been there so consistently for me. One takes one's friends where one can find them, even if they were carved from lumber.

Once we made it to Giro, I quickly disembarked. It was not difficult for me to move relatively fast because I had very few belongings. Two day's worth of clothing, a knife on my hip, and my hand and a half, bastard sword dangled on my back. I was hardly formidably armed, but I could handle myself adequately in a fight, and indeed had done so on any number of occasions.

The Rogytians were attired completely differently from me, and they could not help but stare at me as I passed by. They were very lightly dressed. Some men either wore loin cloths and some lightweight shirts, while the women were mostly attired in simple, straight dresses with one or two straps supporting them. Most of them were wearing tunics of varying lengths, either white or brown, and their legs were bare albeit quite tanned. Many sported broad brimmed hats to provide them protection from the blistering sun.

I walked through the marketplace and noticed immediately that my status as stranger tended to keep people clear of me. Whereas the vendors eagerly approached various individuals, holding their wares in front of them and proclaiming that their prices were the lowest in the landed, they tended to steer clear of me and, at the most, cast suspicious glances my way.

They did not, of course, speak my native tongue. But I had spent several months in Rogypt, living with small bands of wanderers who seemed to find me rather intriguing, and they had eagerly taught me their language. It was not a particularly difficult one to master. Curiously enough, there was no written alphabet at all; instead the written tongue consisted of pictograms that were often rendered in hilarious detail. I had done my best to try and grasp the reading of the pictograms, but they seemed insanely arbitrary, as if different writers came up with their very own languages in order to convey, well, whatever it was they wished to impart.

Nevertheless, I felt the need to attempt to blend in as much as I could. Granted, it would not be to any huge extent, because my hair was red and my skin color, despite my lengthy stay in the Rogyptian sun, was still markedly lighter than any of the natives. So I strode over to one vendor who was selling native clothing and made some purchases with some of the small amount of money I had managed to accrue via some luck at cards. And by luck, of course, I mean that I cheated and was lucky enough not to get caught at it.

Within the hour I had changed into a knee length white tunic and a short black cloak that draped off my shoulders. My sword remained strapped to my back and my staff, of course, was tightly clenched in my hand. The rest of my possessions were safely stowed in a sack dangling off my shoulder, and so it was that I made my way through the city of Giro, seeing what there was to see—which, admittedly, was not much.

By the late afternoon, sweat was pouring from every pore of my skin. There were public baths to be used, but they would have required payment that I did not readily have, since I had spent nearly half my funds on the clothing I was sporting. There was, however, the lengthy Giro river some short distance away and it was to there I hied myself. They could charge all they wished for bathing in the public baths, but I had to assume that splashing around in a river was still free for all.

I walked for about half a mile and found a place that seemed relatively deserted. I removed the cloak and the short toga, stripping to my undergarments. Slowly I eased myself into the water.

It was, of course, relatively warm, which was hardly a surprise. Indeed, considering the circumstances, I suppose I should have been grateful that the water wasn't boiling. I slid in up to my chin and sighed peacefully. Submersing myself was the only time that I had the chance to feel like a normal person since the buoyancy of the water removed the weakness of my leg. If the entire world became submerged, I would genuinely have no problem with that.

Then female voices carried to my ears from a short distance away. They were laughing and splashing about from down around the bend of the river. That was no interest to me. I would not intrude upon them, nor they upon me, and we would all leave each other alone.

Funny how matters never turn out the way you think they will. Because moments later it all went to hell, and it was entirely because I was endeavoring to save a child.

I floated in the water, not even splashing. It was my nature to remain stealthy whenever possible. I had managed to survive as long as I had by not being noticed rather than drawing undue attention to myself. So my instincts and tendency to blend in prompted me to be unmoving in the water. Even a trained sentry would not have noticed me, especially because my head was partially obscured by a towering thatch of some sort of grass that grew straight up from the river bed.

That was when I heard splashing from much nearer by. I froze, not knowing who it was that was intruding upon my bath. I said nothing, fearful as I typically was that the new arrival was some manner of guard who would just as soon kill an unknown individual as look at him.

I quickly saw, however, that it was no guard. Instead it was a young woman. She seemed to be no more than twenty or perhaps twenty five years old at most. She had long black hair that was tied back in a braid and she sported a toga that was similar to mine except in a smaller size. Around her neck she was wearing a thin silver necklace and there was a stylized eight pointed star dangling from it. She was carrying some manner of basket and she was paying no attention to me at all. Obviously she had not spotted me, which was fine since I had done all I could to secure myself. Instead her focus was entirely upon the curve of the river that was downstream from us, where the young women were laughing and bathing, clearly. I had no clue why in the world she was so interested in them.

Then whatever she had in the basket moved.

That surprised the hell out of me. I had assumed she was carrying laundry to wash or something like that. The notion that there was something living within the basket was extremely strange. I could not fathom what manner of creature she had in the basket, nor what she could possibly want to do with it on the river. I remained exactly where I was, unmoving, so that I could see how the next moments played out.

Perhaps it was a small group of kittens. That would not have surprised me. There were many people who had little to no patience with cats and would not hesitate to dispose of an unwanted brood. But it did not seem likely since a basket full of kittens would have been mewing piteously, seeking their mother even as the basket holder prepared to drown them.

Instead a wholly different sound was emitted from the basket. The small, faint whimper of a child.

"I'm sorry, my son," she whispered. "This is the only way."

I could not believe what I was witnessing. A woman was clearly preparing to drown her infant.

Understand that it is not my personality to especially give a damn about the fates of others. My entire priority is geared around my own survival, and in my several decades of life, I have become quite adroit at it.

But my own appalling childhood had left me with at least some degree of sensitivity to the plight of youngsters. I suppose that is inevitable when one grows up as the lame son of a tavern whore, conceived in a stormy night of rape courtesy of a group of knights. Pathetic sight that I was, I was endlessly tormented by other, healthier youths of far less violent parentage. So to this day I remained sensitive to the plight of youngsters who were faced with all manner of bullying. I take pride in saying that on any number of occasions in my adulthood I had not hesitated to thoroughly pummel obnoxious ten year olds who I caught in the act of harassing younger children. The little bastards had it coming.

What I was witnessing now, however, transcended all of the previous instances. Here was a mother who was clearly preparing to murder a helpless infant. Within seconds she would doubtless tip over the basket and send the baby splashing into the water. And unless the child was half fish, capable of immediately learning how to swim, its remaining life could be measured in seconds.

Instantly I reared up out of the water, tossing aside any endeavors to mask my presence. She saw me and her eyes widened in surprise, and she fell backwards into a sitting position on the bank.

"*How dare you?*" I bellowed at her. "Have you no shame? No pity? Have you no internal sense of motherhood at all? How could you do such a thing?"

Frantically she put a finger to her lips and attempted to quiet me. "Please, stop!" she whispered desperately. "The Rama Lama's guards are just around the bend!"

I had no clue who "Rama Lama" was, nor did I care. My furious attention was entirely on the young woman. "Perhaps you don't want your child. In that case, do the decent thing and find another mother for him! To just toss him in the river as if he were some minor piece of refuse! May your soul burn in hell for what you were about to do!"

As I spoke, I splashed my way out of the river, grabbing my staff to bring myself fully upright. I stood there in my sodden undergarment, making no attempt to curtail my rage despite her urgent gesturing that I should silence myself. "I have no idea if you pray to any gods, but if so, I suggest you plead for His or Their forgiveness immediately!"

She was continuing to gesture to me to silence myself, and then she looked to the side and her eyes widened in horror. Seconds later, two large guards approached her. They were bare chested and bare legged, wearing armored kilts and towering helmets that would have obscured the vision of anyone foolish enough to be standing behind them. Both of them were carrying lengthy, curved swords and they were scowling at the young woman. "What is going on here?" demanded the slightly taller of them, although with their high helmets, it was difficult to get any real idea of how tall the men were.

Seeing them as authorities, I pointed at the woman and declared stridently, "She was going to drown that infant!"

"No, I wasn't!" she said desperately. "I was...I was just going to bathe him!"

"Then why did you apologize to him? Why did you tell him that this was the only way?"

"I...I..." She was stammering. She had no answer. What answer could she possibly have, save to admit her determination to drown her child. My suspicion was that she had had the infant in secret and was hoping to terminate the child before someone, such as her father, found out about his daughter's history of slattern behavior and pregnancy.

She was clutching the basket and child to her breast, and her legs were trembling. She was clearly terrified of the guards, as well she should be. I was hardly familiar with Rogyptian law, but I doubted that it was especially sympathetic to homicidal mothers.

"Wait a minute," said the taller guard. His hand speared forward and clasped around the eight pointed star. "She wears the Morgan Trace. She's a Shew. And this is your first born, isn't it."

Reflexively she began to nod, but then she immediately shook her head. "No. No, he's my third. And...and the first was already attended to. So there's no need for—"

"I don't believe you," said the guard and then, to my astonishment, he slapped his beefy hand forward and knocked the basket and child out of the mother's hands. The child let out a startled cry for the first time.

I did not quite understand what was happening. "Wait...hold on just one—" I began to say.

And he slew the child.

I could not believe it. One moment the child was wailing piteously, and the next the guard brought the sword swinging down and around and cleaved the basket in half. There was no question that the child was dead. There was an awful "splutch" sound and an abrupt termination of the infant's cries.

Understand that in my life I have witnessed any number of instances of man's brutality to his fellow man. But never in all my years had I seen something as utterly cold blooded as this. The guard had not hesitated. He had slain a helpless infant as casually as if he were cutting a piece of lumber.

The mother slumped to the ground, sobbing piteously. The other guard stood near her, brandishing his sword, and for a moment I thought he was going to end the girl's life as well. Indeed, he seemed to be considering it. Instead he shoved his sword through his belt, and then drove his foot forward with considerable strength. It caught the girl in the gut, and she gasped and fell over, her arms doubled over her stomach. She was caught in between her reactions, partly sobbing, partly trying to breathe.

"You are lucky we don't just kill you right here," said the taller guard.

I wanted to kill him. I wanted to grab my bastard sword that was lying a short distance away and leap to the attack. I saw myself charging into battle against them, swinging my weapon with gusto. I saw their heads leaping off their shoulders, or perhaps their chests being hacked open and their internal organs spilling into the river.

Naturally I did not move an inch. Instead I simply stood there and watched as the guard kicked the girl a second time, presumably just to be a barbarian. She gasped once more but otherwise did not make a sound.

The taller guard turned his attention back to me. "You are a stranger in these parts, yes?" I managed a nod but said nothing else. What could I say to such a heartless monster? Upon confirmation of my status, he produced a small white ball. "You have performed a service to the law of the Rama Lama. Accept this token of his gratitude. It is very valuable."

He tossed the ball to me and I caught it with my free hand. I turned it over, not understanding what I was staring at. It was constructed of some manner of light wood. My confusion must have been quite evident, because the guard who had tossed it to me said, "I have given you a wish."

"A wish?" I didn't comprehend what he was saying.

"Present that to the Rama Lama, our leader, and ask for something. If it is within his power...and just about everything is...then he will provide it for you."

"That is very generous," I said tonelessly. My attention was no longer on the coin, but upon the sobbing girl. Horrifically, she was clutching the basket to her bosom. The bottom of the basket was thick with red. I was astounded that a child that small could have that much blood in him.

"Enjoy your stay in Rogypt," he said, and then nodded to his companion. The other guard was still staring at the sobbing young woman, and then he turned from her and strode away. The other guard followed him. Moments later it was just the girl and me.

Long seconds ticked away and I could think of nothing to say to her. I suddenly realized that I was sitting. The strength had gone out of even my strong leg and I was seated on the edge of the shore.

Finally she seemed to pull herself together enough to stare at me silently. Searching for words, I finally said, "I...I didn't understand what you were...I don't—"

"Kill me," she whispered.

"What?"

"You have a sword," and she nodded toward my hand and a half sword. "You would not have such a weapon unless you were capable of using it. Kill me. I beg you. My child is dead and I have no wish to live."

"But...I thought you were going to kill him..."

"Of course not, you fool." She said the words without rancor, as if her anger had been burned out of her. As if my name was simply "you fool" and she was addressing me in that manner. Which, I supposed, made a certain degree of sense. "Down there," and she nodded toward the bend in the river, "the sister of the Rama Lama is bathing with her handmaidens. I was going to put my son adrift down the river to her. She was going to find him and I am sure she would have fallen in love with him. Then I would have volunteered my services as a wet nurse. I had it all worked out. And then you showed up. Idiot."

"I...I don't understand. Why did you need to float your baby down the river? I mean, obviously you loved him, despite all evidence to the contrary. So why...?"

She stared at me, confused. "Don't you know anything about anything? We are Shews. We are slaves. All our men and boys are. And the Rama declared that he wanted all first born sons killed."

"But why?"

For the first time, she sounded genuinely sarcastic. "Apologies. I was unable to attend the meeting where the Rama put forward the thinking behind his decision."

She finally managed to get to her feet. Her legs were wobbling and I thought she was going to pass out. The front of her clothing was now thick with blood, but she did not seem to pay any attention to it. It was as if she had mentally departed the real world and instead had deposited herself into some other, alternate realm. She clutched the basket with the bisected corpse to her chest. "What will my husband say?" she asked in a whisper. "Perhaps he will kill me. Perhaps he will lay my body alongside that of my infant. Yes. Yes, that sounds like an excellent idea. I hope he does that. I hope..."

She turned away and I called after her, "What is your name?" I had no idea why I was asking. It was as if I wanted to form some manner of bond with her. As if being responsible for the slaughter of her son wasn't enough.

"Rebeka," she said.

Then she walked away. She continued to mutter to herself, but I could not make out the words she was speaking.

I tried to envision how her husband would react. Indeed, it

seemed to me that perhaps the wisest course of action would be for her to head in the completely opposite direction of wherever he was going to be, but then I discarded the notion.

I next tried to figure out what I could have done differently. Unfortunately nothing really came to mind. The fact was that I thought I was doing the right thing. I had no clue that she was intending to launch her infant on some ill-conceived boating expedition. I thought that my outcry of warning would benefit the child, not instead result in his demise. There was simply no way that I could have anticipated the lethal turn in which my actions would result.

Yet I blamed myself nevertheless.

In retrospect, as I sit here at my writing desk now, much advanced in age but still maintaining my wits, at least, I find myself wondering at what time in my existence matters had changed that I cared about the child at all. There was certainly a time when I would have said nothing at all. I would simply have floated in the water and watched her do whatever she wanted to her son. My reasoning would have been that it was none of my affair. Instead I had apparently reached a point in my life where I felt the need to intervene when I was seeing a wrong done to someone that was in no position to defend himself. In short, I had tried to be a hero.

And look where it had gotten me. Gotten him.

I dressed quickly, the wetness on my body attended to promptly by the sun beating down upon me. Then I just stood there for a time, leaning on my staff, looking at the city behind me. When I had first arrived, it seemed someplace rife with potential. Now I wanted nothing more save to put it to my back as quickly as possible.

The alternative, unfortunately, was the desert. I was not attracted to a sea of blistering sand and yet more sun, but I did not see any sort of choice.

So with that decision made, I drew on my cloak to provide me some degree of shelter from the heat and started walking, without the faintest idea of where I was going.

In retrospect, it was quite possibly one of the most stupid things I have ever done. I had a small amount of water in a pouch that dangled from around my neck, but even with the most sparing consumption, it would only last me several days at the most. I was very likely heading off to my death.

Why?

At the time, I had no idea. I gave it little consideration. All I knew was that I wanted to be somewhere else than where I was.

With the separation of time, however, and the chance to reflect upon it, I have come to a belated conclusion:

I was tired of living.

I had been doing so for something akin to forty years. That was forty years longer than I was supposed to survive if one considers the pathetic, wretched and deformed thing that had slithered from my mother's nethers all those decades ago. The man who owned the tavern in which my mother worked was all for exposing me to the elements, and my mother—damn her—prevented him from doing so.

It was thirty years longer than I had expected I would live when I was aged ten and was constantly harassed and tormented by the village's youths. It was twenty years longer than I had thought I would make it when King Runcible arrested me for the killable crime of refusing to wed his daughter, with whom I had already slept. What else was I supposed to do considering our relationship, I have no idea, but marriage was simply not a possibility. Not that I could explain that to the king, of course. And if I had not been released from prison by an unexpected aide and allowed to flee, that is indeed where my life would have ended.

I had spent the next twenty years wandering aimlessly, having a series of adventures. I had been possessed; I had slaughtered thousands (all without intending to do so). All those lives lost and I had continued to walk the world, steeped in my endless misery and self-loathing.

And yet I must think that it was the slaughter of the infant that finally sealed it all for me. I had tried to do the right thing and instead the result once more was death. It was the proverbial straw that had broken the spine of the equally proverbial camel. What point, I must have wondered, was there in living anymore? When even an attempt to save an innocent life resulted in the termination of that life, certainly continuing to exist simply held no purpose.

I could have, of course, simply thrown myself upon my sword and put an end to it. But the fact was that I remained, as always, a coward. They say that suicide is the coward's way out; I disagree. Finding a means of jamming my sword through my chest was much too cold blooded an ending for a nerveless fool like me. Poison likewise held no attraction for me. I had no desire to pass away with some manner of toxin eating its way through my innards.

On the other hand, collapsing in the desert, slipping into a dehydrated coma and dying…that was something I could live with. I had heard tell that one's life tends to pass before one's eyes during the dying moments. I certainly hoped that would not be the case for me. Existing once was hellish enough. Being forced to relive it was far too much punishment for any mortal man, even when he was a sinner such as me.

There was no path through the desert, of course. No one would be mad enough to build one because no one would be insane enough to try and cross it. I had no clue what waited on the other side, nor did I think about it overmuch since I was not counting on being able to make the trip.

Had I truly been thinking about making it across, I would have waited for the evening to leave. The wise man trekking the desert does so at night and finds somewhere to slumber during the day, at least as best he can. But the concept of doing things correctly held no interest for me. I was anxious to leave Giro behind and, honestly, my life as well although I was not truly thinking about that at the time.

I wore sandals upon my feet rather than my boots since I reasoned that I would be far less likely to wind up with sand inside them. I was determined to be attired as lightly as possible considering the heat that hung upon me like a blanket.

People seem to think that a desert consists of shifting sands, and I'm certain there are some that fit that description. That was not, however, the sort of desert that I was striding upon now, or at least attempting to do what passes for striding when I walk. Instead the land was flat and arid, the ground cracked beneath my feet. It was as if once upon a time, there might have been something capable of growing that could have supplied food. Now, though, there was nothing save for random bits of shrubbery here and there. Bushes, the occasional small stubbly tree without leaves. I saw no manner of what they called "oasis" anywhere nearby. That was fine. As I said, I had water to last me for a bit, so I would have no need of it immediately.

I walked across the desert, my mind wandering aimlessly and yet always drawn back to the same point. No matter how much I tried to leave the sight behind me, I kept picturing the death of the helpless child. By extension, I also considered the slave status of the Shews. I could not imagine an entire people being pressed into slavery. I was no fool; I knew that slavery existed in the world. People were routinely captured and sold into it: free people whose freedom was stolen from them. It happened. But a whole race? That did not seem right to me somehow. I wondered about the origins of their condition, to have been enslaved and then kept in that position for who-knew-how-long? Granted, it was not my concern. I was not a Shew, not a slave, and so their plight was not directly related to anything in my life.

Still…it was wrong.

What do you care? It isn't your problem.

Which it was not. My inner voice was absolutely correct.

Then my thoughts wandered to the Rama. What reason would he possibly have for requiring the death of all first-born male Shews? It made no sense.

At which point the answer immediately presented itself to me. This had the makings of a prophecy. Some idiot at some point must have made some manner of prediction. Probably it was something along the lines of that the first-born son of a Shew would do something that the Rama would dislike. Perhaps he would be responsible for the Rama's death. Or maybe he would free the Shews from their slavery. Perhaps he would wed the Rama's sister. Who knew? No matter what it was, it was obviously something that the Rama did not want to see transpire. Considering that he was willing to slaughter however many innocent children he could find to pursue his goal, he obviously didn't want to see it a lot.

Something unusual began to build in the pit of my stomach with such ferocity that I was honestly not paying the slightest bit of attention to the heat that was hammering down upon me. It took me a few minutes to realize what it was: it was anger. I was actually angry at the situation in which the Shews were obviously trapped. Granted, it was not my problem...

...but maybe it should be.

Shut up, my inner voice railed at me. *Are you out of your mind? You are no hero. Their problems are not your concern. Besides, what will you do? Go before the Rama and demand that he release the slaves? You will wind up being executed and they will still be slaves. It is a complete waste of time and you must eliminate all such concerns from your mind immediately. Is that understood?*

Slowly, reluctantly, I had to admit that my inner voice was absolutely correct. Being a hero had never sat well with me. Twenty years ago I had endeavored to undertake the role of hero by attacking a young man who had never attempted to be anything other than friends with me. I had seized control of his heroic quest and the results had been less than stellar. The endeavor had solidly taught me a lesson about what happened when I, Apropos of Nothing, little more than a side character, a humorous bit of occasional comedy relief, tried to take the reins and steer the heroic endeavors toward an equally heroic denouement. The result was never positive.

So although the plight of the Shews was regrettable, the fact was that it was not within my limited abilities to do anything about it.

I kept walking.

Determined not to wander aimlessly, I unrolled a small map

that I had purchased from the navigator upon the ship that had brought me here. It was not remarkably detailed. Giro was clearly labeled, and there were several spots in particular that were specified, such as the palace of the Rama. The desert where I was walking was much less detailed.

I did notice one place that was marked as Mount Uneks and the word "oasis" was clearly delineated. As near as I could determine, I was heading in that direction, and so I simply kept walking.

As time passed and the heat of the day increased, I slowly became aware of just how intense the sun was. I kept my cloak wrapped around me but now I was starting to feel as if I was suffocating within it. The alternative, though, was to lower the hood and let the sun beat down upon my bare head. I would likely pass out in no time. So I kept walking with the shielding from the sun providing me some measure of protection.

Soon I spotted Mount Uneks. It was not terribly far in the distance and I was reasonably sure I could make it there before I tumbled into unconsciousness. From where I was, I could even see the oasis that was situated at the base. It was actually quite pleasant looking, considering it was in the middle of a desert. With renewed determination I made my way toward it.

The closer I got, however, the more I started to notice something, and it caused my heart to sink. Some fool, or perhaps a malicious bastard, had set the oasis on fire. I dismissed out of hand the idea that perhaps the sun had done it. This was definitely the hand of some fire-setting monster who had, for some deep-seated idiotic reason, decided they wanted to burn down one of the few areas of vegetation in the desert.

I hurried as quickly as my lame leg would allow me. I reasoned that the flames would spread rapidly and could conceivably poison whatever water was there. Fill it with smoke and ash and make it undrinkable.

But then I saw something that made no sense to me. The flame was contained to what seemed to be a single large bush. None of the surrounding area was catching fire. How could that possibly be? It was fire's nature to spread as fast as it could. What was keeping it in one place?

I had been running, or at least running as best as I was capable—more akin to accelerated limping—but now I slowed down and studied the burning bush. My first impression was correct. It was burning, but it wasn't. It was fully intact.

"How—?" I whispered to myself.

And then, as if in answer, a voice bellowed at me, *"REMOVE YOUR SHOES, FOR YOU ARE ON HOLY GROUND."*

I stared, uncomprehending. "What?"

"REMOVE YOUR SHOES, FOR YOU ARE ON HOLY GROUND."

Very slowly I approached the bush, still not understanding. But I knew one thing. I had no intention of going barefoot. "I'm not removing anything. The ground is hot. It's been baking under the sun. I'll burn my feet."

"YOU DISOBEY ME?"

"I don't want to burn my feet, okay? Do you have a problem with that? Do you want me to be in pain? What sort of sadistic bastard are you? For that matter, where are you hiding? Behind the bush?"

"I AM THE BUSH."

"You're a talking bush? That makes no sense at all. What kind of bush talks? You're vegetation! Seriously, where are you really?"

The bush actually emitted an annoyed sigh. *"I AM THE LORD, YOUR GOD."*

"You're my what now?"

"THE LORD. YOUR GOD."

I digested that for a moment. I was quite sure by this point that this was a magic weaver of some manner who was indulging in a strange, elaborate prank. But I decided to play along with him. "The lord, my God?"

"YES."

"To be truthful, I really don't have much truck with gods. They've never answered my prayers in all my years. Honestly, they seem to exist mainly to torment the poor mortals who walk the world. So if you're looking for me to worship you or something, then I'm afraid you have a problem."

The bush appeared to consider that. ***"THIS IS NOT GOING THE WAY THAT I HAD ANTICIPATED,"*** it finally said.

"I don't see how that's my problem. Now if you'll excuse me, I'm just going to fill up my pouch with water and be on my way. So this has been really entertaining, but I'm going to—"

At that moment a lightning bolt ripped down from overhead. It struck the ground three feet away from me with such force that the sand was instantly transformed into smoking glass.

I stared at it and then turned back to the bush. "Or we could continue to converse."

"YOU HAVE COMMITTED A GRAVE OFFENSE THIS DAY, APROPOS," it said. That startled me because I knew I had not introduced myself. It wasn't my custom to give my name to inanimate objects. It continued, ***"IT IS MY DESIRE TO FREE THE SHEWS OF THEIR BONDAGE IN ROGYPT. I HAD SOMEONE PLANNED TO BE THEIR LIBERATOR. TO SPEAK ON MY BEHALF, TO GO TO THE RAMA AND DEMAND THAT HE LET MY PEOPLE GO."***

"Okay. So?"

"SO HE DIED IN YOUR PRESENCE TODAY."

It took me a few moments to understand what the voice was referring to, but then I did. "The baby? He was supposed to be their savior?"

"YES. THE PRINCESS WOULD HAVE FOUND HIM, RAISED HIM. HE WOULD HAVE BEEN PART OF THE RAMA'S COURT. HE WOULD HAVE LEARNED, GROWN, AND BECOME THE LEADER THAT IS REQUIRED TO FREE THE SHEWS. AND NOW THAT WILL NEVER HAPPEN."

"But if you're a god, can't you raise him from the dead or something?"

"I AM NOT A GOD. I AM THE GOD. AND I AM NOT

THAT SORT OF GOD. WHAT HAPPENS IS WHAT HAP-
PENS, BECAUSE OF FREE WILL."

"Yes, well, free will isn't exactly the best idea you ever had. So what now?"

"SO THE SHEWS NEED SOMEONE TO FREE THEM.
YOU ARE RESPONSIBLE FOR THE DEATH OF THEIR
SAVIOR. THEREFORE, YOU MUST UNDERTAKE HIS
BURDEN."

"Excuse me? I'm supposed to do what now?"

"FREE THE SHEWS."

"And how exactly am I going to do that?"

"YOU WILL GO TO THE RAMA AND SAY THAT I,
THE LORD GOD, COMMAND HIM TO LET MY PEOPLE
GO."

"And are you going to be there with me?"

"YES."

"In person?"

"NO. I DO NOT DO PERSONAL APPEARANCES."

"Well, then, hell, how am I supposed to convince him?! Tell him he has to listen to me because some flaming shrubbery told me so?"

"TELL THE LEADERS OF THE SHEWS. GET THEM
TO BELIEVE IN YOU. THEN CONFRONT THE RAMA.
YOU ARE PERFORMING AN ACT OF GOD."

"Which god?" I said in frustration. "I mean, I'm still not one hundred percent sure I don't believe there's someone throwing his voice. What is your name?"

"I AM WHAT I AM."

"I have no idea what that means."

"YOU CANNOT KNOW MY NAME."

"Why not? Is it a secret? Why would it be a secret? What kind of god keeps his name a secret?"

"JUST TELL THEM YOU HAVE SPOKEN TO ME,
THEIR LORD AND GOD."

"But I don't know which god you are!"

He was beginning to sound impatient. *"I AM THE ONE TRUE GOD. THERE ARE NO GODS BEFORE ME."*

"There are plenty of gods before you! I've heard of a couple dozen! In different countries all over the world! And they all have their own origins and names and all sorts of things, and you won't even tell me—"

"BOB," God told me. *"MY NAME IS BOB. ALL RIGHT?"*

I frowned at that. "Bob? What a strange name. I've never heard of anyone named Bob. I mean, it's barely a sound, much less a name."

"YOU WANTED TO KNOW MY NAME. IT'S BOB. SOMEDAY IT'S GOING TO BE VERY POPULAR. HAPPY?"

"Are you sure," I said suspiciously, "that you're not just telling me that to get me to stop asking?"

At which point a second bolt of lightning erupted from on high and struck the ground directly between my feet. I stumbled backwards and fell, staring upward. "Fine. It's Bob," I said quickly. "Your name is Bob. I'm completely in agreement with that."

"GO AND FREE THE SHEWS."

"I still don't know how."

"FIGURE IT OUT OR THE NEXT LIGHTNING BOLT WON'T MISS."

"Understood."

The burning bush immediately snuffed out. The leaves and branches were completely undamaged.

At that point I still had no idea of how to react. The weaver theory still seemed a viable one, but the notion that there was genuinely some manner of sky god who had targeted me to do His work for Him seemed a fully viable option.

So now I had to go and free the Shews.

Or get electrocuted from on high.

No problem.

Chapter 2

Holiday Inn

MANY PEOPLE HAVE BEEN AMUSED BY me, and I have never entirely understood why.

Yes, yes, I know, my name is unusual. Even unique. I, however, did not name myself, and instead have spent the entirety of my existence learning to tolerate the name that my mother hung upon me when I was far too young to have anything to say about it. As a result my name has caused great merriment amongst many who apparently desperately seek something to be diverted by. I have never comprehended it, but that is the long and short of it.

Furthermore I suspect that some will be equally entertained by the details of my life as I have written them in these journals. Again, it is strange. As I mentioned, thousands have died by my hand. I have caused more destruction than most warlords who are in a constant state of combat. Yet people will likely ignore the destruction that I have caused because of my name, or the self-serving, cowardly steps I take to achieve my goals. No hero am I, but simply a fool lucky to be alive.

Upon consideration of the events that transpired in Rogypt, though, I find myself wondering what manner of rational individual could find any of them the slightest bit entertaining or amusing. People died, came back to life, tried to kill me and nearly succeeded. Promises were made and betrayed, and in many ways, nothing remotely funny happened. Yet I am sure that will not deter some from finding the matters of which I will tell you to be funny.

For my part, at the time I was not remotely dwelling upon humorous aspects of the situation, whether existent or non-existent. Instead my concerns were with the fact that apparently some unseen deity named Bob had chosen me to free the Shews because I was accidentally responsible for the demise of the intended savior. The question was, How to go about it? Bob had unfortunately not been forthcoming with a vast number of details other than that I should present myself to the Shews and perhaps form an alliance. Unfortunately I had not the slightest idea how to accomplish that.

I had ceased moving forward through the desert. Obviously I was going to have to return to Giro; there was no choice about it since I had no desire to be blown into nonexistence by a lightning bolt. So that meant retracing my steps. Since I was no longer driven by the sense of vague urgency that had been propelling me away, I did not feel the need to combat the relentless sun. Instead I dropped under a tree to provide some shade, wrapped myself in my cloak to provide further protection against the sun's rays, and drifted to sleep.

When I awoke, the sun had just descended into its rest. Darkness stretched across my surroundings and the air was somewhat cooler.

A small furred creature was staring at me.

I had no idea what it was, nor I suspected did it have any idea what I was. We exchanged looks and I kept its gaze fixed upon me as my hand stealthily crept toward the knife I had on my hip. In one smooth motion I yanked the knife out, brought it around and slammed it through the creature's chest. It let out a startled yelp, kicked several times more in surprise than anything else, and then died.

I skinned it as quickly and efficiently as I could. Then I made my way back to the bush that had, hours earlier, been aflame. I stared at it for a long moment and then shifted my gaze to the heavens. Stars twinkled down upon me.

"Would you mind?" I asked. "If it wouldn't be too much trouble."

For a brief time there was silence, and then suddenly the bush flared back to life.

"Thank you," I said and proceeded to cook the creature. It only took a few minutes because the fire was quite brisk and the creature was small. Once it was sufficiently roasted I devoured the flesh from its bones. It tasted nothing like chicken, which actually surprised me a bit.

I tossed the bones aside when I was done, wiped my face, and then walked away from the oasis. The bush surrendered its flame and restored itself to a standard, ordinary, not remotely holy piece of vegetation.

Then I began walking.

My mind, however, was racing ahead of me as I envisioned what I would do next.

If I was going to free the Shews as I had been instructed to do, then I was going to require an ally. And there was only one person I could think of because she was the only member of the downtrodden race that I knew. That was Rebeka. That meant that I had to find her.

Of course I didn't have the faintest idea of where to look.

As I often did when I was trying to come up with a concept, I gazed heavenward looking for inspiration. I supposed that it was especially appropriate considering that I was being given instructions by a being who dwelled up there.

I was extremely surprised by what I saw. There was a star shining in the heavens high above that I had never seen before. Yes, granted, I was in a country other than where I had grown up, but the stars should not have been so exceedingly different that I was spotting one of that magnitude for the first time. Part of me wondered whether it was something that Bob might have tossed up for my guidance. Was that possible? Was he actually trying to guide me somewhere?

Why not? Gods were certainly capable of accomplishing anything they set their minds to.

With a mental shrug, I decided to surrender to the obvious

and follow the lead that the star provided.

I made my way back a bit more briskly than I had when I had entered the desert. No doubt the absence of the sun pummeling down upon me lent relative wings to my feet. The star remained remarkably low in the sky, and while other stars seemed to move in the heavens, this one remained fixed in place. The longer it did, the more convinced I became that someone from on high had positioned it there. Why they had done so, I could not guess. What was it trying to lead me towards? What was I supposed to do once I got there? It continued to make no sense.

Then again, there was no reason that it should have made *any* sense. Gods are vast, unknowable beings, and we mere mortals cannot hope to process what goes through their minds.

As I walked, I wondered where gods came from. According to all our mythos, gods created us, but who created gods? I had never really pondered that before since gods had always seemed something that was far away and not of much interest to me. That had obviously changed since the confrontation with the burning bush.

So then who fashioned the gods, and from what? Did the gods pray to them as we prayed to the gods? I did not know, and could not help but think that such things were far beyond the mere musings of one crippled mortal. Nevertheless I could not help but dwell upon it.

My path did not take me into the heart of Giro. Instead as I followed the star, I was drawn to a smaller village some distance away from the city. I glanced at my map, trying to discern the details upon it. As near as I could determine, the area was known by its citizens as Jeruslahem. As opposed to the busy city of Giro, Jeruslahem was much more quaint, if that was the correct word. I also could not help but notice that, the further I drew into it, the more places of worship I was able to spot. No single religion seemed to dominate.

I have never deeply discussed religion in any of my previous tomes, nor do I see the need to do so here. There is an old tale involving several blind men who come upon an elephant, and each of them feels some different portion of the creature. Their assessment of the beast's physical makeup varies depending upon what part of the elephant they are touching. The one touching the trunk, for instance, believes that it is akin to snakes, while another, touching the leg, concludes that it is similar to trees because of the toughness of the skin.

It has always been my opinion that the world's religions are the equivalent of blind men caressing an elephant. The elephant, of course, is God, or the gods, or what we perceive as the true answer to the way in which the world functions. There is no doubt in my mind that there is, in fact, some manner of great truth beyond what our five senses are able to perceive. And the different religions are all blind men stroking it and deciding for themselves what actually constitutes its make up. All of them are wrong, just as were the men touching the elephant. The truth, the great ultimate truth, whatever that might be, is simply inaccessible to we mere mortals. Perhaps there is indeed an afterlife wherein, upon death, the real story behind the hopeless, luckless existence most of us survive under is revealed to us. More than likely we simply reside in dirt while worms snack upon us.

Such cheerful facts rattled around in my brain until I felt exhaustion beginning to swim within my head. Fortunately enough there was an inn just ahead of me. I glanced upward and saw that the star was shining directly above it. I discarded the two as being connected; it was simply coincidence, that was all. A trick of the stars that was playing hob with my imagination.

I entered the inn. The man I took to be the innkeeper was standing in the middle of the main room, passing a broom with vague disinterest over the floor. He glanced up at me and said, as if he were sharing a frustrating secret with me, "I can never get the damned thing clean."

"Well, it's a dirt floor," I pointed out.

He sighed and stopped sweeping, leaning on the room. "Can I help you with something?"

"I'm looking for a room for the night."

"Not a problem," he said. He set the broom aside and walked behind a small desk that was set up off to the right. "We have one room left. Your name?"

"Apropos," I said.

He stared up at me as if he thought that I was jesting. Then he saw the deadpan on my face and shrugged. "You must have had a strange mother," he commented.

"You have no idea."

He had rolled open a parchment and tapped a section of it. "Sign here," he said, handing me a pen with ink dripping from the point. I scratched my name on it as best I could and then presented him with the asked-for amount of money required for the room.

"You in town for business?" he asked.

"Just passing through."

"Well, the best of luck to you. Up the stairs, first door on the right."

As I turned to head for the stairs, a young couple entered. The man looked worn and haggard, but the woman was the one who caught my attention. She was profoundly pregnant; she seemed as if she were ready to burst. She was wincing a bit; she might have been in the first stages of labor right then and there. Her brown hair was wet. Clearly she was sweating profusely.

Quickly they approached the attendant. "Do you have a room?" asked the young man.

"Sorry. No room at the inn," said the man behind the desk apologetically. "This fellow just got the last one."

The man's gaze shifted to me hopefully. Clearly he was hoping that I would give up my room for them. A feat of supreme generosity, which I had absolutely no intention of doing.

"I'm sorry," I said. "I'm bone tired and I need to get some sleep. I'm sure you can find another inn somewhere."

The man seemed outraged at my dismissal of their obvious needs, but the woman put a hand gently on his arm. "He was here first," she said softly. "It's all right." She shifted her gaze to the man behind the desk. "Are there any other inns in the area?"

"I'm afraid not."

"Is there anywhere we can go?"

The attendant shrugged. "We have a stable out back. You can go there, I suppose. "

"A stable?" The young man was bristling with outrage. "Look at her! You would have her lie outside with animals! She is not an animal! Her baby is not an animal!"

His phrasing was slightly surprising to me. "Don't you mean 'our?'"

He turned and looked at me. "What?"

"You said 'her' baby. It is yours, too, is it not? You are the father?"

He seemed momentarily thrown off by the question but then he quickly nodded. "Yes. Yes, of course. I am the father. This is my wife. Who else would be the father? Are you daring," and his voice rose somewhat, "to impugn my wife's loyalty?"

"Not at all," I immediately assured him. "I don't know her and I don't know you. Your phrasing was just odd, that's all."

'The stable will be fine," the young woman said quickly. "How much do we owe you?"

"Nothing." The attendant waved her off. "Feel free to just go there."

She nodded gratefully and she and her husband headed out the door. But before they reached it, the attendant abruptly said, "You're Shews, aren't you."

How he could have told, I have no idea. Perhaps it was their attire. Although the attendant was wearing a light toga as many of the Rogyptians did, they were much more heavily clothed in brown robes draped over white, full-length garments.

Whatever the reason, the man quickly said "no" at the exact same moment that the woman began to say "yes." He fired a warning look at her and immediately she corrected herself, also saying "no." Then the man continued, "We are not Rogyptians. We are passing through, returning to my home."

"Well, good journey to you," said the attendant.

The man fired me a last angry glance before he strode out with her. I heard her moan softly as they disappeared through the door and then immediately erased them from my mind.

I headed upstairs to my room.

It was quite small. A single dresser with a single drawer stood off to the side, and there was a chamber pot that at least appeared clean, so I was thankful for small favors. A single cot with a straw-filled mattress occupied the wall on the opposite side of the room. If the young couple had had this room they would not have been able to share it unless she lay atop him. And considering that was doubtlessly how she had gotten into trouble in the first place, I didn't consider that to be a huge likelihood.

I tumbled onto the bed and the straw rustled beneath me. I waited for sleep to overcome me.

And I waited.

And waited.

I have no idea how long I lay there, staring up at the ceiling. I wondered if the star had moved on in its path or if it was still hovering over me for no reason.

But my mind kept wandering back to the poor young woman. Not the man; I didn't give two damns about him. His wife, however, whom I noticed had been leaning against him for support...

She seemed so wan, so haggard, and yet there was an air of peace that she seemed to wear like a cloak. I could not get over it, how calm she seemed. Perhaps it was the pregnancy that brought her such obvious tranquility. For all I knew, when she wasn't carrying a child, she was a complete harridan. But that was mere speculation. All I could know for sure was what my observation at the moment told me. It might well have been my imagination, but there seemed to be a sort of glow around her. I had heard tell that pregnant women supposedly glowed, but never actually witnessed it.

The more I thought about her, the more I concluded how much more comfortable she would be in the bed that I was occupying. I felt an unusual sensation coursing through my veins and came to the horrific realization that it was guilt. I was actually feeling guilt for having had the good fortune to occupy the last room at the inn. This was extraordinarily unusual for me. Guilt was not something that was ordinarily in my emotional vocabulary, and the fact that I was feeling it in relation to the pregnant woman was extremely odd.

Perhaps you are growing up a sarcastic voice suggested to my inner consciousness, and I quickly endeavored to shunt it aside. I had no interest in second-guessing myself and even less interest in developing something as pointless as a conscience.

Yet the poor woman was out there, huddled in a stable, desperately trying to get some sleep while I lay upon a bed. Not a terribly comfortable bed, but still...

"Damn it," I muttered and rolled off the bed. I dressed quickly, grabbed my sack with my possessions, my staff and weapons, and made my way down the short flight of steps. The attendant was not visible; there was no one in the main room. That was not surprising. He had likely gone to bed. Anyone who was sane was asleep by this point.

I made my way out the front door and around to the back where I knew the stable would be. I had expected it to be dark. Instead, to my surprise, there was a lamp burning within that was providing light. To my even greater surprise, I heard the soft whimpering of an infant. I was astounded. Apparently she had given birth out in the stable. I wasn't sure there was intrinsically anywhere superior for such an endeavor. Most people were born in their place of residence with the aid of a midwife, a mother, or on their own. At least she had the company of some animals to provide additional warmth.

At that point whatever residual emotions I had remaining in the situation were set aside. Of course she could have my bed. The woman had just given birth, for the love of the gods. She and her infant deserved a decent bed, not some blankets or sheets tossed together in a stable to provide some manner of cushion. With my shoulders set, I walked to the stable and entered.

I was quite surprised to discover that the place was far more populated than I could have imagined. The smell was thick with hay and, of course, animal fur. There was a donkey and a cow looking on, but what was curious was that three men were standing there as well. They looked as if they had just crossed the desert, and were gazing in what appeared to be wonderment at the child. All of them were dark skinned with thick beards. Perhaps they were brothers, although I had no way of knowing for sure. They were dressed in flowing robes of varied colors and their expressions were not just of wonderment (as I mentioned) but also of—I know of no other way to put it—reverence. What in the name of all that was holy did they have to be reverent about? It was a damned baby.

I stared at the baby. Its mother, lying nearby, looking exhausted, had placed it in a manger.

The baby stared back.

I tried to figure out what the three men were seeing in this child that I could not. Had they never seen an infant before? It made no sense.

It wasn't even especially cute. No one had wiped the remains of whatever a child must pass through in exiting the womb from its face. Its eyes were open narrowly, and it had stopped its whimpering. Now it just seemed to be staring out at the world with great fascination, as if it were trying to determine how and why it had been evacuated from its previous comfortable residence into this new, vaster place. And it was indeed looking right at me. This struck me as quite odd, because newborn children did not generally focus on anything in particular because typically they could not see anything.

I tried to imagine what it saw when it stared at me. I could not even begin to.

Yet something in its gentle expression actually caused me to relax. I had no idea why that would be, but I actually felt as if I was drawing some manner of comfort from the little creature.

"Hello," I said to the child.

It didn't respond. Naturally.

The father looked up in surprise and he frowned. "What are you doing here?"

"I, uhm," and I shrugged. "I couldn't sleep. I'm not going to be keeping the room. So I felt that you would be able to make better use of it."

"That…is very kind of you," said the man. He was obviously touched by the gesture. "My wife and son could use the rest."

"Son. Congratulations." I glanced at the three men. "Who are you?"

And then, before they could answer, I heard the sound of feet marching toward the stable. Not only that, but I heard metal slapping against flesh. The sound that armed men made when their swords bounced off their bare thighs.

Soldiers. Soldiers were coming.

And there was a newborn Shewish boy lying five feet away from me.

"Get him out of here," I said immediately.

They stared at me in confusion. "What? Why?" said the father.

"If you don't want your son to die in the next ten seconds, you'll do as I say."

The new father was astounded and confused. "Are you *threatening* him?"

"No, I'm not threaten—will you just go!?"

I was too late. I heard the footfalls directly behind me and spun to see two of the Rama's soldiers. It wasn't the same ones whom I had seen earlier kill the boy in the basket, but they might as well could have been. They looked right past me and straight at the boy. "That's a Shewish boy, isn't it," demanded one of them.

Immediately the reason for their presence made itself clear to me. The man in the inn, the attendant. He had summoned the authorities upon realizing that two members of a race who were not in good standing in Rogypt had materialized with a soon-to-be first born child on the way. The attendant was laboring under the exact same rules that the Rama had put forward. Perhaps there was even an award for providing such services to the leader of Rogypt.

The mother was staring uncomprehendingly. "What...why would you...?"

The one a step behind him yanked out his sword.

The mother screamed.

And I snapped.

I would like to say, in retrospect, why I completely lost control of myself. It was one hundred percent averse to my nature. It was not only contrary for me to risk myself for someone else, but I in fact endeavored to watch out for my own wellbeing at all times.

The answer was simple and obvious: I was not going to witness a second child being slain in the same day. I was not.

"Get out!" I bellowed at them once more and activated the trip button situated in my staff.

There was a sculpture of a dragon wrestling a lion mounted upon the top of the staff.. It appeared simply to be ornamental. If that was all anyone believed it to be, so much the better. But upon the trip of a button, a vicious tongue snapped out of the dragon's open mouth. A tongue that consisted of four inches of tapered, sharp steel.

I swung the staff toward the throat of the closest guard, the one who had pulled out his sword. Had I made contact cleanly, as I intended, I would have laid open his throat. But the soldier was formidable at battle, of course, and reflexively he brought the sword up and deflected the thrust of the staff. Had he not managed to do so, he would have died almost immediately.

Unfortunately for him, he did not clearly see the blade itself, merely the staff. So his concentration was purely on that and, as a result, he deflected the staff upward toward his face.

The blade ripped open his right eye.

The man let forth a shriek that was positively deafening. He stumbled backwards, grabbing at his face, dropping his sword and then—even better—tripping over it. He hit the ground gasping, writhing, howling a string of profanities in his language that he should have resisted saying considering there was a lady present. I, however, was hardly in the mood to scold him.

I spun to face the other guard. He had pulled out his own sword and was coming straight at me. I was not enamored of the idea of having a head to head sword battle with the brute, but I didn't seem to have any choice. I yanked my bastard sword clear of the scabbard on my back and held it securely in my left hand, balancing myself on my staff with my right hand. The soldier stopped and stared, for my blade was longer than his and seemed much more formidable. The fact that the man wielding it was significantly less of a threat than he was had not yet entered into his mind.

The father had grabbed up his wife. He was not even attempting to have her walk. Instead he was cradling her in his arms. One of the three men had lifted the child, whose gaze still seemed focused on me. I was reasonably sure I was imagining it.

The soldier realized that the others were attempting to flee. His particular focus was upon the child as he shouted, "Stop where you are!"

I took that moment to attack, charging forward as fast as my leg would allow and swinging my blade.

He saw me coming and, bringing his sword up, intercepted the blow. The blades clanged together loudly, the sound ringing through the stable. The cow mooed in alarm, or perhaps just irritation, and the donkey brayed as another one of the three men pulled it along. Obviously it belonged to one of the three of them, or perhaps to the new father and mother.

He came at me then, and as I surmised, he was in far better shape than I was. I backpedalled as quickly as I could, managing to deflect his assaults. And then, in a particularly low point in my career of self-defense, he struck my blade with such force that it caused my sword to ricochet and strike me in the head. I stumbled and fell.

Quickly he turned to pursue the fleeing people, and that was his mistake. I still had my staff, and I shoved it forward so that it caught between his legs and tripped him up. He hit the ground, landing hard on his elbows.

I slammed the staff forward with as much force as I could

muster. The dragon's head slammed into his and it landed with a most satisfying thud. The soldier gasped, his head clearly reeling.

I sat up and quickly twisted the staff in the middle. It split into two handheld batons, and I lunged forward, swinging my left hand. It struck the soldier and he fell backwards. He caught himself and tried to force himself to sit up. The baton in my right hand lashed out and caught him from the opposite direction. His eyes rolled up in his head and he slumped backwards.

Quickly I snapped the staff back together again. It clicked into a single device and I used it to haul myself to my feet as quickly as possible.

I knew one thing of an absolute certainty: I had to get the hell out of there. There was no way I was going to allow myself to be captured because they would most certainly kill me as soon as look at me. I had half-blinded one soldier and knocked the second unconscious. If they captured me, I would not be long for the world.

I turned quickly to leave the stable and that was when the frying pan slammed across my head.

I fell backwards, the staff rolling out of my hand. I hit the ground and lay there, staring up at nothing.

Then something came into my view.

It was the attendant. He was glaring down at me.

"Idiot," he muttered.

And I blacked out.

CHAPTER 3

The Rama Lama Ping Pong

SLOWLY THE DARKNESS BEGAN TO LIFT. There was a bit of light filtering in through somewhere that warmed my face, which meant that I'd been unconscious for a while since daytime had resumed.

I started to sit up and the world swirled around me. It caused me to wretch for a few moments before pulling myself back together again. I managed to sit up and look around. Much to my lack of surprise, I was in a cell.

There were sigils written upon the wall in my language and I immediately was able to discern that past prisoners had scribbled them there. They were not especially heartening. They said cheerful things such as "Prepare for doom" and "All who read this will die" and "The Rama shows no mercy." Yes, very comforting and not at all helpful in settling my jangled nerves.

I rubbed the back of my head and felt a lump growing there. How wonderful. I glanced around the cell and saw that it too had a dirt floor. That was certainly popular enough hereabouts, although I didn't know for certain where hereabouts was.

There was a small window on the far side of the cell. Sun was filtering through it. There were no bars over it, but it was much too narrow for any living being to slide through. A foot wide and six inches high. Standing on my toes, I was able to bring my eyes up to it and peer outward.

I was accustomed to cells being in the lowest rooms of any

structure. That was not the case here. I was at least two hundred feet in the air, looking down upon the whole of Giro. I had apparently been removed from Jeruslahem to this place, wherever this place was. It was certainly impressively high. I stretched my memory back to when I had first arrived and gazed upon the city, endeavoring to remember what structures had towered so high into the air. None were coming readily to mind, but even if I were able to muster the image in my head, it would not do me any good. I didn't know which buildings were which or what they represented.

At least I wasn't handcuffed. That was positive. Not only that, but I still had all my possessions. My sword was back in its sheath and my staff was lying against the floor a short distance away. I limped over and picked it up. The entire situation was extraordinarily strange. They had me cold; they could have killed me back at the stable. Why had they dragged me, unconscious, back to Giro?

I moved around the cell for a time, trying to see if there were some means of escaping, but nothing was presenting itself. There was no lock upon the door keeping it closed. If there had been, I might have been able to pick it. Instead the door was some quite strong wood, and it was barred on the other side by something that was keeping it shut: a solid slab of wood, perhaps. I pulled at the door experimentally but it did not appear to be the slightest bit interested in moving.

And so I remained imprisoned, wondering if I was going to be left there to starve to death. Time passed as it has a habit of doing, and then there was finally some noise from the door. I had been sitting at the time but now got to my feet and waited. If they were going to walk in and execute me, at least I would be standing.

The door opened wide and four soldiers strode in. Their faces were locked into sour expressions. It seemed as if they would indeed be perfectly content to cut me down right where I was. They all had their swords in their hands as if expecting me to attempt to engage them in battle. I stared at them instead and actually managed a small smile. "How lovely to see you," I said with false cheer. "And what can I do for you?"

The foremost one pointed his sword at me and said, "You will follow us."

"To where?"

"To where we lead you."

I shrugged as if I were utterly indifferent over what was to happen to me. "Lead the way, then."

I followed them as they led me down the hallway.

It was different hallways than any I'd ever seen. The walls were not bricks, or at least did not seem made of bricks. Instead they were solid sheets of some manner of masonry, all of them pale brown, as if they had constructed from the desert itself. There were glyphs everywhere. I glanced at them as quickly as I could. As near as I could determine, they demarcated the history of the families who had ruled in Rogypt for who-knew-how-many years. Everything was there: births, marriages, deaths, war and conquest. They certainly seemed to enjoy dwelling upon their past.

I had never been much for that. Thinking about the things I had done in my life never brought me much joy, so I tended to dwell mostly upon the future in general and specifically how I might continue to survive it. Nevertheless, it was certainly quite the accomplishment to have so much of one's history decorating the wall in that fashion.

I was ushered into a vast room and stopped in amazement. It was clear what this place was the moment I set foot in it. It was the throne room of whoever the person was who was the ruler of Rogypt. The Rama Lama, I think they called him. The room was extremely opulent, but not opulent in the way that I was accustomed. Throne rooms in my old world had been festooned with tapestries, ornate drapes, statues, that sort of thing.

This place was filled with gold. Gold in the statues, gold in the decorations, gold in the lace, gold everywhere. If the sun had been coming in at the right angle, the reflections would have burned out my eyeballs. I had never in my life witnessed so much gold in one place. It was staggering, breathtaking. Where in the name of the gods had they managed to acquire all this damned gold? It was astounding. If I could have walked out of there with a couple of bowls, I would have been set for life. It was beyond all my dreams of avarice.

All the concerns of the Shews flew from my head. The commands of the burning bush were no longer of any relevance. The only thing I cared about in the world at that moment was the fortune that surrounded me. Whoever had this much gold must have cared for nothing else that the world could possibly offer him. Why would he? He was surrounded by a king's ransom...no, all the kings. Every king in the world could be ransomed for the amount of fortune that was surrounding me.

I had stopped walking and was brutally reminded of the fact by a guard shoving me in the back. I stumbled forward and caught myself with the aid of my staff before firing him an angry glance. He did not appear the slightest bit intimidated by the prospect of my wrath.

Suddenly they dropped to their knees. I stood there in confusion for a moment, not understanding the abrupt display of reverence. Then one of the guards near me struck me in the knees with a swipe of his hand. "Down!" he snarled. "Genuflect!"

I had never been much for bending of knee, but in this instance there seemed to be no way around it. So I dropped to one knee, still clutching the staff so that I would be able to rise to my feet should the need come up. The others were staring intently at the floor, but I reasoned that since they were doing that, none of them could be watching me. Instead I gazed up toward the throne, for I had assumed that the person who typically sat there was about to arrive, and hence all the kneeling.

I was utterly astounded by what I saw.

A young boy was making his way to the throne.

And he was lame in his right leg.

It was not a birth defect like mine, that much I could discern. Instead he had clearly sustained some manner of injury that had never healed properly. It was deeply scarred and I could even see signs that infection was still present. It was really quite awful to look at, but since he was clothed in a short toga that came to above his knees, it was impossible not to see.

He could not have been more than twelve or thirteen years old. His face was round and immature, and yet there was something in his eyes that indicated he had seen far more things than any thirteen-year-old boy should be required to witness. I had no idea what color his hair was because as near as I could tell, it had been shaved off. It almost made him look more like a statue than a human being.

He did not have a staff. Instead he was walking with a cane. It was gold, of course, but I suspected it was not solid because gold is quite heavy. A boy would not have been able to wield a cane made of pure gold. Hell, I likely would not have been able to manage it. So the odds were that it was instead simply adorned with gold on the exterior. Either way, even his walking implement was worth a fortune.

He made his way to the throne and slowly lowered himself into it. Moments later, a young man entered as well. He seemed to be about twice as old as the youngster, and his skin was the same dark caste as more or less everyone else in Rogypt. His hair was likewise shaved off and I wondered if perhaps he was the boy's hair stylist. There was a sinister look to him that I could not quite articulate. He had not spoken a word to me, or to anyone, yet I could already determine just from gazing upon him that he was not to be trusted. It was a disconcerting concern, but there it was.

Finally he spoke: "All hail the Rama Lama."

"All hail," echoed everyone in the room save for me. I did not think that it was required that I repeated what everyone else was saying. It was enough that I was kneeling.

"What have we today?" the boy said. It was the first words that he had uttered. He sounded bored. My fate was in the hands of a bored young lad. It was tempting to simply pull out my sword and throw myself upon it. It would save me some time.

The lead guard, or at least the one who I assumed was the lead, stood up and bowed once more to the young Rama Lama. "This man," he said, and pointed to me as if I were not obvious enough, "has committed crimes against us. He speared out the eye of one guard, downed a second, and all to help a couple of Shews violate the law."

That pronouncement seemed to capture the Rama's attention. "Which law?"

"She gave birth to a son. The soldiers were simply trying to do their duty."

Normally when a ruler is informed that a law has been violated, his reaction is predictable. He is typically officious over the notion that someone has taken it upon himself to act in a way other than what he and his advisors have conscripted.

That was not the Rama's reaction at all. Instead, although he did the best he could to cover it, it was clear that this piece of news clearly scared him. Youths are not especially good at covering their emotions in general, and fright was nearly insurmountable to tamp down. The Rama tried but his eyes were wide and his voice actually trembled slightly. "Where are they? Where is the baby?"

"Our sources say that they have fled Rogypt."

"Fled? You are certain?"

"Quite certain, Rama. They were apparently nomads simply wandering through."

Upon receiving that information, the Rama slowly sank back into his chair. Relief clearly swept through him. "If they have departed Rogypt, then they are no longer of any concern."

"Are you sure, Rama? We have men pursuing them even as we speak…"

The Rama waved off the notion. "You need not concern yourself. If they are not present here, then there is nothing to worry about. They are not the individuals for whom the law was written."

I was having trouble tracking what the Rama was talking about. Of course, I should have said nothing. I was on trial for my life. Except I was not really; I knew they were going to kill me, or at least attempt to. It wasn't as if I didn't have some contrarian ideas to oppose that notion, but I needed to handle one thing at a time. So while everyone else was cowering or being supremely deferential, I drew myself to my full height and said, "Then for whom *was* the law written?"

There were gasps from throughout the court. Courtiers had managed to file in once the Rama showed up, and it seemed to my discerning eye that they were there mostly to react to whatever was going on. They certainly did their jobs as they all seemed to inhale air simultaneously upon hearing my question.

"*Quiet, you!*" snarled the nearest guard.

I ignored him since his opinion was of no relevance to me. "I was simply wondering what sort of brute makes a law for the slaying of helpless infants and what the thinking might have been."

That was it for the guard. He drew back his fist and swung it at me.

I stepped back and countered the blow with my staff. His fist glanced off the sturdy wood and I immediately slammed the staff's dragon head forward. I didn't bother to snap out the tongue because I wasn't out to kill anyone. But the dragon head struck an extremely solid blow to his skull. The guard staggered and I slammed a second shot that sent him tumbling to the ground.

Then I was hit from behind before I could move to prevent it. I stumbled forward and fell to the ground, landing on my hands and knees. I blinked several times to shake off the sensation of the world spinning around me.

"Stand him up," the Rama ordered. I was hauled to my feet and managed to focus my gaze upon him. He scowled at me and demanded, "Who dares to question why our laws were written?"

"I do."

"You are not one of our people. Who are you?"

I could have lied to him but saw no point in doing so. "My name is Apropos."

The Rama seemed to roll my name around on his tongue. "I have never heard that name before."

"Neither have I," I admitted.

"There are answers to your question, but they will not be provided you. You are a lawbreaker."

"I'm someone who fought for the life of an infant child unable to defend himself," I said. "The kind of person that a true leader would be fighting himself to save instead of condemning him to death."

Once more all of the courtiers gasped. The Rama actually drew himself up, his eyes widening in surprise. "You truly do not care whether you live or die," he said in obvious astonishment.

"We have not known each other all that long. So were I you, I would not presume to tell me what I do and do not care about." I fired an angry glance at the guard behind me. "Try attacking me face to face next time and see how well you do," I muttered.

"Do you have any idea," said the Rama, "all the ways that I can kill you? Or have you killed?" He was slowly approaching me, leaning on his cane as he did so. He winced as he walked. Not only was his leg not supporting him, but it appeared to be keeping him in pain. At least my leg was simply twisted and useless; it did not hurt when I moved. "How imaginative are you? Perhaps you have questions as to the details of the various ways you can be executed."

"I have only one question, actually."

"Really?"

"Yes. The question is: can you be trusted to keep your word?"

He seemed stunned that I would ask such a question. "Why would you care about such a thing?"

"That is my own business. If you are in the mood to answer a question, let it be that one.'"

"Very well," said the Rama after considering it for a moment. "Yes, of course. I, the Rama Lama, will always abide by my word. That is the decent thing to do. Does that answer your question?"

"Indeed it does," I said.

"Good." He nodded to the guard behind me and pointed to me. "Execute him."

I didn't have to turn to see the grin that must certainly have spread across the guard's face. I heard his chuckle. He was looking forward to cutting down the obnoxious stranger who had dared to speak so rudely to their leader. Instead I reached into the folds of my clothing and produced the small, white ball that the guard had given me earlier. I knew that I was staking my future on the word of a young boy, and such creatures were notoriously unreliable. It was, however, the only option I had available to me. I held the ball high so that all could see it and declared, in as stentorian a voice as I could, "I wish for you to release me and harass me no further."

Once again everyone in the place gasped. They were becoming somewhat predictable in that regard. Even the guard behind me sounded astounded, or at the very least genuinely put out. I said nothing but simply stood there with the ball held up so that it remained in the view of all and sundry. "That is my wish. Are you going to grant it?"

Rama Lama stared fixedly at the ball. "That is a ping pong."

"A what?"

"A royal wish. Do you not know what it is that you are holding?"

"I know that it is supposed to compel you to grant the wish of whoever is holding it. That is the extent of my knowledge of this... ping pong."

"Where did you get it? Who is the dead man who gave it to you?"

My gaze shifted ever so slightly and I saw across the way that one of the guards was sweating profusely. I recognized him instantly. He was the tall guard who had slain the boy. The infant's murderer was standing right there, and in addition to the rivulets of sweat that had materialized on his face, his dark skin had suddenly gone deathly pale.

Fortunately for him, no one else had noticed his reaction. Their attention was all focused on me.

The Rama was obviously irritated that someone had handed me a means of getting out from under the death sentence he had cavalierly set upon me. If he was not going to kill me, then clearly he wanted to take the life of whoever it was that had afforded me the ability to avoid his condemnation. Which meant that I had the bastard. The guard who had mercilessly cut down a helpless infant was now going to be put to the death by the very individual whose laws he had been obeying.

His life was in my hands. All I had to do was give the word and he was dead. The Rama could cut him down, possibly right where he stood.

A slow smile spread across my lips. I envisioned him being cut to pieces by one of his own associates. Or perhaps it would be a gloriously slow death. I had seen some men executed by being buried up to their neck. That would certainly be a horrific way for him to die, being left to roast in the unforgiving rays of the sun.

All of that flashed through my mind.

My gaze continued to rest upon his face.

He was terrified. Very slightly, he was shaking his head "no" and mouthing the word "Please." It was clear what was happening. He was begging me for his life, appealing to the mercy that I did not possess.

Except…

Except…

He was just doing his job. He was obeying the law.

Cold fury rampaged through my mind. Yes, granted, he was doing job, but what sort of horrific job was it? Going around killing infants? What sort of unfeeling monster did that? Did he go home in the evening to his wife and children and they would ask how his day had gone, and he replied, "Oh, it went splendidly. I killed three helpless babies today. Their mothers wept buckets. What is for dinner?"

Except…

Was it true? Did he in fact have a wife and child? Or children? Would my words make the wife a widow, the children fatherless? Was he going to die because he carried out the law? Did he approve of the law? I could ask him, I suppose, but I was not going to have the opportunity since he would be dead.

Dead for doing his job.

Damn it. DAMN it.

The baby's soul cried out to me for justice, and yet I was hesitant. Why in the world was I hesitant? The guard had done the deed. I had seen him do it. I had heard the baby's cry be abruptly terminated by one slice of this man's sword. Yet now, when his life was literally in my hands, I wasn't closing that hand and squeezing the life out of him. What in the hell was wrong with me? Had I lost my edge? I had survived into my fourth decade because I had never hesitated to screw with anyone who irritated me or got in my way. Now I was balking at having the slayer of an infant dispatched.

Kill him. Just kill him. Point him out and put an end to this...

I have no idea how long I stood there silently. The guard knew that I knew him; he was waiting for me to point him out. Once I did, he would be obliged to admit to the accusation. Even if he tried to deny it—and I doubted he would—his general disposition and outward appearance would certainly verify his identity. He would not be able to lie his way out of it.

"Well?" said the Rama.

I blinked my eyes several times. It brought me back to the real world and then I cleared my throat and said, "I'm sorry. I can't identify him."

I saw the guard out of the corner of my eye. He visibly sagged, clearly astounded. I could not blame him. I was almost as surprised.

"Why can you not?" the Rama asked.

"It happened quite quickly, and I did not get a good look at his features. He claimed to work for you but provided no specifics."

"Was he a guard? A minister?"

"He did not identify himself."

"And may I ask what service you provided him that he granted you a Rama Lama ping pong?"

"I saved the life of a child," I said smoothly. We were in the realm of lies, a place where I was quite serenely positioned. "His mother was not paying proper attention to him and he tumbled into the river. I swam in and fished him out. Your man witnessed it and felt that I deserved a reward. Was he wrong?"

Slowly the Rama shook his head. "No. He was not wrong.

Saving a child is indeed a worthy endeavor. I commend you for your bravery."

"Thank you." I bowed slightly.

He studied me for a time. I did not dare to say anything because I was fully cognizant of the fact that I was still dealing with a thirteen year old, and such creatures were routinely motivated by whimsy to do truly awful things for no reason other than that it amused them. Then he extended his hand. "Return the wish to me. You have used it and have no further need for it."

Slowly I approached him, never dropping my gaze from his. The look he fixed on me was quite intense, as if he were endeavoring to take apart my face with it. Not out of hostility, but more curiosity. That made sense, I supposed, since my features were quite different from what he was accustomed to.

I placed the ball in his outstretched hand. Then he asked me a very strange question: "How do you survive?"

"I'm sorry, what?"

"With your deformed leg. I am surprised that you were not drowned at birth."

"I'm told that it was actively discussed."

"Yet you are here. How did you come here?"

I provided him the succinct tale of how I had wound up in Rogypt. I kept it brief as I was concerned that I might say the wrong thing and set him off upon me. I was not still fully confident that he would honor the wish that I had presented him. But he appeared to be listening to me quite intently, nodding at certain points to indicate that he was truly paying attention. When I finished, he once more allowed the silence to extend.

It was at that point that the young man standing next to him leaned in toward him and whispered into his ear. The Rama nodded slightly and then turned his attention back to me. "I am impressed by you. You will stay here in my palace for a time as my honored guest." He clapped his hands and called out, "Ahmway!"

To my surprise, the guard whose face I had been watching immediately snapped to. He brought one arm up and hurriedly wiped away the sweat that had beaded upon his forehead and strode up to the Rama. "Yes, your excellency," the newly named Ahmway said quickly.

"Escort Apropos here to guest quarters."

Seeing the opportunity, I said quickly, "I could use an aide to serve me during my stay here." I nodded toward Ahmway.

The Rama cocked an eyebrow. "Do you mean sexually?"

"What? No!" I said quickly. "Not sexually! Just to provide help as the need arises."

"Yes, of course. Ahmway, you are to remain with Apropos and serve him in whatever need he requires."

"By your command," Ahmway said. He then nodded to me to indicate that I should follow him.

I did so.

I strode after Ahmway as he led me through the vast hallways. This place was much larger than any building that I had ever been in, and that included royal castles. More glyphs lined the walls, but I did not bother to study them. Instead I kept my eyes fixed on Ahmway, who was walking quickly but not so briskly that he would leave me behind. Eventually he turned sharply right and entered a room. I followed him.

It was marvelously ornate. A huge bed, the biggest I had ever seen, was against the far wall. There was so much exhaustion in my body that I could scarcely wait to collapse upon it. In the middle of the room was what appeared to be a small pool of some manner, and I could feel warmth radiating from the water. It was clearly a bath of some sort. "Looks nice," I said casually, gesturing toward the pool.

Ahmway ignored the comment and turned to face me. "Why did you not give me up?"

"Give you up?" I tried to sound as innocent as possible.

"Do not engage with me. We both know you remember that it was me that gave you the wish." His eyes narrowed. "Did you not care about the child that I slew?"

"Care?" My mood shifted abruptly and I advanced on him

so quickly that the much larger man actually backed up, clearly startled, perhaps even slightly afraid. *"Care?* That you slew a helpless infant? Of course I cared, you monster. What sort of insane, unfeeling creature would not have cared under that circumstance?"

"I had no choice," he said defensively.

"Yes, you did. You had a choice. You could have turned away."

"And my partner would not have. If I had refused to obey the law, my partner would have slain the child, and then reported me to our commander. And he would have had me executed for dereliction of duty! Would you have explained to my parents why their son had to die in a pointless endeavor to protect a child who was also dead? Would you?" There was no belligerence in his face. Instead it seemed that he desperately wanted me to understand.

I suppose to some degree I did. Everything he said made an odd sort of sense. It was entirely possible that his partner would have indeed slain the child and then done exactly what Ahmway said he would. So if he had attempted to save the child, he would have been effectively ending his own life. Should he have done so? Would I have?

Of course you wouldn't.

I sighed deeply and sank onto the edge of the bed. "All right," I said softly. "All right. I understand. I cannot say I approve of it, but I understand."

Ahmway let out a low, relieved sigh and sagged against the wall. "I am pleased to hear you say that."

Shaking my head, I said, "I don't understand, though. Why is there such a law in the first place? What possible reason is there to slay the first born children of the Shews?"

"You do not know."

"Of course I do not know!" I made no attempt to hide my annoyance. "Obviously I am new here! How would I possibly know?"

"The law was created in order to save the entire future of Rogypt."

"What?" I did not understand. "Why is the slaying of children supposed to have the slightest impact on the future of Rogypt?"

"There is a story involved."

"Of course there is a story involved," I sighed. "There is always a story involved. Fine. Tell me the story."

And he did.

This was the story.

Chapter 4

Curse of the Moomy

MANY, MANY YEARS AGO THERE WAS a Rama who was known as the Rama Yana.

At the time when the Rama Yana came to power, the Shews were not slaves. They were instead simply another race that lived in Rogypt. They farmed, they marketed, they contributed to the general upkeep of the land. They coexisted with the Rogyptians, and the Rogyptians with them.

Now the Rama Yana had a beautiful wife. He treasured her above all others and his devotion to her was without bounds. Her name was Usana and her desires were limitless.

In those days, there were no pyramids anywhere. Rogypt was a relatively flat land, with the sole exception being the great coliseum where vast games were routinely held.

Usana would stand in the balcony of their residence and look out upon the land before her, and she would see vast tracts of nothingness. Finally Usana went to the Rama Yana and said, "We need monuments."

"Monuments to what?" he asked.

"To you," she said, meaning to herself. "To your greatness," she said, meaning her own greatness. "We should have vast pyramids erected so that all who set foot in Rogypt know of your wonder," she said, meaning her own wonder. For Usana was a young woman who was absorbed with her own beauty and abilities to provide pleasure, but she was also wise enough to know the ways in which she could accomplish her desires.

"Pyramids?" said the Rama Yana. "Those are ambitious undertakings. Who would build them?"

"Slaves," said Usana.

"And from where would I get these slaves? We would need hundreds, perhaps thousands."

Usana shrugged and said, "Conscript the Shews."

"The Shews?" The idea had never occurred to the Rama Yana. "Why would I conscript the Shews? They have done nothing to warrant it."

"I have heard many things," said Usana, her voice filled with darkness and fear, which was quite the accomplishment considering she was hurriedly fabricating everything she was saying. "I believe that they are plotting against you. That they wish to overthrow the proper succession of the Ramas and make you the last of your line. What better way to control them than by forcing them into slavery?"

The fact that she was lying to his face never occurred to Yana. He was filled with both outrage and concern.

Still, he could not be certain. And so he went to his greatest advisor.

He consulted the Moomy.

The Moomy was a being of mysterious origins. Some claimed that he was immortal, although there was no concrete proof to that. Some claimed that he had magical powers, capable of transforming objects and people and supposedly casting formidable curses.

All anyone knew about the Moomy of a certainty was that he was quite tall and formidable, and he had been the Rama's advisor for as long as anyone could remember. Indeed, it was the Moomy who had selected Usana to be the queen of all Rogypt. Usana had began as nothing, a poor girl from the most humble origins, and the Moomy had raised her up and brought her to Yana's attention. And Yana had fallen in love with her and shared everything with her. His throne. Rogypt. Everything.

So the Rama Yana went to the Moomy and asked the towering advisor for his opinions on the subject. The Moomy did not hesitate: "Do as your queen advises, great Rama," said the Moomy. "If it is her desire to see slaves build monuments to your greatness, who are you to deny her the opportunity?"

"And what of enslaving the Shews?" asked the Rama. "Is that truly the best way to treat them? They who have committed no offense against us that I am truly aware of?"

"I have heard," said the Moomy, "that they are conspiring to remove you from power."

Well, that was all the impetus that the Rama required.

He unilaterally declared that all Shews were now slaves of the Rogypt empire, and dispatched soldiers to enslave them. Had the Shews fought back, they would likely have been able to maintain their independence, for they outnumbered the soldiers. But the Shews were a relentlessly peaceful people, and their religion preached peace and living a life where they never went to war. So rather than battle against those who would enslave them, they submitted, convinced that the Rama's mood would pass and he would eventually free the Shews.

Which did not happen.

Instead the Shews were pressed into service and under the lashes of the slave drivers, they proceeded to build a vast pyramid to celebrate the Rama's greatness. And they built a variety of other statues and monuments to celebrate the gods and the Rama's family and whatever else occurred to him.

The Rama watched the progress over the next years and was quite pleased at what he saw. He was also relieved that the imaginary schemes against him had been brought under control, despite the fact that he had never been presented with any actual proof. Which made sense since there was none.

Time passed, as it always did. A son and heir was born to the Rama, and he was most pleased about that. And Usana's beauty remained untouched by the passage of time. No surprise, of course, for she had a bevy of handmaidens who constantly attended to her and made certain that her beauty remained undiminished.

Then one day the Rama set forth on what was intended to be a lengthy overview of the lands under Rogyptian control. Once the journey was under way, he noticed that one young servant kept looking away from him, refusing to make eye contact. Some rulers would have been quite content with that, for they feel that commoners should never look directly at their ruler. But the Rama was concerned over why one who was as young as this lad was endeavoring not to gaze directly at him. So he took the lad aside and questioned it.

His answer to the Rama made no sense to him: "I am reluctant to look at you because you are being shamed and do not know it. And I am afraid because now you will ask me why I would say this, and you will not believe me and slay me for my honesty."

"What are you talking about?" demanded the Rama. "Tell me why you would say such a thing."

"Because the queen is secretly the lover of the Moomy. They have been lovers for some time, and now that you are out and about, their congress with each other will be without anything to contain them."

And the Rama roared with fury, and pulled out his sword and struck down the young man right there and then for daring to say such things. No one asked the Rama why he had cut down the lad because one simply did not pose such questions to a ruler. Yet even as the lad's body was carted away, the Rama stayed right where he was, blood still dripping from his sword, and pondering what the young man had said.

He called for camp to be made in that spot and even though they had only departed hours earlier, his word was immediately carried out. Once darkness had descended upon them, the Rama draped a cloak over himself to disguise his features and returned whence he'd came.

He quietly made his way into the palace, and once inside up to Usana's royal bedroom. They always slept separately save for the times that they chose to have intercourse. The Rama opened the door ever so softly, convinced that she would be alone.

She was not. She was naked in her bed, asleep, her body covered with a thin veil of sweat. Next to her was the sleeping form of the Moomy, also naked.

Had the Rama reacted properly, he would have backed out, summoned guards, had them arrested and then brought before the chancellors. But he was in anything but his right mind. Instead he let out an infuriated roar and charged them, pulling out his sword as he did so.

His determination was quite simple: He was going to cut down the Moomy and then deal with his queen separately. He had not yet decided, in the horror of discovery, exactly what he would do with her, although doubtless it would not be anything positive.

But as he came at her, she woke up and saw him coming, and more, saw the target of his sword. With a horrified cry, she leaped upon the Moomy and threw her hands up, attempting to ward off her husband's wrath.

The Rama saw her intercede, but it all happened too quickly for him to stop the sword's descent. It cleaved down into her, slicing her heart in twain, which might actually have been symbolic of the moment. She had time to unleash one horrific dying cry and then pitched forward onto the bed.

The Moomy let out an awful shriek and grabbed her dead body to himself. Guards came pouring in at that point, uncertain of what in the world was happening. They saw the body of their queen and the agonized Moomy on the bed. They moved to attack the man with the sword until he turned to face them and they realized that it was the Rama, and then they dropped to one knee and awaited his commands.

Having just slain his beloved wife, the Rama was mentally paralyzed. He stood there for a time and then ordered the Moomy to be arrested. The guards moved forward and grabbed the grieving Moomy off the bed, dragging him away. He said nothing. His face had gone ashen and it was as if all emotion had fled his body. The Rama gazed upon the body of his faithless wife.

And he rewrote history.

On some level, he must have known of his wife's faithlessness. But he convinced himself that it had not been her at all, but instead entirely the work of the Moomy. That the Moomy must have used his dark arts to seduce her and that Usana was entirely blameless. His heart hardened toward the Moomy and so, when the Moomy was dragged before him some hours later, the Rama made it clear that there would be no trial. That the Moomy would simply be executed. The one bit of mercy he extended was that he would make certain that the execution would be swift.

The Moomy stood in the throne room, facing the Rama, and when he spoke his voice was low and dangerous. And what he said was, "I lay a curse upon you, Rama. The first-born son of a Shew will bring the entirety of Rogypt down. Nothing you can do will stop it. As I have spoken it, let it be written in the book of fate. Rogypt will fall, and it will be because of you! You!"

Everyone within hearing of the Moomy was clearly terrified of what he was saying, but the Rama was still filled with such outrage over the death of his queen that he ignored the curse. Instead, he angrily strode toward the Moomy and declared, "I need not wait for someone else to attend to this!" He pulled out his sword, swung it, and chopped the head off the Moomy. The head rolled across the floor, slid to a halt, and then—to the fear of all concerned—began to laugh uproariously. No one had ever heard or seen anything like it. Different people claimed different lengths for how long the laugh went on: Some said a second or two, others claimed a full minute. Either way, eventually the laughter tapered off and stopped, and then the head simply lay there, the eyes rolling up into their sockets. It was as dead as any other decapitated head would be.

The Rama stared down at the head of the man he'd come to view as his great enemy and the despoiler of the queen. Then he turned to his servants and said, "Remove this thing." Then he said to his counselors, "Come with me." He strode out of the throne room and the counselors followed in his path.

Moments later they filed into the central meeting room and the

Rama turned to them and said, "Do you believe in the curse that the Moomy laid upon us?"

They all looked at each other, each of them afraid to speak. The Rama snarled at them. "I depend upon you for guidance! Do not be afraid to speak your feelings!"

Thus encouraged, they said, "Yes. We believe in the Moomy's curse. How could we not? He laughed even after his head was severed. Someone who can do that can do anything!"

"Then how do we counter it? How do we prevent it?"

The question, once posed, had a remarkably simple answer.

When the Rama emerged with his advisors, they put forward a new decree that immediately became law: All first-born sons of the Shews were to be executed. Not only that, but it became law that from that point onward, any newly born first sons of the Shews were also to be terminated.

The new ruling appalled the Shews, and they begged for mercy. But there was no mercy forthcoming from the Rama, for he was interested only in saving the fate of Rogypt. So the law was declared, and the children sought out and slaughtered. The soldiers systematically cut them down, and their bodies were piled upon great smoking heaps. The black smoke reached toward the skies and the stench of so much burning flesh floated throughout the entirety of Rogypt. The wailings of the mothers was massive, filling the air day and night, but the Rama turned a deaf ear to it all because he knew that what he was doing was correct and just and in the best interests of all concerned.

And the law is enforced to this day, because even though much time has passed, the curse of the Moomy hangs over Rogypt and on some level everyone still waits for it to take effect and for the first born son of a Shew to destroy us all.

CHAPTER 5

Mummy Dearest

ONCE AHMWAY HAD FINISHED HIS STORY, he then lapsed into silence. I sat and thought about what he had told me.

So on the surface of it, the existence of the law was purely to save the entirety of Rogypt from the curse of a long dead madman. Therefore it made sense to the Rogyptians and to all of the Ramas who were responsible for enforcing the law since then. They obviously believed that they were acting in the best interests of the country. It was impossible to reason with someone who thought that they were behaving on behalf of their entire people.

My gaze shifted to Ahmway. "What do you think? Do you set any store in this ancient curse business?"

"None at all," Ahmway said firmly. "Tales of such things become distorted over the years. Unfortunately it's not for me to fly in the face of the law."

"What about the Rama? Would it be possible to talk to him about reversing it?"

"The Rama?" Ahmway frowned, obviously considering it. "It depends, I suppose, on the idea of someone managing to talk sense into him. But there are very few people that he listens to."

"To whom does he listen?" To my mind, relieving the Shews of their status as slaves was no longer a priority, despite the fact that a piece of flaming shrubbery had assigned the task to me. But if I could get the Rama to revoke the law, at least that would be something to benefit them. Perhaps that would satisfy their unknowable god.

"Well, he has counselors and advisors," Ahmway said thoughtfully, "but in truth, there are only two individuals who truly have his ear. The first is his main counselor. You saw him in the throne room with him earlier. His name is Mane. He first arrived here several years ago and wormed his way into close proximity with the Rama's father, the previous Rama. He was with the Rama when he died. It was the Rama's last wish that Mane serve as advisor to his son."

"He probably killed him," I said.

Ahmway looked astounded at the notion. "How could you say that?"

"Because it would be the simplest way for him to benefit himself," I said reasonably. "Was there anyone else in the room when the Rama passed?"

"Well…no," Ahmway admitted.

"Was the Rama's death unexpected?"

"He had not been feeling well, but he did not seem fatally inclined."

"Killed him," I repeated with conviction. "So this Mane is definitely someone that we will want to watch out for. Who is the other?"

"The Rama's nurse."

I blinked in confusion. "I'm sorry, what? His nurse? Isn't he a bit old for a nurse?"

"Well, she is somewhat more than a nurse. The Rama's mother died in childbirth. The infant was given to the nurse and she effectively raised him. He is as devoted to her as he could possibly be to his own mother. And with the death of the Rama's father, her rank has only risen since then."

"What kind of woman is she?"

Ahmway thought about it, pursing his lips as he considered a response. "She has always cared very deeply about the Rama. And about others, as well. That has always irritated the Rama somewhat, which I suspect is influence from his father."

"So is it possible she will listen to me about trying to get the Rama to change the law?"

He shrugged. "I do not know her well enough to predict what she will do. Plus she is a female, and they are inherently difficult to predict no matter what the circumstance."

"That is certainly true enough. Would I be able to speak with her?"

"Of course. She is quite easy to access. Now that the Rama is much older and no longer requires her daily services, she spends much of her time at the Shewish care center."

"The what?" I frowned. I had never heard of such a thing.

"It is something that the Shews established some years ago. It is a place where anyone who sustains injuries during the construction of the pyramids is able to go to receive healing. They call it a hospical."

"That sounds rather convenient," I said. "They should make more hospicals. Make them available to everyone."

"Well, that seems like quite a good idea. Perhaps that is indeed something they will undertake in the future. But that is where she is, if you wish to go and speak to her."

"Can you bring me there?"

"Of course," said Ahmway. "I was assigned to attend to you in all things. Being a guide for where you want to go would certainly fall under my responsibilties. However," and his voice dropped to a warning tone, "if I take you out of here and you attempt to flee, I will be forced to hunt you down. The Rama was quite clear that he wanted you to stay around."

"Yes, he was," I said thoughtfully. "And I wish I knew why." I thought about it a moment more and then shook it off. "What is the woman's name?"

"Nuskin," he said.

"Nuskin? That does not sound likely a feminine name."

"It is what it is."

"That is true. All right." I had been sitting for a time, but then

I stood and slapped my legs. "Let us away."

We awayed.

The journey to the hospical was without incident, which suited me just fine. It was nice to spend time in a place and not have it all turn to shite within minutes.

As we departed the palace, I had my first opportunity to study it from the outside. It was certainly majestic. It was several hundred feet high easily, and ornate statues of various Rogyptian deities decorated it. I was impressed by the imagination that went into depicting them. Most statues of gods that I had seen simply presented them as idealized human beings. These things, however, were bizarre mixtures of humanity and animal. Half-crocodile, half-jackal, half-eagle. All manner of beasts. I wondered what their backgrounds were and decided not to think about it overmuch.

We made our way through the streets and minutes later were moving into one of the seedier sections of town. In this part of the city, there was no view of the palace or any other more majestic buildings. Instead the shadows seemed to stretch everywhere, which on some level was quite soothing since it provided at least some relief from the incessant sun. The structures surrounding me were far more ramshackle, as if they had been slapped together with some sort of sticky substance rather than actually being built by people who knew what they were doing.

Ahmway indicated one building that was directly in our path and that was where we headed. We strode in and I was surprised by how deep and wide the place was. It consisted of one large, long room, and straw mattresses lined both sides. There were people lying upon the mats in various states of discomfort. Some were actually sleeping, but most were moaning softly while various individuals appeared to be doing their best to heal them of whatever was bothering them. Most of it seemed based in massaging, rubbing their shoulders or backs or various other body parts that had been damaged through excessive use.

"There," said Ahmway, and he pointed toward one mat at the end. I saw the woman who was there rubbing the neck of a particularly haggard looking worker. What struck me most about him was his age. His hair was stringy white and hanging around his shoulders, and his face was worn and tired. I was amazed that this man could possibly be a worker.

The woman doing the neck rubbing, on the other hand, was stunning. I knew from the description of the Rama's background that, if this was Nuskin, she had to be around my age. The unfortunate truth is that most women who tend to be as old as I am wind up looking much the worse for their years. Women's looks tended to fade the moment they left their teen years behind. That was not the case in this instance, however. She seemed extraordinarily beautiful. Nor was she someone who tended to spend hours obsessing about various make-ups to enhance her features. She wore no make up of any sort; her face was clean and clear. Her thick black hair hung around her shoulders and there were streaks of gray in it, but somehow that gray actually complemented her appearance. Her face was triangular in shape and she had quite an elegant nose, with deep blue eyes on either side that were focused on the man she was massaging. Apparently she was doing quite a good job because he was sighing in relief and pleasure. For some reason I suddenly found myself jealous of him. I shook my head briskly as if to clear my thoughts and ordered myself to focus.

I wanted to speak up right then but could not force myself to interrupt her. So instead I simply stood there and watched her fingers working over his shoulders. Eventually, though, she became aware that I was watching her and shifted her attention to me. Suddenly I felt the need to look everywhere except directly at her. When I finally allowed my gaze to return to her, I saw that she was still staring at me, her face an amused question mark. I nodded briskly and she returned her focus to her patient.

Thus it went for another few minutes until she completed her therapy with that particular slave. She shook out her hands as if to restore feeling to them and then strode toward me. "You are not a Shrew."

"I am not, no."

"Nor are you Rogyptian. Yet you have a Rogyptian with you as a guard," and she nodded toward Ahmway. "A member of the royal elite, if I am not mistaken."

"You are not mistaken."

"Then may I ask who you are?"

I bowed slightly for no reason that I can determine. "I am called Apropos."

"Really?" She cocked one arched eyebrow. "By whom? People who are determined to make sport of you?" She asked it with no meanness. She seemed genuinely interested.

"It is the name given me by my mother."

"I see," she said casually. She had strolled over to me and was looking me up and down appraisingly. "She was quite imaginative."

She imagined me accomplishing great things in my life, so I would say yes, that is certainly an accurate assessment. I nodded. "She was."

"Dead?"

"For quite some time."

"Natural causes?"

My voice dropped, becoming unaccustomedly hoarse. "I'd rather not discuss it, if that's all right with you."

"As you wish. So," and she clapped her hands and rubbed them together briskly as if she were about to begin treatment on me. "What can I do for you?"

"Well, I'm not quite sure we should discuss it here, Nuskin, if that's all right with you."

"All right." She gestured toward the exit. "Let us go for a walk."

We walked out of the building and began a leisurely stroll toward the marketplace. Ahmway followed, of course, but made sure to hang back some paces so that we would be alone. Nuskin glanced over her shoulder, taking in the discreet distance that Ahmway was maintaining. "He was assigned to you by the Rama, was he not?" It was phrased as a question, but wasn't, really.

"That's right."

"And may I ask how you came by this honor?"

"I'm not entirely sure," I admitted. "I was holding a talisman at the right time and that opened quite a few doors."

"Ah. You had a ping pong."

"I did indeed."

She laughed softly at that, shaking her head. "That would be my doing, I'm afraid."

"Yours...?"

"It was something I instituted when he was very young. I assume that you are aware I raised him, yes?" I nodded and she continued. "As the young Rama, naturally he was entitled to whatever he wished. But his father did not desire for him to grow up with such an entitled attitude, with the notion that all he had to do was ask for something and it would be provided him. So I instituted the concept of the ping pong. When he would behave himself well, he would earn one of the balls and that would entitle him to a wish. He typically used it for something trivial...an extra piece of cake or some such. But he became enamored of it and wound up recreating it as part of his reign."

"That's very charming."

She stopped at the stall of a fruit seller and purchased a nectarine. She glanced at me questioningly and I shook my head, indicating that I was not hungry. She shrugged and bit into the nectarine, and the juice flowed from it and down around the edges of her mouth. Insanely, I found that attractive. Granted, it had been an unconscionably long time since I had been with a woman, but the notion of becoming attracted to a nurse seemed absurd. Especially when I considered her an option for my use.

"I need to speak to you about something."

"I suspected as much," she said, "considering that you obviously sought me out. May I assume that it has something to do with the Rama?"

"It does indeed. It is about this law that first born Shewish sons should be executed."

She kept her face carefully impassive, as if she were doing so through years of practice. "I cannot say I am surprised. You are not the first to be concerned about it and will doubtless not be the last."

"That sounds to me as if you are resigned to it."

"Do you know the reasons behind it?"

"I have been informed of it, yes."

"Then that should be enough to inform you that the Rama is not likely to back away from it. He believes that he is endeavoring to preserve the future of Rogypt. He is not about to toss aside the future of his country simply to spare the feelings of his people."

"People you obviously care about," I pointed out. "I mean, you're here tending to them."

She shrugged. "Everyone has to be somewhere."

"But you must have a reason," I insisted. "What is your connection to them?"

Nuskin chuckled at that. "My connection is that I am a human being and they are human beings, although granted there are some who do not view them in that respect. I am simply looking to occupy my time. I would not advise reading anything beyond that into my activities."

I began to respond when suddenly I heard a very distinctive sound. One that I had heard enough times in my life that I knew immediately we were in danger. It was the sound of an arrow being fired from a bow and hurtling through the air.

With absolutely no warning, acting purely on instinct, I grabbed the startled Nuskin and threw my body around her protectively. I have no idea why I did that. What I should have done was immediately sprint from the area as fast as my lame leg would allow me to move. Instead, as if I were a damned hero, I sought to shelter the startled Nuskin, who gasped in confusion against my chest.

I spun to see what was happening behind us and my eyes widened in shock. Ahmway was staggering, trying desperately to reach around behind his back. There was no hint of pain on his face, but rather just pure determination to get his hand around there. Then the blood drained from his cheeks as he stumbled forward, at which point I could see what was clearly lodged there: a still quivering arrow. Ahmway was clearly not dead because he was still trying to reach the weapon, but he wasn't even coming close to it. Instead his fingers were grasping at the open air.

At that moment Nuskin let out a startled cry. Something yanked her out from my arms. I turned and saw that two men had grabbed her. Everything was happening far too quickly. What I should have done was allow them to take her. I had only met her minutes earlier and had not had the time to develop any sort of emotional investment in her. But instead I actually began to reach around to my back to extract my sword from its sheath.

Before I could do so, though, something was dropped over my head. It was a canvas bag, obscuring my vision. I released my hold on my sword and tried to yank the bag off my head, and then something struck me. It might have been a fist or perhaps some manner of bludgeon. All I knew was that I totally lost my balance—a delicate thing even under the best of circumstances—and tumbled to the ground.

"Kill him!" I heard a voice growl from nearby.

"No, bring him along," came a response.

Nuskin cried out my name and I lurched forward on my hands and knees, trying to put some distance between my attackers and myself. In this endeavor, I failed utterly. There was a second blow to my head and this one did far more damage. The world changed to black around me and for the second time in roughly two days I slid into unconsciousness.

CHAPTER 6

Really Big Shew

THIS TIME I WAS NOT ALLOWED to wake up on my own. Instead I was jolted from my slumber by a sharp boot in the gut. I gurgled and sat up, automatically reaching for the sword that was customarily strapped to my back. But it was not there.

The bag had been removed from my head so that I could see where I was. I was in some small building somewhere. It was likely someone's home, but I had no idea whose. The room that I was in was very sparse, with scarcely any furniture visible. The floor was dirt, which was hardly atypical.

The room was quite full, however. There had to be at last ten people in there, all dressed quite simply, and several of them visibly wearing that same necklace that Rebeka had been sporting. So I was in a room with a group of Shews. I had no idea what they wanted of me, and I certainly wanted nothing from them. The fact of the matter was that I was on their side, but they had no way of knowing that and I wasn't sure that they would believe me.

Nuskin was on the other side of the room. She was on her knees and there was a man standing behind her with a blade to her neck. I quickly realized that the blade was mine, and that offended me somewhat. I had never in my life used the blade to kill a woman or even threaten one, and very much disliked seeing it put to such use now. But I was hardly in a position to do anything about it.

"You awake?" said the man who was holding my sword, and

then said "Good" without giving me the opportunity to respond. "What are you to this woman?"

"He is nothing to me," said Nuskin. Much to my surprise, she did not sound the least bit frightened or concerned. It was as if she had foreknowledge that she would be able to get out of this situation intact. "I met him perhaps five minutes before you grabbed me. He has nothing to do with this, whatever this is. You might as well free him now."

"So that he can return to the Rama and tell him exactly where you are? I think not."

"I have no idea where I am," I pointed out. "You stuck a bag over my head before bringing me here. So I would actually be the worst person to provide any sort of rescue. I'm assuming that's what you're concerned about. Rescue."

"I am not," said one man. He was the tallest man in the room, the oldest and most broadly built. His upper body was bare and I could see scars from lash beatings all over his chest. I assume his back was likewise decorated. He was glaring at Nuskin and then said, "I do not understand why she is still alive. What is the point in not simply cutting off her head and sending it back to the Rama?"

I definitely was not thrilled by his point of view.

"Because that is not the plan, Simon," said the swordsman. "That was never the plan. We all know that the Rama is still fond of this woman. We are to use her as a bargaining chip."

"You are a fool," said the one who had been addressed as Simon. His glance took in the entirety of the room. "You are all fools. You truly believe that the Rama will somehow be convinced to change the laws of Rogypt. That he will stop killing our first-born. You do not know him at all. The only thing that will convince him is threats, not bargaining. And he will not respond to threats unless he knows that they are genuine. The way to make certain that he is aware of our sincerity is by sending the head of his beloved nurse back to him." He took a step toward Nuskin and snarled at her, "Are you prepared to die, woman?"

Nuskin simply stared at him. "Always," she said calmly. "Do

what you feel you need to do."

"Wait," I said. "Are you really just going to kill a helpless woman?"

"And her friend," said Simon meaningfully.

"But why—?"

"Because," and Simon's voice rose, "the laws killed my grandson! One of the Rama's barbarian guards cut him down with his sword! This madness must end!"

Suddenly the timing of this was starting to make sense. "Was the child's mother named Rebeka?"

My response was startled silence. The swordsman managed to nod slowly and Simon approached me. I couldn't help but notice the formidable dagger that was attached to his hip. His hand was hovering near it as if he were prepared to extract it and use it imminently. "Yes," he said with a rumble to his voice. "How did you know that?"

"I was there. And the guard who was with me when you took me...someone put an arrow in his back. He's likely dead, so if you're seeking vengeance, then that has been attended to."

"Get Rebeka here!" ordered Simon. He didn't address the command to anyone in particular, but it prompted three men to flee the tent immediately, presumably to fulfill it. "What is your name?"

"Apropos."

He didn't react to it at all, other than to nod slightly. "And what are you doing in our country?"

"I was just passing through. But I seem to have been caught up in local events."

"Indeed." He was now standing face to face with me and his breath washed over me. There was alcohol on it. I had no idea whether it was clouding his judgment or not, but there was certainly quite a bit of it. If I had been able to light a flame near his face, he likely would have been immolated. "And how did you come to be in the company of the man who killed my grandson? Was he a friend of yours?"

The wrong answer would likely have gotten me gutted right then. "More of an acquaintance," I assured him. "He was assigned to protect me by the Rama." I glanced around. "Didn't do a particularly good job of it, obviously."

"Are you endeavoring to be amusing?"

"Not endeavoring. It just comes and goes."

There was motion at the doorway and moments later Rebeka entered. Her eyes rested upon me and widened. Oh yes, she definitely remembered me. "It's you," she said and then turned to the swordsman and said, "Tommen, it's him. The man I told you about. The man responsible for our son's death."

Immediately the dagger was in Simon's hand. Clearly he was prepared to slice me from crotch to sternum right then. I put up my hands quickly and said, "Whoa, whoa. All I was responsible for was trying to stop a woman preparing to drown her child! I had no idea that she had some sort of involved plan about sending it floating down the river to some royals!"

This was clearly news to everyone else in the room. All eyes shifted to Rebeka. "What?" said Tommen. There was a slight stammer to his voice. "What is he talking about?"

"I...I don't know," Rebeka said quickly, trying to cover for herself and not doing a particularly good job of it. Clearly she had not told her husband or the grandfather—whether he was her father or her husband's, I could not tell—the full truth of what has transpired. "I have no idea..."

"Yes, you do." It was Nuskin who had spoken. "The princess, some handmaidens and I were bathing in the river the other day. I heard some manner of scuffle going on up around the river bend, but I did not investigate." Her voice was firm and full of conviction. "You were going to float your son down the river in hopes that she would become enamored of him and bring him back to the palace. That was your plan, was it not?"

Rebeka was rapidly shaking her head, but as she did so tears poured down her face. She was not exactly the most convincing of liars. "I don't know what she is..." Then her voice trailed off as she was unable to finish the fabrication.

Tommen had allowed the sword to slide off Nuskin's throat as he was so distracted by his wife's sobbing. Nuskin, who had been kneeling, slowly got to her feet. There was nothing but sympathy on her face. "It might well have worked," she said. "You did nothing wrong except to attempt to save your son. It is commendable that you at least tried."

Simon spun and faced her, his expression twisted in anger. "What do you know or care? What interest do you have in the fate of the Shews? As far as you are concerned, they can continue to slaughter our newborn sons until the end of time!"

I saw the opportunity to make my move at that point. "You're thinking too small," I said. "Dreaming of managing to end the law about your children being slaughtered. Even if you manage to accomplish it, what kind of lives are you preserving for them? They grow up to become slaves? To build monuments to the people who want to enslave you? What kind of lives are you fighting for them to maintain?"

"What would you have us do?" demanded Simon. He did not seem especially impressed by my argument. "We are slaves. There is no changing that."

"Yes, there is. You can demand that the Rama release you."

The men exchanged looks for a moment and then, to my surprise, there was a roar of laughter. I considered that odd since I had not been attempting to make any sort of jest. When they had managed to compose themselves, one of them said, "It's ridiculous. The army of the Rama far outnumbers us. Plus they are trained fighters. If we attempt to rise up against them, they will slaughter us. No one can free us."

"I can," I said firmly.

Their expressions were incredulous. "You?" another of them said, and then Simon spoke up. "You are a fool."

"I don't dispute that," I said. "Nevertheless, it is up to me to free you. And I'm telling you that if you do anything to this woman, you will be crippling my ability to accomplish that."

"And what in the world makes you think," said Simon, "that you can possibly free us?"

A dozen possible lies crossed my mind, because the truth seemed simply too ridiculous. What was I supposed to tell them? That a piece of ignited shrubbery had given me the instructions to free the Shews because I had been inadvertently responsible for the death of their actual savior? Certainly I could come up with something better than that.

Yet I paused. I didn't doubt that I could manage to carry off some manner of fabrication. In my several decades of life I had become exceptionally skilled at lies. I was possibly the most easily disingenuous person who was walking the surface of the planet. And yet something caused me to hesitate.

"Well?" Simon said challengingly.

My hesitation fell away and I looked him full in the eyes. "God told me to," I said.

Simon stared at me incredulously and several of them began to laugh. I didn't tolerate it. Instead I turned a harsh gaze on them and said sharply, "Do you find your god's words to be amusing? His chosen messiah to be someone that you would laugh at? I wonder how He would feel about that?"

My tone immediately shut them down. Even Tommen seemed surprised. Simon, however, was hardly deterred. "And in what form did the holy of holies appear to you?"

"A burning bush," I said. I felt awkward in saying so because I was speaking the truth, and doing so was an unaccustomed habit for me. "A burning bush in the desert. He told me," and I paused a moment before continuing, "that I had to do it because I was accidentally responsible for the actual messiah being slaughtered. That would be your child," and I nodded toward Rebeka. "Again, I am sorry for that. It was certainly not intentional, and had I known what you were attempting to do, it never would have occurred to me."

"I still want to know what put that idea in your head," growled Tommen.

Rebeka had not lowered her gaze. Instead it was fixed on me and there was clear astonishment in her voice. "God did," she whispered.

"Oh for—!" Simon began to say.

"No," and her voice became harder, firmer. She was speaking with such conviction that even Simon was silenced. She was still staring fixedly at me. "God came to me in my dreams, while I was pregnant. He told me that it was going to be a boy and he was a child of destiny. He was the one who told me when and where to go after he was born, to the place where she," and she nodded toward Nuskin, "would be. Unfortunately He told me nothing of Apropos being there or what he would do."

"Yes, well, I tend to have a habit of being exactly where I should not be at exactly the wrong time," I said ruefully.

Simon seemed to be having trouble finding what to say. "So you're claiming that you are divinely designated to...what? Free the Shews?"

"Apparently I am, yes. Unless, of course, you kill me. Or her," and I indicated Nuskin. "But the fact of the matter is that if you have any hope of freedom, then you need me, and I need her."

"Why do you need her?"

"Because if I'm going to free you all, I'm going to have to persuade the Rama to listen to me. At the moment he just sees me as a diversion, an entertainment. But if you slay her, then I'm going to be the one who stood there and let his mother figure die. How do you think that's going to fly with him? So my suggestion is that either you kill us both or let us both go. I'm not seeing much middle ground."

I was going all in on a roll of the die that I was not in control of. For all I knew, Simon would be perfectly sanguine with cutting down the both of us and considering it a good day. Perhaps both my head and Nuskin's would wind up being sent back to the Rama as a warning of...of what? Of imminent war? The Shews battling the Rogyptians with their freedom on the line? That did not seem to me the most likely means by which to free them.

Then again, I suppose that I was even far less of a likely savior as far as Simon, at the very least, was concerned.

To my surprise, Simon turned away from me and strode over to Rebeka. He pulled his dagger from his hip and placed it to her throat, which more or less eradicated for me the notion that he was her father, but rather her father-in-law. A father-in-law who seemed at that point quite content with the idea of eliminating his daughter-in-law. "Do you swear," he said, "that what you've told us is true? That God came to you in a vision and instructed you to do what you did?"

"I swear," she said, her voice trembling slightly but holding steady. "I swear on my life, on the life of my husband and my parents. I swear on the soul of my child. What I have said is absolutely true. And if this man says that God appeared to him, then I believe it."

There was dead silence then. It was obvious what was happening: everyone in the room was waiting to see what decision Simon would make about the matter. I did not know if he was officially their leader, but he was certainly someone to whom they listened very closely.

Simon looked at Rebeka, then me, then back to her again. Then he pulled the blade from her throat and I could see a small trail of blood dribbling from where he had been holding it against her. He had not been jesting. He absently wiped the blade clean on the side of his tunic.

"All right," he said as he slid the blade back into its sheath. "What is the plan?"

"You let us go," I said immediately. "I return with her to the palace and inform the Rama that I saved her from a bunch of unknown ruffians. This will earn me his undying gratitude. And I will use that gratitude into manipulating him to making all of you free."

They hesitated to reply. I understood why. It was quite a leap of faith that I was asking them to make. Yet I could see from the eyes of some of them that it had a certain allure to it. I decided to try and push it further down the road. "You must have dreamed of it," I said. "Even slaves have dreams. It's the one thing that the Rama cannot take from you. You must have dreamt about being able to live free of someone telling you what to do. Of walking away from the construction of endless temples and memorials to men who have done nothing with their lives except to stand on the backs of your labors. You must have dreamt about giving a greater future to your children than you have for yourselves. I am here," and I thumped my chest, "to provide you with that opportunity. Because I have a dream as well, my friends." The rhetoric began to soar within me, and for once in my life, I did not feel like a poor peasant bastard. Instead I felt like a king. "I have a dream that on the red hills of Rogypt, the sons of former slaves and the sons of former slave owners will be able to sit together at the table of brotherhood. I have a dream that the state of Rogypt will be transformed into an oasis of freedom and justice. I have a dream that one day every valley shall be exalted, every hill and mountain shall be made low, the rough places will be made plain, and the crooked places will be made straight, and the glory of the Lord shall be revealed, and all flesh shall see it together!"

"Free at last!" cried one of the slaves, and another shouted, "Free at last!" and a third cried out, "Thank God almighty, we will be free at last!"

I smiled then, for I knew I had them. I turned to Simon then and waited for his approval.

Instead he scowled at me, took two quick steps forward and clamped his large hand around my throat. I gurgled in surprise but that was all that I was in a position to do at that moment.

"If you lead these people down a false path," he snarled in my face, "if you make promises of things that you are not able to achieve, I swear that I will hunt you down and send you straight to our God so that you can explain your failure to Him in person. Do you understand me?"

I wasn't able to respond because he was cutting off my air, and I could not nod because my head was clamped in place. So I simply managed to make a soft grunting noise.

That appeared to convey the thrust of my response, because he released his grip upon my throat and I fell to the floor. My staff was still lying there and I used it to shove myself back up to standing.

"Do not lead my people down a false path, stranger," Simon warned me. "If you do, it will not end well for you."

It rarely ends well for me, I thought grimly, but kept that opinion to myself.

Instead I drew myself up as tall and commandingly as I was able and said, "Am I free to leave and take Nuskin with me?"

"Go," said Simon, and then could not help but add, "But if you betray us, I will find you and make you pay for that betrayal."

"Yes, you have made that more than clear. Come," I said to Nuskin and headed for the door.

But then a hand clamped on my shoulder once more. It was Simon, of course, and he said with soft anger, "Do you truly believe that we will simply allow you to leave here and see the whereabouts of this place?"

"I had given it no thought at all one way or the other. If you have to cover our heads yet again, feel free to do so."

As it turned out, that was exactly what they did. They pulled a bag over my head and presumably Nuskin's as well and prepared to lead us out. As they did so, a voice spoke softly in my ear. I recognized it immediately as Rebeka's and she whispered to me, "Avenge my son."

I didn't respond save to briefly nod and then I was thrust forward. I felt something being shoved onto my back and realized that it was my bastard sword. Obviously my belongings were being returned to me, and I at least felt grateful for that.

Now, though, I had a very serious problem. I had talked a good game, but the Shews were going to be expecting results. Which meant that I was going to have to find a way to convince the Rama to release the Shews.

And the truth was that I still didn't have the faintest idea how to do that.

We were walked through the city for a time. I had no clue why no one we passed asked something relevant such as, "Hey, who are those people with bags over their heads?" It almost made me wonder if they had a weaver who had managed to render us invisible somehow. Eventually we were halted and the bags yanked off. I was able to see then that it was night, quite possibly rather late, and there was no one walking the streets. Nuskin was indeed standing right next to me and we stared at each other, scarcely able to believe that our captors had set us free. Without a word the Shews who had escorted us here disappeared into the shadows of the city.

"We're alive," Nuskin whispered.

"Right." I did not whisper. "And now all I have to do is find a way to convince the Rama to free the Shews, because if I don't, they're going to kill us." I had had my back to her, but now I turned to face her. "Is there anything you can do? Do you have any influence over him?"

"None. He reveres me as much as a young man can revere the woman who raised him, but he would not lend an ear to my opinions about freeing the Shews."

"All right, then. So I'll have to come up with something else."

She rested a hand on my shoulder and said, "I have confidence in you."

People tended to say that to me a lot. I wished they would stop saying that because it generally did not end well for them, either.

CHAPTER 7

Sister Act

WE MADE OUR WAY QUICKLY BACK to the palace. As we approached the large entrance, several guards spotted us and immediately ran down the stairs toward us. There was clear alarm on their faces. The moment they drew within hearing range one of the bigger ones said, "We were told that you were kidnapped!"

"Where did you hear that?"

"Ahmway!"

That was news I had not expected. "I thought he was dead!"

"No," said one of the guards, shaking his head vigorously. "No, he survived. The arrow was extracted from his back and, as near as we can determine, did not puncture anything vital. He is weak but very much alive."

"Unless the Rama has slain him," said the other guard. "He was most irate when he heard that you had been kidnapped and his first inclination was to slay the person he deemed responsible for it."

"Well, let's make certain to stop him from doing that," I said.

Quickly we entered the palace and were brought straight to the Rama's throne room. There we waited, glancing uncomfortably at each other, neither of us certain how to proceed. Then the large doors at the far end of the room were thrown open and the Rama entered. There was clear relief on his face when he saw Nuskin standing there. Clearly he had not wanted to believe that she was safe until he saw her with his own eyes. "Nuskin!" he cried out and limped as quickly as he could toward her. He wound up becoming tangled in his own feet and tripped himself, crashing to the floor. Several accompanying guards attempted to reach down and pick him up, but he waved them off angrily. "I can stand! I'm not a child!" he called out childishly and, some moments later, had managed to haul himself to his feet. He stumbled the remaining distance and Nuskin managed to subtly catch him.

The man whom Ahmway had referred to as Mane ran into the throne room as well. There was clear surprise on his face when he saw us. "You are alive!" he exclaimed.

"Yes, it is a nasty habit that I have gotten into," I replied.

"How did you do it?" I noticed that Mane sounded more suspicious than anything else. "We had assumed that we would never see you again."

Nuskin's gaze shifted to me. It was clear she was going to say nothing, but instead simply agree with whatever I came up with.

I saw no point in telling the Rama that the Shews had orchestrated the kidnapping. All that would accomplish would be to harden his heart even further against them. My mind racing, I said, "We were kidnapped by a group of mercenary men. They were Rogyptians, as near as I could determine. They were intending to ransom us. But I was able to get the drop on them and fight our way to freedom."

"You got the drop on them? How?" said Mane suspiciously.

"They thought that they had disarmed me, but as it turned out, they were wrong." I nodded toward the dragon head of my staff and touched a button. The bladed tongue snapped out and the Rama gasped in almost childish delight. "I cut their throats before they even knew what happened."

"Marvelous!" declared the Rama, clapping his hands in joy. "Oh, well done, Apropos, well done! Do you see, Mane? Do you?"

"Very clearly, yes," said Mane. He was now genuinely smiling, and that surprised me greatly. I'd encountered many men like Mane before. Typically they were schemers, always endeavoring to try and figure out how they could usurp power for themselves. In this case, however, he seemed actually happy that everything had transpired the way that I said it had. I wasn't sure if he was intentionally trying to lull me into a false sense of security, or if he truly felt that way. "Well done, Apropos. You are a genuine hero. Nuskin owes you her life."

"And I owe you a debt I can never repay," said the Rama. His smile broadened. "And I know exactly how to reward you. You will be married at once!"

I blinked in confusion. "Excuse me? What?"

Mane likewise seemed confused. "Rama? I am not quite sure I understand."

"My sister!" said the Rama, bubbling over with pleasure. "We have been wondering what to do with her! This is the perfect answer! He can marry her and become my brother in law!"

Nuskin seemed a bit concerned at the notion that I was having my bachelorhood tossed aside by the Rama. "I...am not sure that is wise..."

"He protected you, did he not? He will be able to protect her as well!" He switched his attention back to me. "You have not met her yet, have you? Come! I will introduce you!"

It was one of the few times in my life that I had no idea what to say. My mouth moved but no words emerged.

"Rama," Mane said, "perhaps we should discuss this first..."

"Nonsense!" said the Rama. "This will well attend to my sister and I will no longer have to give her any thought. She believes," and once more he shifted his gaze to me, "that she will be the next ruler of Rogypt after I pass. This will attend to that."

"I don't understand. She is your older sister? Then why is she not the ruler now?"

It was Nuskin who replied: "Because according to Rogyptian law, as long as there is a male heir, it is the male who inherits. Females are shunted aside in favor of the men, always."

"That sounds fair," I said sarcastically. Nuskin could not help but smile, perceiving the tone of my voice.

The Rama, however, took my comment quite seriously. "Yes, isn't it? Thank you for understanding, Apropos. My sister never has. Come. Let us meet her together. She will doubtless be in her room; she is always in her room."

Interlocking his arm through mine, the Rama led me down one of the countless long hallways in the palace. I kept looking at Nuskin in confusion, still uncertain what in the world was happening. I had only met the Rama bare days before. How had he become so enamored of me in such a short time that he wanted to marry me to his sister? None of this was making any sense. Then again, I suppose that when one is dealing with a teen, things don't have to make sense. The fact that he had had the idea at all was enough for him to convince himself in his own mind that it was a superb notion. Perhaps that was all that was required.

"Here," he said, striding up to one ornate door, and he pounded on it authoritatively. "Clea! Open up! I want to introduce you to someone!"

An annoyed teen voice sounded from the other side. "Why would I want to meet someone that you want to introduce me to?"

"Because I am your ruler and I am ordering you to."

There was a brief pause and an aggravated sigh, and then the door was literally flung open. An annoyed teen girl was standing there.

She was the most beautiful young woman I had ever seen.

I could scarcely believe it. I had not been at all sure of what to expect, but it was certainly not this vision of loveliness standing before me.

But her beautiful features were twisted into nothing but irritation. It was almost sacrilegious to see such a gorgeous face have anything save a glowing smile painted upon it.

She stared at me impatiently and it was only then that I realized my jaw had dropped open. I closed it and it made an audible click as it did so.

"Clea," he said proudly, "this is Apropos. Your future husband."

She actually laughed scornfully. It was as if someone had fired an arrow into my chest. "This?" she said dismissively. "Are you out of your mind, Lama? He's ancient!"

I was taken aback by her dismissal. "I'm older than you, I grant that, but I'm hardly ancient."

"I don't care what you have to say," she informed me and then said to her brother, "And I don't care what you have to say, either. You are not going to select my husband for me, and it's of no relevance what y—"

The Rama's cane swung so fast, so viciously, that Clea had no chance of getting out of its way. It slammed across the back of her knee and sent her crumbling to the ground. She cried out, grabbing the injured leg and calling out a list of what I assume to be imprecations so quickly that I could not understand a word she was saying.

The Rama brought his cane around again and slammed it on the floor just to the right of her head. When he spoke his voice was utterly calm. "That could have smashed in your pretty face just then," he said. "Without your face, what would you have then?"

She didn't reply because she was busy gasping in pain as she wrapped her hands around her leg.

"I think you need a further lesson," he said and brought the cane around to strike her with it yet again.

I could not abide his actions any further. As he drew back the cane to bring it swinging down, I grabbed it and yanked it from his hand. The movement was so violent that the Rama stumbled, bereft of his cane, and only the quick action of Mane prevented him from tumbling to the floor. The Rama's head snapped around and he looked upon me with clear betrayal in his face.

I did not hesitate. "No future husband will tolerate a man beating his future wife. Even if that man is the ruler of all Rogypt."

To my surprise, a look of understanding seemed to pass across his face. He then bowed slightly to me and said, "Yes. Of course. Quite right. May I have my cane, please?" and he put out his hand expectantly. Seeing no way around it, I returned it to him. He then said to Mane, "Come. Let us leave the happy couple here to become acquainted with each other."

He then turned away and strode out the door as well as his lame leg would allow. The others followed and the doors swung shut behind them.

Clea was still on the floor, nursing her leg. I walked over to her and stretched out a hand. "Let me help you," I said.

She stared at the hand as if I was cradling a handful of offal, but then she managed to fight down her revulsion and take my hand. I pulled her to her feet and she was clearly favoring the leg that the Rama had just kicked. "Come," I said, "let's get you on the bed." Her eyes immediately narrowed in suspicion and I rolled mine in response. "Just to give you somewhere to lie down. I'm not about to try and..." I couldn't even complete the sentence. I gestured toward the bed and gave her a stern, not the least bit romantic look.

She eased herself onto the bed but was still staring fixedly at me. "My brother could have had you killed for interfering," she said. "That was brave of you."

"I didn't think he would kill his future brother-in-law."

"You thought wrong," she said, her voice flat. "Did you believe that you were the first person he's ever brought to me? He keeps trying to make up for the first one."

"First one?"

Her eyes seemed to drift far away. "His name was Alo. I was fifteen. I loved him more than anything in the world. He loved me. He was the leader of Lama's guard. He asked Lama for my hand. Lama was in a bad mood that day, it turned out, and had him cut down on the spot. He was immediately sorry for what he had done. And so began the endless dance of him deciding that he was going to find a new great love for me. Every six months or so he brings me a new future husband. I never become attached to them because sooner or later, they do something to irk Lama and he has them slain. So whatever protection you feel your status provides you, I can assure you that it does not. Sooner or later, you will die at Lama's hand, and there is nothing that you can do about it." She cocked her head and raised an eyebrow. "What did you say your name was, again?"

"Apropos." I sounded strangled when I spoke because her passionless prediction of my terminal fate was causing me to become choked.

"Hunh." She frowned. "Interesting name. Perhaps you are even an interesting person. Well, it is of no importance. Your fate is sealed and there is nothing you can do to avert it." She nodded toward the door. "You may leave now."

I hauled myself to my feet and started out of the room. But then I stopped and turned to face her. "Just so you know," I told her, "I have no intention of marrying you. None. You are far too much of a child for me. I cannot envision that we would have anything in common. And I will be damned if I allow myself to become related by marriage to your lunatic of a brother. Just so we are clear on that."

Her eyebrows knit together. "Are you aware that I could have you condemned to death for speaking to me in that manner?"

I had absolutely no patience for her at this moment. I walked over to her and practically snarled in her face, "Then do it. Call a guard in here, tell him to kill me, and let us put an end to this idiocy. Because I am unsure of just how long I can tolerate the sustained foolishness of your hatred for me, whom you do not know, and the arbitrary lunacy of your brother. If you wish to terminate my life, then do it. But do not threaten me with it if you are not going to see it through. Is that understood?"

I glared at her and she stared at me with what seemed genuine surprise. I stalked away from her then and to the door, and threw it open. A guard was standing there. I was unclear as to whether his job was to keep others out or her in. He turned and looked at me blandly, waiting for an order, I supposed. Defiantly I looked to Clea and said, "Well? Do you have an instruction to give him?"

I would not have been startled if she had ordered him to slay me right then and there. Instead she slowly shook her head. Deciding not to question my good fortune, I left the room and headed back for my chamber.

It was only when I was well away from her that I began to

tremble violently. Despite my words, I was hardly the bravest of individuals and I did not truly wish to die that day. The fact that I had managed to handle both the Rama and his sister so bluntly and live to talk of it was nothing short of miraculous, and I had no idea how much longer my luck would hold out.

I was tempted to bolt from the palace at that point. No one had been instructed to keep me a prisoner there, so I was reasonably sure that I could get out without being observed. I disliked the notion of fleeing, but this entire business was spiraling out of control. I was no closer to determining how to convince the Rama to set the Shews free, and if that wasn't enough, now I was engaged to a teenager who had nothing but contempt for me. Which I supposed I couldn't blame her for, truth to tell. Still, I was hardly thrilled with being the target of her wrath.

"Apropos!" a voice called from behind me. I recognized it immediately. It was Mane.

I turned and forced a smile, trying to hide any indication that I had been contemplating fleeing the palace. "Mane. It has been an exciting evening, hasn't it."

"It has indeed." He seemed to be studying me with great interest. "Let me walk you to your room."

I was about to tell him that it wasn't necessary, but then a couple of guards stepped out of the hallway behind him and regarded me fixedly. There was no explicit threat here, but implicit? Most definitely.

"The Rama seems to have taken a fancy to you," he said as he fell into step alongside me. I still was not entirely familiar with the massive layout of the palace and so allowed him to guide me. "It is quite impressive. I have never seen him take to any relative stranger so quickly."

"What can I say? I have a way with people."

"Yes, you certainly do. I was wondering if I might be able to ask a favor of you."

"Of course," I said, not really seeing how I had any option to refuse whatever it might be.

"Tomorrow is the anniversary of the death of the Rama's father, the previous Rama. There is to be a ceremony held within the pyramid where his body lies in state. I think it would mean a great deal to the Rama if you attended it with him."

I blinked in surprise. I hadn't been certain what to expect from Mane, but this request seemed rather reasonable. Naturally that was enough to raise my suspicions even more, but I worked hard to keep them in check. "Of course," I said. "I would be honored."

"The Rama will likely be emotionally vulnerable during the visit, so I ask you not to judge him too harshly if he should burst out wailing or have some other unmanly reaction. You'll be pleased to know that your fiancée will be in attendance as well."

"Oh yes. Thrilled to hear that."

"How are the two of you getting along?"

"Wonderfully. Couldn't be better."

He clamped a hand on my shoulder then, and although there was still a smile on his face, there was no affection behind it. "Do not lie to me, Apropos, and I will extend you the same courtesy." He sounded quite formidable, which was something of an accomplishment since he was half my age. "You are not getting on well with the princess because no one gets on well with the princess."

"We are getting on as well as can be expected."

He released his hand on my shoulder and nodded in approval. "That is certainly closer to the truth, I will admit that. All right, then. Who knows? You may accomplish what her previous suitors were unable to do."

"You mean survive?"

He smiled. "That is exactly right. Ah. Here is your room." He gestured and the guards opened the doors for me. "Have a good night's sleep. I'll be leaving these two guards here to make certain that you are not disturbed."

I knew, of course, the actual reason they were going to be there. They were going to make certain that I stayed right where I was. So whatever notions I had of deserting the palace, however fleeting they might have been, were destined to remain exactly that: passing fancies.

I didn't do anything to tip that off, naturally. Instead I bowed slightly to Mane and then strode into my room. The doors were closed behind me.

To my astonishment, Ahmway was sitting in the room. Immediately, albeit slowly, he rose to his feet. There was clear surprise on his face. "You survived! Is that why I have not been executed?"

"I suspect it is. How is it that you are alive?"

"The arrow lodged against my shoulder blade. It was a matter of seconds to pluck it out, but by that time you were long gone." He swung his right arm in a circle and winced. "I've lost some movement in the arm, but I imagine that will pass."

"You are exceedingly fortunate. I'd have to attribute a portion of your still being able to stand here and talk as indicative that the arrow was not very well made."

"That is certainly true."

I crossed the room and sagged into a chair. My weak leg was feeling quite tired. Ahmway advanced on me and demanded, "Was it the Shews? It was, wasn't it."

"Yes. It was."

"And how did you get them to spare you?"

I saw no reason to lie to him. He already owed me his life; I did not think that he was going to turn on me. "By promising that I would convince the Rama to free them."

"That will never happen," he said immediately.

"I am aware of that. And there is every possibility that they are aware of it as well. And if that is the case..." My voice trailed off.

"How long have they given you to accomplish the goal?"

"Nothing was discussed, but I doubt it will be terribly long. So I'll have to move as quickly as possible." I frowned and then said, "Just out of curiosity: what would happen if the Shews were freed? I mean, what impact would it have on Rogypt?"

"We would have no one to build our temples and monuments."

I nodded. "Okay. And?"

"And? What do you mean, 'And?' Isn't that enough of an issue for not freeing them?"

"Well, no," I said, trying to sound reasonable. "So you don't build any more pyramids. I'm not sure how that is a big deal."

"Whenever we built pyramids, the Shews have always done the building."

"If you want them so much, then why can't you build them yourselves?"

Utter confusion crossed his face. "Because we've never done it ourselves. It has always been the job of the Shews."

"Only because they are forced to do it. It isn't as if they are gainfully employed to build these things. And I assume that if they tried to flee Rogypt, they would be hunted down by the army and compelled to return, yes?"

"Of course," said Ahmway with a shrug. "That is the way things have always been since the time of the Moomy."

"Then things have to change," I said firmly, "and I'm going to have to figure out a way to change it." I drummed my fingers on my leg. "I just wish I had the faintest idea how to go about it."

Ahmway said nothing for a moment, and then said, "Perhaps you could blackmail the Rama somehow."

"Blackmail him?" I wasn't certain I had heard him properly. "With what? What would you suggest I threaten him with? What would he care about enough to make certain that no one finds out about it that he would be willing to free the Shews? For that matter, if I did indeed learn of such a secret, what would stop him from having me executed before I could tell anyone?"

"Nothing," Ahmway admitted. "It was a foolish idea, I suppose."

"Then I will just have to come up with a better one," I said confidently. Except, of course, I hadn't the slightest notion what that would be.

CHAPTER 8

Father's Day

I BRACED MYSELF AGAINST THE NARROW, dirty hallway of the pyramid, my heart pounding against my chest. Lama was on one side of me, and Clea on the other. They were as terrified as I was.

From down the corridor, we heard the roar of the creature's voice. It was coming for them.

Briefly I considered the possibility of turning and knocking the two of them unconscious and then fleeing into the shadows. That certainly seemed a reasonable way in which to handle the situation. Before I could do so, however, Clea reached over and wrapped her arms around mine.

"Save us," she whispered.

"Not a problem," I replied, and wondered how in the hell I had gotten into this situation considering the day had started reasonably well...

I did not slumber much after Ahmway left me, and when I awoke I was surprised to see that there was an attractive young woman nearby me. She was pouring water into what was clearly the small in-ground tub a short distance away. She glanced over at me and, seeing that I was awake, simply nodded in acknowledgement of the change in my status.

"Is that for me?" I asked.

She nodded again and gestured for me to come over. I eased

my self out of the bed and walked over to her, swaying slightly on my lame leg.

To my astonishment, she proceeded to remove my clothes. I grabbed her wrists roughly and said, "What are you doing?"

"I am undressing you," she informed me. She had a lovely voice. It was almost musical when she spoke.

"I think I am perfectly capable of undressing myself," I said.

She shrugged, stepped back, and bowed slightly. "I did not mean to offend you," she said. "If you find my presence disconcerting, I will depart while you undress."

"Yes, thank you."

She walked out of the room and I waited until she was gone before I removed my garments. I then eased myself into the water. I had to say, she had done a superb job of warming it. It was wonderfully hot, although not so much so that I found it to be at all scalding.

I allowed the ease to cascade through my body and slowly sank under the water. I floated there for long moments, unable to remember the last time I had felt so relaxed. Then I allowed the water's buoyancy to bring me back to the surface.

I gasped, because the young woman was back. She had disrobed completely and was stepping naked into the bath with me. She was holding some sort of brush in one hand and a cloth in the other.

I tried to say something but opened my mouth too wide and wound up swallowing water and then choking on it. As I desperately tried to compose myself, she moved around to my back. "Just hold still," she said.

"I told you I could bathe myself!" I managed to sputter.

"No, you told me you could undress yourself, which obviously you could. Now allow me to attend to the rest."

"But—"

I was unable to get any other words out because she was already running the brush thoroughly over my back. And somewhat to my surprise, it actually felt quite wonderful. I didn't know whether it was the composition of the brush or the way in which she was holding it, but it was extremely relaxing. I felt as if my body were melting under her ministrations.

"How does that feel?" she asked.

"Good," I had to admit. "Very good."

"I am pleased to hear it."

And then she worked her way around to my front, using the cloth.

I gasped as she put aside the brush and began running the cloth over me. She was half smiling as she proceeded. "You seem tense," she said.

"Well, there's a naked woman in the tub with me," I managed to say, sounding as if someone were throttling me. "That's tensing me up a bit."

"We need to relax you, then."

She set aside the cloth and reached down below my waist.

I let out a loud and extremely unmanly squeak. Obviously, however, she liked what she was feeling. "There you are," she whispered. "Now you're feeling like a man."

"Am...am I going to have to leave money on the table for you?" I said. I was starting to feel a burning in my temple, and other places as well.

"Why ever would you have to do that?"

"I...I'm just not sure what the custom is."

"I imagine it is the same as in other places."

She was nibbling the side of my neck, rubbing against my body with hers. Her breasts were small but quite firm, and her nipples were fully erect. So was I.

"Your body is sufficiently clean," she whispered into my ear. "But now we need to cleanse your soul."

Her body undulated onto mine and I was out of quips and did not even have the energy to push her away from me. Sitting up and facing me, she slid herself onto me and I cried out into her ear. She smiled, sliding up and down upon me, our hips moving in total synchronization. She appeared to be enjoying it and I certainly knew that I was. It had been quite some time since I had been with a woman and this one was certainly more than enough. When I finally exploded within her, I felt as if the top of my head was blowing up. For long seconds I continued and then I remained within her for some time after that.

Finally she disengaged herself from me. "A sufficiently enjoyable bathing experience?" she asked.

I managed to nod. It took me seconds to recover my voice. "Very much so," I finally managed to say. "Quite possibly the best I've ever had. May...may I ask, just out of curiosity...who sent you here?"

"The high counselor, Mane. He said he wanted you prepared for the day." She had clambered out of the tub and had retrieved a large set of towels for me. She gestured that I should emerge from the water, which I did. Ignoring her own wet body, she focused on toweling down mine so aggressively that I felt as if I should be shining when she was finished. Drained of any energy, I fell back onto the bed and stared up at the golden ceiling. I reminded myself to be sure to thank Mane for the young woman, although I was not entirely sure how to phrase it.

She had pulled her simple garments back on, and still had not dried herself off. Her stomach and I assume her back were still lined with water. "Have a pleasant remainder of your day."

"Thank you."

She headed out, leaving me naked on the bed. I reached down and started gathering my clothes, putting them on once more. I couldn't help but wonder if that was how everyone in the palace was awoken on a typical morning.

Minutes later, more servants walked in, carrying breakfast foods. It was mostly vegetarian, with tomatoes, peppers, carrots, various greens and a large glob of what appeared to be white cheese in a bowl. On the side was some manner of flatbread. It was hardly my typical breakfast, but at that point I was so famished that I likely would have wolfed down a pile of sand if they had brought it to me. I devoured it hungrily and washed it down with several swigs of what appeared to be some sort of wine. "Thank you," I said to the servant, who nodded and smiled in a distracted manner but otherwise never spoke. Then again, considering what the previous servant had done for me, he certainly had a hard act to follow.

I emerged from my room and the guards who were standing there—different than the ones I had seen the previous night—bowed to me. "This way," said one of them, and I obediently followed, reasoning that I didn't have a choice. At least I was fully armed, with my sword on my back, my knife on my hip and my staff in my hand.

We passed through the palace and out the back. Certain smells came floating to me and I immediately realized that we were heading toward somewhere that horses were kept. Sure enough, there was a large corral in the back of the palace and I saw that the Rama was already there. He was moving through the corral and endeavoring to interact with quite simply the four most magnificent white horses I had ever seen.

They seemed to have no interest in him. Instead they were firmly moving away from him at the slightest opportunity. He wasn't trying to do anything cruel to them; he was simply trying to pet them, as if they were oversized dogs. But they didn't have the slightest tendency to interact with him at all. They consistently distanced themselves from him.

"Greetings, Rama," I hailed him.

He turned and saw me coming. "Well met, Apropos. I was endeavoring to get a handle on my horses to get them affixed to my chariot, but they do not seem cooperative this morning. Or ever," he added with a slight grimace.

I still had the carrots left over from my breakfast; I had not eaten them but instead shoved them into my pocket to save for later. Seeing an opportunity, however, I leaned over the fence that comprised the corral and extended my hands, filled with carrots, to the horses.

Immediately one of them headed in my direction. Granted, I had always had a natural affinity for animals. I had no idea why, but by and large, they seemed to like me. Except, of course, for that herd of unicorns that had endeavored to trample both the Princess Entipy and me to death, but that was quite a long time ago. Besides, I tended to ascribe that mishap to her presence rather than anything that I had done to provoke it.

Seeing the one horse move toward me, the others followed suit. Within moments they were practically fighting each other to devour the contents of my hand, and when the carrots were gone, they stayed right where they were. I petted them, stroking their lustrous white manes. "They are magnificent," I breathed. "I've never seen the like."

"You never will again. Pure-bred Rogyptian horses," said the Rama proudly. "A gift to me from a distant Sultan. They seem to like you, Apropos. Far more than they like me," he added, his voice taking a slight downturn.

I shrugged. "I just have a lot of experience in dealing with horses."

He pointed to the far side of the corral. There was a chariot there, and it was an impressive vehicle. It was trimmed in gold, and the wheels were huge and solid black. It was quite large for such a vehicle, seemingly capable of transporting at least three individuals. "Do you think you can hitch them up?" he asked.

"I can give it a try, if it would please you."

"It would indeed."

It didn't take me long at all. My typical affinity for animals truly served me in good stead. As little taste as the horses may have had for the Rama, they seemed to take a very quick shine to me, and it was only a matter of minutes to get them hitched up to the chariot. While I was doing so, I noticed that another set of eyes had arrived to watch me go through the procedure: the princess Clea, my "fiancée." She watched silently. I wasn't certain if she was impressed or not, and I certainly knew better than to ask.

Mane joined us moments later, and there was a large, sturdy individual next to him. Mane seemed quite surprised as I strapped the fourth of the horses into its harness. "Rama," he said, "I have brought your charioteer to bring you to the pyramid. But I see you already have the horses ready to go."

"Yes," said the Rama. "Apropos will drive us there."

"He will?" said Mane.

"I will?" I was likewise as surprised.

"Are you capable of steering a chariot?" he asked.

I saw no reason to downplay my abilities. "More than capable, actually. I have some experience." Which was technically true. I had steered horse drawn vehicles on a number of occasions in my life. I had never steered chariots that were identical to the Rogyptian styling, but I reasoned that it was certainly similar to others. All I had to do was maintain control of the team and there shouldn't be any serious issues.

"That's good to hear," said the Rama. He turned to Clea. "Are you coming?"

"Of course," she said.

The Rama made no effort to hide his surprise. "You are? You never come."

"I felt you could use the company." But as she spoke, she kept her gaze fixed on me. It was as if she was assessing me, out here in broad daylight without having our engagement being forced upon her.

As for me, I still had not the slightest interest in wedding her. She was much too young for my preferences. That did not deter me from inclining my head to her in a gesture of acknowledgment. No reason we couldn't all be polite to each other.

Mane bowed slightly and said, "The procession is waiting for you, Rama."

"Excellent."

"Procession?" I said, making no effort to hide my confusion.

"Yes, of course," said Mane as if we were discussing things to which I should readily be privy. "Whenever the Rama goes anywhere, there is always an escort. For security reasons."

"Of course," I said, and I supposed it made a certain degree of sense. Even monarchs who were beloved still took care when

it came to allowing for possible assaults from those who were dis-
satisfied with their reign. And considering that the Rama oversaw
a kingdom where he enslaved a portion of his population and slew
their first-born children, it was logical to ensure that the chances
of attacks upon him were minimized. Then, sounding cautious, I
asked, "Is there a chance of an attack?"

"There is always a chance, but it is very dubious," Mane said
confidently. The Rama nodded as well, apparently satisfied with
that assessment.

With the Rama and Clea in the chariot, I snapped the reins
and the horses immediately set off.

We left the courtyard and rode through the streets of the city.
People spotted us coming and scrambled to get out of the way.
The wheels were large and absorbed the jaggedness of the road,
so the shaking was minimal. I tried to keep my attention focused
forward as we proceeded. I noticed that no one was making direct
eye contact with us. Instead everyone was bowing almost in half
upon seeing the Rama. The youngster in turn bowed and nodded
to his people in response, but every so often I would glance back at
his face, and I saw no warmth in his eyes. He clearly either did not
like, or was disinterested in, the people who were attempting to pay
deference to him. Clea was likewise disinterested, although there
was no hostility in her eyes. She wasn't even looking at them but
instead appeared to be gazing inward, locked in her own thoughts.
I had no idea what those thoughts might be, but she was obviously
fully engaged in them.

There was a trail of soldiers striding quickly behind us. The
reason for their presence was obvious: they were guards for the
Rama. Anyone who might have been foolish enough to attempt an
attack would be cut down before they managed to make it even a
few steps.

I watched the reactions of the crowd as we rolled past them. It
was hard to determine what was going through their minds because
they were resolutely averting their gazes. One man, however, did
not. It was Simon. How he managed to wind up in the crowd when

he should have been slaving to construct whatever in the world the Shews were busy building, I could not begin to imagine. But there he was, and his gaze was not at all lowered. Instead it was fixed directly on me, and he did not seem especially happy to see me. I suppose I couldn't blame him. Here I was, supposedly the best bet for freeing his people from the strictures of the Rama, and instead I was effectively acting as his personal driver. I'm quite sure that didn't go over especially well with him. I could just see him reporting back to the others: "Apropos is serving the Rama. Why did we trust him? He's obviously betrayed us. Let's kidnap him again and next time we send him back one piece at a time." Yes, that was going to go over quite well.

I snapped the reins and hurried the horses along. The Rama nodded approvingly of how I was handling the horses while Clea remained resolutely indifferent. Within moments Simon and whoever else might be with him had been left behind.

We stayed steady on the road and soon we were leaving the vast city behind us. I had to say that I was pleased to do so. Honestly, at that point I was tempted to simply send the horses galloping forward at full speed, find a cliff that I could send them over, leap out at the last moment and watch Lama and Clea plummet to their deaths. That, I dared say, would solve all my problems in one shot. Unfortunately that really was not an option, or at least not one that I was anxious to pursue.

I had no idea where I was going, but the Rama was perfectly happy to guide me in the correct direction. It soon became evident that one of the great pyramids in the distance was our goal. "Your father is entombed there?" I asked.

"And a great many of my ancestors with him," said the Rama. He sounded rather proud. "They rest together, talk together, dine together…"

"Dine?" I shook my head in confusion. "They're dead. What do they need to dine on?"

"The lost hopes and dreams of the Shews, I suppose."

"Well, that sounds charming."

We drew close to the pyramid long minutes later and disembarked from the chariot. The Rama sprung out as quickly as his lame leg would allow him to, and Clea stepped out after him. She continued to seem bored, absorbed instead with whatever was cascading through her head. The convoy drew up behind us and then marched to a halt. They did not seem the least out of breath; I admired how fit they were. I would have been exhausted. Then again, I was hardly someone who could consider himself to be remotely in good shape. I made my way down from the chariot, leaning on my staff as I customarily did.

There was a large archway in the base of the pyramid that seemed to invite us in. The Rama and Clea were heading for it and so naturally I fell into stride behind them. I had to admit to being curious about what I would discover in there, having never had the opportunity to enter a pyramid before.

We entered and I was immediately staggered by the mustiness of the place. Not to sound melodramatic, but I could smell death all around me.

I was surprised, however, that I could see the large chamber that awaited us when we first entered. That was because there was a flaming pit in the dead center of it. It was about ten feet wide and fire was burning across it as if it were a swimming pool filled with flame instead of water.

"Magic?" I asked.

The Rama laughed at the notion. "Magic? No, no, don't be absurd. Natural gas keeps the fire going. It provides us with a means of illumination." He was reaching toward a stone shelf that was off to the side and it had extinguished torches lying upon them. There was a large bucket of pitch nearby them and the Rama shoved the torch into the pitch and then thrust it into the flames. The torch immediately ignited.

Clea and I followed suit and moments later the three of us were slowly making our way forward. There were various chamber entrances to our right and left, and as we passed each one, the Rama nodded to them as if greeting them with silent respect. I have to admit, I admired his dedication to those who came before him.

As we made our way down the hallway, through a series of corridors that twisted and turned back on each other as if we were in a maze, I commented, "I would not be so dismissive of magic were I you. Certainly the curse of the Moomy, of whom I have heard tales, would qualify as magic."

"They are exaggerations," the Rama said as if the tales were irrelevant. "They are nothing to concern oneself about."

I saw a means of entrance there. "If that is the case, then why do you feel the need to perpetuate an ancient law that stems from his threats? What reason is there to slay the first-born sons of all Shews? Certainly they pose no threat, either to you or the people of Rogypt. Doesn't it make sense, then, to remove that law from its place of reverence?"

"I cannot."

"Of course you can. You are the Rama. You can do whatever you wish."

The boy king shook his head firmly. "I promised my father that I would uphold all of the laws, just as he did in his time and his father before him. I cannot simply decide that a certain law be tossed aside because it no longer seems relevant."

"And who would gainsay you? Who would dare?"

Clea chose that moment to speak up. "One must always be cautious of backstabbers. They do not announce their presence, but they linger in the background and wait for the right moment to strike." She actually looked at me as if noticing me for the first time. "Of what concern is it to you? Do you have friends among the Shews who desire you to speak on their behalf? When you and Nuskin were kidnapped, were they Shews who released you in exchange for your efforts to have the laws changed or even have them freed altogether?"

Damnation, but she was fast. She was, of course, absolutely right, but I was hardly in a position to admit that to her. Fortunately enough I was able to lie to her with facility, for I had spent decades lying routinely and thus was exceptionally practiced at it.

"Of course not," I said as if it were the most absurd notion in the world rather than the absolute truth. "I was just thinking aloud, that is all. I have nothing of particular invested in the fate of the Shews. They are a slave race and what happens to them is of no consequence to me. Enslave them, do not enslave them. Kill them, let them live. Either plan does not mean that to me," and I snapped my fingers and praised whatever unnamed god I had encountered in the burning bush that Simon was not around to hear me be so dismissive of his peoples' future.

"Of course he doesn't care, Clea," said the Rama, unknowingly coming to my aid. He dropped his voice to a low whisper. "Do not concern yourself about her words. She is but a female after all and what she says is of no consequence."

Despite his lowered voice, Clea could naturally hear every word he said. Her lips thinned tightly but she did not bother to respond to his charge. For that, I was extremely grateful. Especially, of course, because she was correct in her assumptions, but her brother's arrogance left her assumption behind in the dirt.

"Here," the Rama said abruptly. He had stopped in front of one entranceway that frankly seemed identical to all of the others, but he was clearly quite sure that he was where he was supposed to be. His voice sounded different even though he had spoken only a single word. He sounded hushed, saddened, aware of whose presence he was in. He took a moment and inhaled deeply before striding in. Clea and I followed, her resigned, me dutiful, dwelling on the content of our discussion. It was obvious to me that the Rama clearly wasn't all that fixated on the importance of the law that was sending unknown numbers of Shewish children to their deaths. Obviously I had to be able to use that to my advantage. If I could somehow convince him to step away from the pointless promises that he had made to his predecessors—convince him to stand up for himself and become his own man—I might well be able to turn him around on this business.

We strode into the room in which the Rama's father was entombed. I was surprised to see that he was not within some manner of crypt, unless one considered the entirety of the pyramid to be a crypt. His father's body had been completely mummified. He had been wrapped from head to toe in strips of white linen. "Is that all they do when they mummify you?" I asked.

Lama shook his head. "No, it's an entire process. First they remove your internal organs. Then—"

I put up a hand and kept a smile pasted on my face. "That's... all right. I don't really need to know much more than that."

"It's a very interesting procedure."

"Not that interested."

The Rama shrugged at my indifference and instead went to his father. He wrapped his hand around the hand of the corpse and spoke in a soft, reverent whisper, "I hope you are walking well alongside the gods, father. I am trying my best to rule in the way that I think you would want me to. It is difficult for me having no idea if you approve of the way I'm handling things. If there were only some way that you send me a sign, that would be wonderful."

He squeezed the mummy's hand, which I thought was both kind of sweet and also amazingly creepy.

And suddenly he cried out. "Where did—*ow!*" he shouted and slapped at his hand. I immediately saw why.

Some manner of large, round insect had come out of nowhere and crawled onto the back of his hand. Perhaps it had been residing in or on the mummy and was annoyed by his touching it. Wherever it had originated from, it had scrambled onto the Rama's hand and had apparently bitten him or stung him.

The Rama smacked the creature and it flew off his hand and landed on the mummy. Perhaps offended by the creature's very existence, the Rama swung his cane around and crushed the little beast on the mummy's chest. Apparently the insect had drained some blood from its bite because a small bit of what was clearly human blood spread on the linens. It was not much, perhaps a drop or so. Yet amazingly the linen immediately soaked it up and the blood actually disappeared into it.

"That's odd," I muttered.

The Rama brushed off pieces of the shattered insect from the mummy and retook his father's hand in his and squeezed it once more.

And the mummy squeezed his hand back.

The Rama let out a startled and terrified yell. I was unsure what he was howling about because I hadn't been in a position to see what was transpiring since his body was blocking my view. But then the Rama backpedalled and I saw to my horror that the mummy's hand was still firmly grasping his. As the Rama backed up, the movement brought the mummy to a sitting position.

Clea, upon seeing what was happening, moved much faster than I would have. My instinct was to back up, to retreat, to get the hell out of there. Clea, instead, ran toward the two of them and grabbed the Rama's forearm and wrist firmly. She yanked as hard as she could and the Rama's hand came loose of the mummy. I figured that in causing it to release him, the mummy would simply slump backward on its slab.

Instead it not only remained sitting straight up, but it slowly swung its legs over to the side and stood up.

This caused all three of us to scream, although I'd swear that my voice was of the highest register. The Rama backed up, stumbled, and fell against Clea. She tried to catch him but his weight and backward motion caused the both of them to fall to the ground.

At that moment I wanted nothing more than to flee, to leave them to their fates. But the place was a maze; I was uncertain of how to get out of there. And if this monstrous thing went in pursuit of me, the last thing I needed was to get lost in endless corridors. So my only choice was to bring the Rama and Clea with me, which meant I had to find a way to stop the mummy from advancing upon them.

I thought initially that this was some manner of bizarre and sick joke. That a living person had had himself wrapped up in the linens of a mummy and laid himself upon the slab for the purpose of attacking the Rama, or perhaps giving him a heart attack. But as the mummy rose from its slab, some of the linens that covered its face fell away and I was horrified to see the drained and eyeless face of the dead Rama visible beneath it. Although its mouth was still covered with the bandages, I was able to hear a deep, meaningful growl emerge from somewhere within the creature's chest. Slowly it stretched out its arms, flexing its fingers, reaching toward the Rama.

To my shock, Lama seemed to have recovered his wits. He was gazing in rapt amazement rather than fear at the monster, and he whispered, "He wants to embrace me."

"Are you insane?!" I demanded. "It's a monster!"

"He's my father! He loves me!" said the Rama.

Clea was no more enamored of getting near the thing than I was, but the Rama paid her no mind. He shoved her aside rather roughly and walked toward the towering creature. "Father," he said in a voice filled with awe. "You've come back to me. You've—"

The mummy's hands speared forward and locked onto the Rama's throat. Lama tried to keep on speaking, but was unable to as the breath was being choked out of him. He yanked at the creature's hands, trying to pry them off, but was unable to do so.

I did the only thing I could. I lunged forward, yanking out my sword, and swung it blindly. I might well have nearly killed Lama in my attempt to save him, but fortunately enough my aim was true. My blade swung downward and sliced through the mummy's right wrist. It cleaved the hand from it and the hand tumbled free of Lama's throat. Its abrupt unhanding clearly surprised the mummy and it staggered back, releasing the Rama from the grip of its left hand. In what was a somewhat humorous fashion if one was able to maintain one's sense of humor in this situation, the creature reached over to its right wrist with its left hand and felt in the air for the hand that was currently lying on the ground.

The Rama stumbled toward me. Clea was already there, watching the creature with wide eyes, clutching onto my arm and whispering, "Get us out of here, get us out of here."

The creature ignored them. Instead it reached down and picked up the hand, which I could see was still spasming. It held the hand against the wrist and seconds later it was somehow reattached.

"Yes, out of here," I agreed. I shoved the sword back into the scabbard, grabbed up the fallen torch, and moved as fast as I could out of the room. The Rama and Clea were right behind me and, even more problematic, so was the mummy. I had no idea how heavy the thing was, but it seemed to me as if the ground shook from every step it took.

We were out in the corridor and the Rama shouted, "This way!" I wasn't sure that he was correct, but he seemed most determined, and so I felt as if I had no choice but to follow him. Clea was running right alongside him, although I noticed that she had slowed her gait so that she would not be appreciably ahead of him. I was bringing up the rear, looking frantically over my shoulder to check on the mummy's progress.

It was advancing slowly but steadily. Its eyeless sockets were fixed on us and there was no doubt in my mind that if it got its hands on us, it would not hesitate to tear us to pieces.

Lama went to the right, then left, then right again.

And then stopped.

There was a dead end directly in front of us.

"This isn't right," muttered the Rama.

"I thought you knew which way to go!" I shouted.

"I'm being chased by my dead father! Forgive me for getting mixed up!"

We backtracked quickly and got back to where we had entered the dead end. But we had managed to give the mummy time to catch up with us. It wasn't running the way we were, but its slow and shambling gait was implacable. It was about twenty feet behind us and gaining.

"Come on!" I shouted. I no longer cared which way we were going, as long as it was in the opposite direction of the mummy.

We ran blindly down the corridors, moving in one direction and then another almost at random. If we were trying to lose the creature, we didn't seem to be having any luck for it continued to follow us relentlessly. I had no idea how it managed to stay so resolutely on our tail, but it was clearly doing so.

The Rama was staggering even more than his lame leg was responsible for. I caught him from behind as he stumbled and he sagged against the wall. He was clutching at his chest and his breath was coming in ragged gasps. "I just...I need a few moments..."

"We don't have a few moments!" I said in a hoarse whisper.

"Fine. Leave me. Get away while he kills me."

It was a surprisingly noble expression of sacrifice, and I was more than happy to take him up on it. But Clea, damn her, shook her head "no" fiercely. "We are not leaving you behind. You have ten seconds and then we keep going."

The Rama managed a nod.

I braced myself against the narrow, dirty hallway of the pyramid, my heart pounding against my chest. Lama was on one side of me, and Clea on the other. They were as terrified as I was.

From down the corridor, we heard the roar of the creature's voice. It was coming for them.

Briefly I considered the possibility of turning and knocking the two of them unconscious and then fleeing into the shadows. That certainly seemed a reasonable way in which to handle the situation. Before I could do so, however, Clea reached over and wrapped her arms around mine.

"Save us," she whispered.

"Not a problem," I replied, and wondered how in the hell I had gotten into this situation considering the day had started reasonably well.

I heard shuffling at the far end of the hallway. The mummy was almost upon us. I grabbed the Rama and Clea and said, "Go!" and then turned to face the advancing creature. My legs were shaking violently because the thing was striding toward me and I knew that if it got its hands on me, I was dead. I could have stepped aside and let it pursue the fleeing Rogyptians, but for all I knew, it might turn its attention to me and kill me just for being there.

I faced the monster with the torch blazing in my hand. "Come on," I said softly, "come on."

It stood there for a moment, as if expecting some sort of trick and then it came right at me.

I was ready for it and when it drew close enough to grab me, I thrust the torch straight at it.

The linen immediately caught and began to go up. The mummy looked down and began to frantically beat away at the fire. I lunged forward once more with the torch, looking to set its lower body on fire, but the mummy moved with astounding speed and smacked the torch out of my hand. It fell to the ground and rolled away from me. I tried to get to it, but the burning mummy stepped in between, blocking my path to it. It continued to beat away at the flame and it was clearly managing to extinguish it.

"Damn it," I muttered as I turned and ran. Without the torch I now had no illumination, but it wasn't necessary to worry about because I could see the torches of the Rama and Clea ahead of me. I sprinted after them as quickly as my lame right leg allowed me.

The torches ahead of me stopped. I didn't understand why until I drew near them, and then I did.

Through sheer dumb luck, the Rama and Clea had found their way back to the area that had provided us entrance to the inner pyramid. But where it had been open before, a large stone door was in place that blocked our egress.

I heard noises on the other side and realized it was the voices of the guards, shouting at each other. Their voices were muffled, but I was able to make out the gist of what they were saying. They had not placed the stone there to block us in; they were trying to determine a way to remove it. Ultimately, though, who was responsible for the blockage was rather beside the point. The situation we were faced with was that we were unable to extricate ourselves from the pyramid, and the mummy was closing in on us. By the time the soldiers managed to extricate us from our imprisonment, there would be nothing left to rescue.

I spun and saw the mummy striding toward us. It knew that it had us. The Rama and Clea backed up as far as they could and their backs bumped into the door, blocking their way out. The flame pit was blazing nearby and the large bucket of pitch was off to the right.

My mind racing, I did the only thing I could think of: I grabbed up the bucket of pitch. It was horrifically heavy and I grunted as I lifted it, but fortunately enough the strength in my arms served me well. The mummy drew closer, closer still, and with a prayer for accuracy in my aim, I hurled the bucket of pitch directly at the creature.

The gods, or God, or whatever were with me, for the black, foul stuff struck the mummy directly and spilled all over its upper body. The mummy let out an angry roar as its white linen became soaked with black. The pitch dribbled down its torso and legs. It was enough to halt its forward motion briefly as it clawed at the pitch, trying to remove it from its body.

I circled around the flame pit to the far side and held my staff up as if it were a javelin, balancing it carefully, having a care as I moved since I wasn't using it to support my lame leg. The mummy saw where I was standing and advanced on me.

Timing it perfectly, I hurled my staff. The mummy, seeing it coming, raised its arms as if to brush it aside, but it misjudged my target. Instead my staff struck between the creature's legs, causing it to trip. It stumbled forward and plummeted directly onto the fire pit.

I swear, it was as if the flames leaped up to greet him. Doubtless it was the pitch that served to attract them, or perhaps they simply recognized a soul that was destined for the pits of hell and were simply eager to drag it down to its final destination. Whatever reason it may have been, the flames wrapped themselves around the mummy within seconds. The mummy lurched upward, trying to climb out of the fire pit. I stumbled around it and fell to the floor on top of my staff, and then slammed my good foot forward into the creature's "face" as it had managed to climb halfway out of the pit. The mummy fell backwards, its arms waving frantically, and it unleashed a roar of protest that I will carry with me to the end of my days. The creature was now an inhuman torch, its arms thrashing about, and I was sure that it was feeling no pain because it was incapable of doing so. It was, however, royally angry that such an unseemly fate had befallen it, and were it capable of emerging from the pit and wreaking vengeance upon me, it would unquestionably have done so.

But it was unable to because its legs burned away before its torso did. As its ability to support itself dissolved, its upper half sank downward into the flames, and within seconds the rest of it had been burned…well, "alive" is probably not the best way to phrase it, but it was certainly incinerated. The last thing I was able to see was the creature's face, or whatever the remains of it were, as it sank into the flaming pit with a look of pure dead fury upon it.

I lay upon my staff, gasping for air. I could not believe that I had accomplished it; that I had managed to defeat the thing. It was damned near heroic, and that was certainly not a condition to which I was accustomed. I was no hero. I was Apropos of Nothing who, when confronted with some sort of imminent danger, typically found a way to distance myself from it as quickly as possible. Yet here I had actually rescued the Rama and his sister, my supposed fiancée. I tried to clamber to my feet but the strength in my legs went out as the nearness to an abrupt death that had tried to befall us landed squarely on me. In other words, the pure panic that I had managed to bottle up so that we could survive rebounded upon me and I lost all my energy, to be replaced by violent shaking and trembling. It was going to take me some time to recover from our major brush with mortality.

Then Clea was standing by me and helping me to my feet. I managed to get my budding panic under control and allowed her to get me standing. "Are you okay?" I asked her.

She was staring at me with open wonderment. "You risk your life to save ours, and all you do is ask if I am okay?"

It didn't seem like too much of a big deal to me. I knew that I was fine, so there was no harm in offering police social graces and asking after her state of being. I shrugged. "Just checking."

To my utter astonishment, she reached up and brought her lips to mine. It was a rather clumsy kiss as kisses went. I suspected she did not have an extended amount of experience at it. But I gamely stood there and allowed it to run its course. When she broke for air, I could see that she was continuing to gaze at me with what might well have been pure adoration in her eyes.

I thought, *Damnation. The stupid teenager is falling in love with me.*

This was simply not grief that I needed. She was of more use to me when she made it clear that she was not remotely interested in wedding me or even spending time with me. If she came to see me as a hero, if she fell in love with me...

That was when I thought, *Well, now, wait a minute. What would be so wrong with that, really? If I do wind up wedding her, if I become the brother-in-law to the Rama, would that not elevate me in power? Despite what Ahmway said, I very much doubt that the Rama could just dispose of me if I was literally part of his family. And once I was in a position of power, how much easier would it be for me to change the laws from within? My gods, this could actually work. A brother to the Rama—not literal, but close—would have much more influence than an outsider. Of course, it might well initially cause me to lose credibility with Simon and the others, but surely I would be able to make them understand.*

And yes, she is less than half my age, but it isn't as if I am forcing myself on her. Instead she is somewhat forcing herself on me.

I managed to pry her off me and I forced a smile. "Thank you, highness," I said to her, endeavoring to sound subservient. "That was very kind of you."

Now on my feet, I went over to the large stone that was blocking our egress. I look it up and down and determined quite quickly that this was no random block of stone that had dropped down by happenstance. "This is a door," I said firmly. "Something caused it to slide into place. Something..." and then I paused. "Or someone."

"Who would have wanted to trap us in here?" said Clea.

The Rama had the immediate answer. His voice was flat and

angry. "Whoever it was that somehow brought that mummy to life. This entire thing was a trap. When I get out of here, I'm going to launch a full investigation. Whoever was responsible for this is going to pay with his life."

"I like your thinking," I said. I was continuing to inspect the area around the door. If there was one thing I was familiar with, it was hidden passages and hidden doors. The first one I had encountered was when I was quite young, serving as a squire in the court of King Runcible. There was a secret door that led down into the King's wine cellar and I had availed myself of its contents on numerous occasions. Since then I had had a knack for discovering such hidden entrances in many of the castles that I had had reason to reside in over my life. I applied that knowledge to the situation now as I ran my fingers over the bricks that served as the entranceway. It took me only a minute to discover one brick that was unaligned with the others. I pushed in on it and was immediately rewarded with an internal clacking noise from the wall. Seconds later the door slowly rolled upward and the light shone in from outside. I never thought I would be so happy to see the broiling sun of Rogypt as I was at that moment. The Rama let out a sigh of pure joy and Clea wrapped both her arms around mine as if I were a savior who had led them to the promised land.

As the door slowly rose, the soldiers who had escorted us came charging forward as if they were meeting an enemy in combat. And amongst them, with a look of great concern on his face, was Mane. "Where is the Rama?" he called and then spotted Lama standing there with a smile on his face.

Mane was clearly surprised.

And in that moment, I knew instantly. He was surprised because he had expected the Rama to be dead. Which meant only one thing was possible: Mane had somehow arranged for the mummy to come to "life" and attempt to kill the Rama.

Which meant he and I needed to have words.

CHAPTER 9

Mane Line

I KEPT MY OWN COUNSEL ON the ride back to the main palace. The Rama and his sister, however, did the exact opposite. They leaned against the edges of the chariot and informed any soldier within shouting distance of my epic bravery within the pyramid, defending them against the attempts of a monster to kill us all.

It was nonsense, of course. If I had had a means of escaping by myself and leaving them to their fates, I would have done so in a heartbeat. Unfortunately that had not been an option and so I had basically managed to save myself, and the Rama and Clea had accrued the benefits of being with me when it happened.

As we rolled through the streets, we encountered many of the same individuals that we had passed as we had initially proceeded on our way. During the trip, the Rama repeatedly shouted, "All hail Apropos! All hail the hero who saved your beloved Rama!"

The thing is, when someone riding a chariot and who is your absolute ruler shouts orders to you, it is the tendency of all within hearing to immediately obey. So was it in our case as the confused but willing Rogyptians bellowed, "Hail Apropos!" at the tops of their collective lungs. They naturally had no idea of the details as to why they were being commanded, but that was wholly beside the point. The Rama ordered it and he was accompanied by guards, so naturally everyone did what they were told.

Except for Simon. Of course.

I spotted him easily enough as we passed along, and his perpetual scowl was constantly in place. There was actually more to his expression than that: There was pure hatred in his eyes. My becoming a hailed hero was certainly not within the realm of what he had wanted me to accomplish.

I managed to catch his eye and mouthed the words, *Don't worry. It's under control.* Unfortunately I had no idea if he was able to discern what I had said, or if he cared about my sentiments. If he had come to view me as an enemy—admittedly it would not take much to tip him in that direction—I had no doubt that I would wind up being kidnapped again and this time my triumphant return would be as a head stuffed in a bag.

Within the hour we had returned to the palace. Apparently word had been sent forward as to my activities and my status as hero. Yes, everyone "knew" that I had rescued Nuskin, but that accomplishment paled in comparison to having saved the life of the royal family. As I walked through the hallways, everyone I encountered bowed to me and acted in a subservient manner. Even guards who had scowled at me when I had first arrived were now utterly obsequious. I had to admit, it was rather impressive to see this sea change in their deportment. I somewhat liked it.

I made my way back to my chambers and stood there for long moments, wondering what my next move should be. And then, by superb serendipity, my hesitation as to what I should do next was resolved by Mane striding into my chambers, big as life.

"Greetings, Apropos, and congratulations on—"

That was as far as he got before I charged forward and grabbed him by the shoulders. His eyes widened in shock and astonishment, but I did not care about that. Despite the lameness of my leg, my arms were more than powerful enough to deal with Mane as I slammed him up against the wall, shoving my forearm across his throat and causing his breath to choke in his throat.

"You did it," I snarled into his face. "I know you did. You sent that mummy to attack the Rama and Clea. Why do you want to kill them?"

His reaction to my words was extremely important because I was all too aware of the mindset of the type of person I was dealing with. The fact was that many of these sorts of individuals were quite self-obsessed and proud of their ability to deceive others. When confronted with proof of their perfidy, there was always a flash of satisfaction in their eyes that they were unable to hide because they were pleased with all that they had accomplished.

I looked for that now in Mane's eyes.

Instead all I saw was fear and confusion. Borderline panic.

It was possible that he was truly insane. That there was one part of his personality that was operating independently of the other part. But I didn't think that was the case. He might be many things, but totally crazy didn't strike me as one of them.

"What are you talking about?" he managed to say, his voice barely coming out as a hoarse whisper. That made sense, since I was pressing my arm against his throat.

"The mummy that attacked us. You were the one who cast the spell that enabled it to do so."

He barely managed to shake his head in the negative. "I don't know what you mean…I serve the Rama…I would never…I…"

Then his eyes were starting to roll up into his head. He was on the verge of passing out.

I withdrew my arm and stepped back, and Mane sank to the floor, coughing and gasping. He stared up at me in total bewilderment, clearly unable to understand what I had been talking about.

Still, I was not willing to let it go just yet. "Admit it," I said. "You wanted the Rama dead and you wanted me dead. Perhaps you have designs on Clea, perhaps you don't. But you need him out of the way, and if I die as well, so much the better."

"You don't know what you're talking about." His voice was more or less returning to normal. "I have nothing but reverence for the Rama. I have dedicated my life to serving him."

"So you say."

"Yes, so I say. And I have done nothing to undercut that dedication. Whatever you think about me, Apropos, you are wrong."

He removed his hand from his throat and coughed several times to clear it. "I simply came here to congratulate you on your accomplishment. Not to be accused of...of crimes that I could not commit, even if I wanted to. I do not know any spell that could revive the dead. And if I did, I would certainly not use it against the Rama or anyone he cared about."

"Oh really," I said, one eyebrow cocked.

"Yes, really," he said firmly. "I have no idea how in the world the mummy came back to life." Then he paused, frowning. "This may seem like an odd question, but did the Rama bleed on it?"

I was about to dismiss the question out of hand, but then remembered that he had indeed done so. That that large insect had bitten him and, when crushed on the mummy's chest, a small spot of blood had resulted. "Well...yes," I said. "But I do not see what—"

"That's it, then," Mane said immediately. "It must have been part of the curse of the Moomy."

"The Moomy cursed the mummy?" I said with incredulity. "How is that possible?"

"How is *any* of this nonsense possible?" he said. "Who knows how the magic of a wizard works? All I do know is this: many curses are blood activated. That's why I was asking if the Rama had bled upon it. That blood must have triggered the curse. You were lucky to escape alive."

"Lucky," I said shrugging. "One tends to make one's own luck."

"All I know is this: you have narrowly avoided death several times since you arrived here. Whatever gods you have watching over you are doing a superb job." He rubbed his throat once more and then cleared his throat again. "If it is all the same to you, I will refrain from informing the Rama about your assault upon me. I am certain that it was a rather strenuous endeavor and certainly played hob with some aspects of your judgment. Yes?"

"Yes. Right." I rubbed the bridge of my nose, still trying to sort out what sort of miraculous powers this generations-old wizard must have possessed to be able to somehow ensorcel a dead human being to come staggering back to life. "That is very kind of you. It was certainly an unexpected attack."

"Of course it was. Who could possibly anticipate a mummy returning to life?" He clapped a hand on my shoulder. "Thank you again for rescuing the Rama. My thanks, however, will not remotely have to be enough. I am quite sure the Rama will find his own ways to reward you."

"I'm sure he will, yes."

Mane walked out of my room at that point and I staggered over to my bed and fell upon it face first. The mattress beckoned to me and I sighed as I sank into it. I closed my eyes but moments later started awake as a vision of the mummy rampaged through my mind and jostled me to consciousness.

Except it was not moments later. It turned out that I had slept for far longer than I had anticipated, because darkness was crawling across the sky.

Ahmway was standing there, resolutely guarding the door. And even more surprising, the girl who had bathed me in the morning was pouring steaming water into the tub.

"What are you doing here?" It was a general question to both of them.

"I am here to protect you, as I have been assigned to do," said Ahmway.

"And I am here to bathe you," the girl said in that odd combination of chipperness and silkiness in which she customarily spoke. "The Rama wishes for you to be clean tonight."

I stared at her. She smiled.

"Ahmway," I said softly. "I think I would appreciate your waiting outside."

He bowed to me in a most formal manner and exited the room, the large door closing behind him.

"Undress, please," she said.

I quickly did so and, as she gestured for me to do, slid into the tub. Moments later she had dropped her scanty clothing to the ground and eased herself in beside me. She proceeded to wash my back. Then my chest. Then the lower half of my body, and I was not remotely capable of holding back my arousal. Nor did she make the slightest effort to restrain hers as well.

This time there were no doubts, no questions in my mind. I was sitting up as she clambered atop me and began to move slowly but then faster and faster.

The door creaked open at that moment and to my shock and embarrassment, Clea strode in.

I gasped into the girl's mouth (not hard since her lips were atop mine) and I tried to shove her off, but the efforts of the upper half of my body were in direct conflict with what the lower half was in the midst of.

I expected Clea to start shouting immediately. Or to scold me or have a fit or storm out or react in some sort of violent manner. After all, her fiancé was in the midst of having sex with some random slave girl.

Instead, to my utter astonishment, she simply drew closer and cocked an eyebrow. "Continue," she said casually, as if she had walked in while I was reading poetry to a group of children.

"C-continue?" I managed to get out. My voice sounded so strangled it was as if Mane was endeavoring to return the favor of my earlier strangling him.

"Yes," she said and sat down on the edge of the tub. She dangled her legs into the water. "I have never had sex before, and I wish to observed it being done well so I can emulate it. *Is* it being done well?"

"Oh...yes...no complaints," I managed to say. The heat building within me was impossible to ignore.

The slave girl smiled.

"All right, then. Go to."

We went to. The last time I had had sex with people watching, I had been tied to a bed and there was a magic ring on my member. That was certainly not one of my more pleasant memories. This, however, was simply strange. Clea watched with fascination as the girl bounced up and down upon me, her small but firm breasts dancing in front of my eyes. I refrained from sucking on them because that seemed to be a bit much considering we were being observed. I built and built and then exploded into her and she seemed to be quite taken with the moment as well. My head sagged back so limply that I struck it on the flat stone tiling that surrounded the bath and nearly knocked myself unconscious. I managed to hold myself together and the slave girl clambered off me and extricated herself from the tub. I sat there gasping, staring at Clea, who appeared to be taking mental notes of some manner.

"That was satisfactory to you?" she asked after considering what she had just witnessed.

I managed a nod.

"All right. Thank you," and she was addressing the slave girl. "That was very educational."

"I was happy to help, your highness," said the girl, and she bowed to Clea.

And never saw the knife that was in Clea's hand.

"*No!*" I screamed, but it was too late. Clea's hand came down and drove the knife into the slave girl's back. The slave girl gasped and staggered and tried to stand, at which point Clea swung her arm down and around and slammed the blade deep into the girl's chest. It sounded awful, like an overripe melon. The girl doubled over and blood seeped from her mouth. She was utterly stunned, unable to grasp what was happening to her.

The door was thrown open and Ahmway entered. What a sight must have greeted his stunned eyes: Me, stark naked and dripping water, staring in horror at Clea as she yanked a knife clear of the chest of a naked young woman who was also sopping wet.

The slave girl managed one final look at me with a gaze full of confusion and betrayal, and then she toppled backwards. She fell into the large sunken bathtub, splashing water in all directions. Immediately the water in the tub turned crimson as she bled out her life into it.

I said nothing. I was too stunned. I just stood there, staring, leaning against a column to support myself.

"Guard," said Clea. She had not even turned to see who was standing behind her. She just simply assumed that the guard she must have passed when she entered the room had now come into it himself. "Remove this." She tilted her head toward the floating corpse.

Ahmway said nothing but instead simply nodded. I backed up, stumbling over to the bed and sat down upon it. I grabbed up a sheet and wrapped it around my middle as I watched. Ahmway waded down into the water, reached the girl's wrist, and pulled her toward him. There was no sign of movement as the water grew redder with her life's blood. Ahmway drew her to him and picked her up in her arms. She must have weighed next to nothing because he did not so much as grunt as he carried her out of the bath. Without a word he strode out of the room, leaving the door open behind him as he exited.

"How could you do that?" I whispered. I was so appalled by what I had seen that I could barely form the words. "You murdered her."

"Yes. She was a slave. Her life was mine to take as I saw fit."

"No, it wasn't!" I shouted at her. "Slaves are human beings as well! They are entitled to rights! Not to be cut down for doing nothing wrong!"

"She had sex with my fiancé. How is that not wrong?" She sounded utterly innocent in asking the question, as if she could not fathom a response.

"You watched! You sat there and watched!"

"So that I could better serve you on our wedding night."

"But why did you have to kill her?"

"Because," she said so matter-of-factly that I was having trouble believing that we were discussing a cold-blooded murder, "of you."

"Me?"

"Of course you. You were clearly enjoying your time with her. So much so that you would inevitably have been comparing my performance to hers. I have no doubt that she was far more proficient at sex than I would be because obviously she was far more practiced at it. In which case you would inevitably be drawn back to her. Before we are married, naturally you can be attracted to whomever you wish, but afterward that is not permissible. So I decided to solve the problem in advance by removing the temptation. Which I have done."

I could not understand it. "But...she was a human being!"

"No. She was a slave. She owed her life and continued existence to my good graces. If I decided that she needed to die, then she needed to die." She shook her head and actually chuckled. "You really do not understand how things work here in Rogypt, do you?"

"Not how matters of life and death work." I stared in horror at the bath that was filled with red water. I cleared my throat and then said, "Clea, could you...could you leave me now?"

She blinked in surprise and then nodded. "Of course," she said. Then she walked over to me, cupped my chin in her hand, and said, "You just need time to understand the way things are done here in Rogypt. You will adjust."

"And if I don't?"

She smiled. "Why, then I would have you executed, I imagine. But I'm sure it will not come to that." Then she patted me on the cheek, turned, and walked out of the room.

I sat there, shivering violently, trying to process all that I had just witnessed. Was she mad? Was that it? Was Clea simply insane? No, definitely not. There was no hint of madness in her attitude and deportment. She was simply disconnected from the reality of what she was saying. She wasn't attached to the depth of her actions. She had slain poor...

What the hell was her name?

I was appalled that I didn't know that. How could I not know that? I had had sex with her twice. It had been the last thing she ever did before Clea stabbed her to death. How was it that I had never asked her name?

Because she was a slave. You didn't think of her as a person. She was nothing but an entertaining sex toy...

"Stop it!" I said angrily to my own mind. I was furious with myself for even contemplating such a thing. That mindset might have been the Rama's or Clea's, but it was definitely not mine.

Isn't it?

If I could have opened up the top of my head and scooped out the offending portions of my brain with a spoon, I would have done so.

I dressed as quickly as I could and bolted for the door, having no idea where I was going but wanting to get there as quickly as possible. Ahmway was standing there on guard, as always, but I spun and faced him. My lips taut with anger, I said, "I just need some time alone. Stay here."

"But—"

"Stay here, damn you!" I snarled, and Ahmway froze where he was. I had never been more grateful so see another human being not moving.

I started walking. I had no idea where I was going in the vast palace, but I knew I just needed to distance myself.

No. No, I did not. I needed to seek answers to determine how in the world I was supposed to deal with the Rama and his sister. The Rama was detached from people and Clea was just a flat out murderess. For some reason she caused my thoughts to fly back to the Princess Entipy, whom I had initially concluded was murderous and out of her mind. Eventually I had realized that I was wrong, although the reality of the situation—namely that we were related in ways I could not have imagined—surpassed anything I could initially have come up with.

And as my mind raced, I came to the conclusion that there was only one individual to whom I could speak about them. The one who had been with them the longest. The one who had practically raised the Rama from childhood.

Nuskin.

I felt as if I already had a bond with her. We had shared the experience of being kidnapped together, after all. Certainly she might well have some insight into some way of handling these two homicidal youths.

What if she caused it?

I had been walking quite briskly, but that stray thought brought me to a halt. If she had indeed raised the Rama, was it not entirely possible that he had learned many of his attitudes from her? Were there things she had said and done that had put him on this path where he felt more loyalty to ancient prophecies than he did to the lives of his people? Was it possible that she had somehow failed to teach the Rama to think for himself? Was she actually to blame somehow?

No, that was ridiculous.

Wasn't it?

I passed a guard and asked him for directions to Nuskin's chambers. He pointed and indicated that it was down the hall, then a right, then the second door on the left. I nodded my thanks and headed where he had indicated.

Even as I walked, my mind continued to spin. Was Nuskin going to be of any help? Or was I seriously barking up the wrong tree? Was I going to be consulting with the woman who was genuinely responsible for the creatures that the Rama and Clea had grown up into? For all I knew, the act of doing so might trigger some manner of fit or vengeance that she might try to take upon me. Anything was possible.

I put all of that from my mind. I couldn't second-guess my conversation with Nuskin. I saw her as an ally in all of this and I would get myself nowhere if I worried about what she might or might not say.

I got to the door of her chambers. It was closed. I raised my fist to knock upon it, and then from within I heard a female voice cry out in what sounded like pain. I had no idea what was going on in there, but if she was being injured, beaten, perhaps killed, I was not going to accomplish anything by standing around on the other side of the door.

Once upon a time, hearing someone in danger, my instinct would have been to turn and run the other way. Perhaps I might have summoned guards to show up and take care of what was going on. But I had come to like Nuskin, and if she was in some manner of jeopardy and I was on hand to provide assistance, then I was not going to hesitate to do so. In retrospect, that was an alarming development in my personality, but I suppose it could not be helped. Slowly but surely I was beginning to metamorphose into an actual hero.

Naturally the fates, upon seeing this transition in my personality, felt compelled to remind me of the folly involved in such a change.

I slammed my shoulder into the wooden door that prevented entrance into her chamber and at first it held. This surprised me; it indicated that the door was locked. Perhaps her assailant had entered and then bolted it behind him. I struck it again with even greater force and this time the door gave way to my assault against it. The door burst open and I half stumbled into the room, calling out her name even as I reached down to the dagger I kept on my hip. I had not expected to find myself heading into battle and so my bastard sword was back in my chamber, but the knife came with me everywhere. If nothing else, one never knew when one might encounter some bread that required carving.

I yanked my blade from the scabbard and began to shout warnings, to whom I knew not since I had no clear idea what was transpiring. Then I skidded to a halt, realizing my error to my embarrassment, because there were two people upon the bed and they were engaged in the throes of what was obviously heated lovemaking. I could not have misinterpreted the situation more thoroughly, and I have no doubt that my face flushed red with chagrin.

"Sorry," I muttered, and was about to backpedal and vacate the room, leaving it to the pair of lovers upon the bed, when they sat up together and gaped at me. I stared back and my jaw dropped in shock.

One of them was Nuskin, which I suppose I should have realized would be the case.

The other was Simon.

CHAPTER 10

Simon Says

I COULD NOT BELIEVE WHAT I was seeing. The man who had kidnapped us, the man who was threatening to kill us, was in bed with Nuskin? None of this made the slightest bit of sense.

Anger threatened to overwhelm me at that juncture. If I had been wise, I would have sheathed the knife, but wisdom was no longer holding any sway in my mind. I swung my staff around and slammed shut the door as I drew closer, my face twisted in fury. "What was it?" I demanded. "Some sort of tortured joke? The entire kidnapping: you were working *together*? Are you out of your mind, Nuskin?"

"It wasn't like that!" she said, gathering the blankets around herself to protect what was left of her modesty. Then she sighed. "All right, it was like that. But we had to—"

"To what? Trick me? Make me think that Simon and his men were going to kill me?"

"That option is not entirely off the table," said Simon. He had reached for his clothing, which was dangling off the edge of the bed and was slipping it on under the covers. As if I gave a damn what a naked man looked like.

"Oh, shut up," I snarled at him. "You threatened her and didn't mean a word of it. How long have you two been together, eh?"

They glanced at each other. "A year," said Nuskin.

"Year and a half, actually," Simon corrected.

I studied the both of them, endeavoring to get past the anger and try to deal with this logically. "You wanted my aid in convincing the Rama to...what? Stop killing the Shews? Free them, perhaps?"

"That was the plan," said Simon. He clearly was not thrilled to be admitting it, but obviously saw no choice.

"Great plan, that. And it did not occur to you simply to ask me?"

"Of course not." Simon stepped out of the bed and I was reminded just how much bigger the man was than me. If we got into a battle right then, I would not wager heavily on my odds of defeating him. But that did not deter me the slightest in my fit of rage that was directed at him.

"Why not?"

"Because you are a stranger and we had no clue as to your plans."

"Then you could have asked," I said, but I was addressing Nuskin rather than Simon. "You could have inquired as to my intent, instead of colluding with your lover and endeavoring to either frighten or pressure me into acceding to your desires."

"You're right," Nuskin said, lowering her head. At least she had the good taste to seem ashamed. "You are very right. I should not have..." Her voice trailed off and then she turned to Simon. "You need to leave. I need to speak with Apropos alone."

He began to bluster a response, but then he belatedly seemed to hear the determination in her voice and decided to give in to her request. He tossed me one final, annoyed look and then headed out, leaving Nuskin and me alone in her room.

"Would you—?" and she spun her finger in a small circle. Realizing what she wanted me to do, I turned and presented my back to her. I listened as she clambered out of bed and heard the shuffling of cloth as she quickly clad herself. "All right," she said finally and I turned to see that she was attired once more. "So... I suppose we should talk."

"I'm not entirely sure what there is to say."

She didn't seem the least bit put out by my ire. Instead she gestured toward a short couch nearby, indicating that I should take a seat in it. I reluctantly did so, settling in. She remained standing, folding her arms across her breast. "Why did you come here?" she asked.

It took me a moment to remember. "I wanted to discuss the Rama and Clea with you. But it doesn't matter."

"No, it does," she said firmly. She came and sat next to me. "What do you want to discuss about them?"

I hesitated and then decided there was no reason I couldn't be honest, at least about that. I told her quickly what had happened in my chambers minutes earlier. I felt slightly embarrassed over the circumstances of my love-making, but got past that as quickly as I could so that I could focus on Clea's actions involving the slaying of the girl. Nuskin listened to all of it with her face carefully neutral. At one or two points she nodded but gestured for me to continue until I had managed to get through the entire story.

"And so I decided to consult with you," I said finally. "To learn why she would do this. Is she cold hearted? Indifferent? Insane?"

"Some of all three, I imagine," said Nuskin after a few moments of consideration. "She simply does not prioritize human life in the same manner that you or I would. To her, humans exist simply as objects to be manipulated. Do you play chess, Apropos?"

I blinked in surprise over the notion that the game had worked its way here to Rogypt. "Yes, of course."

"When you capture the pieces of other players...when you take them from the board...you are effectively terminating their existence. What else is death, really, except being removed from the board of life? Yet do you ever feel any compassion for them?"

"No. Naturally not. They're just playing pieces."

"Exactly. And I suspect that is how the Rama and Clea view the world around them. They see them as no different from playing pieces to be removed from the board as they see fit."

"But that's ridiculous!" I protested. "Because when you're done playing the game, the pieces just get put back, the same as before!"

"And the Rama and Clea believe that anyone they kill will return in the next life. So that is why they are unconcerned about taking anyone's life now. They just assume that they are sending them on their voyage into their next existence."

"That's insane."

"No, that's their religion."

There was something in the way she said that that caught my attention. "But not yours, is it. You're Shewish, aren't you."

Slowly she nodded. "Yes. I mean, I have never made a secret of it, but it is not something that I typically discuss. It's a subject that the Rama can still be sensitive about, so I try to speak minimally about it."

"And you worked with Simon to try and convert me to your cause."

"From my understanding, you are already converted to our cause," she pointed out. "You said that God spoke to you. Was that simply a lie on your part?"

"No," I said defensively. "Most definitely not. But I still have no idea how to convince the Rama to do what I wish. I had begun to think that perhaps marrying Clea and working my way in from the inside would be the way to go, but now I am not exactly convinced of that."

"It might be a way to proceed," she said slowly.

"Perhaps, but I'm not convinced."

"Do you have an alternative plan?"

I shook my head. "Not really. I was hoping you might come up with something."

"Not readily. I have been an advisor to the Rama for the entirety of his life, and have not yet discerned a means by which I could convince him of my point of view."

"And I'm supposed to?"

She shrugged. "God wants you to."

"It's not as if He's given me any guidance."

"Perhaps He expects you to think for yourself."

"Or perhaps He simply has no idea and expects me to come up

with ideas that He Himself can't even begin to conceive."

"That could be the case. It's impossible to know how He thinks."

I growled low in my throat. The conversation was going nowhere. In fact, it was going in circles. I was no closer to coming to a conclusion than I had been earlier.

"All right, then," I said finally. "I will just have to go with the plan. To join with Clea in marriage and hope that I can use my new position to somehow influence her. But I am not enthused that the plan will succeed."

"Nor am I," said Nuskin.

The way she said that caught my attention. I stared fixedly at her and said, "What do you think will succeed?"

"Honestly?"

"That would be preferable, yes."

She paused and then said, "I think something very bad is going to happen. I think the prophecy is going to come true no matter what the Rama attempts to prevent it. I think the entirety of Rogypt is doomed to destruction, and there is nothing anyone can do to prevent it."

"What a cheery opinion," I said.

She shrugged. "You asked."

"That I did. And you are making me regret it."

She rose from the couch then and patted me on the shoulder. "The best of luck to you then, Apropos. I will be praying for success from you."

"But you won't be counting on it."

"I have learned to count on nothing in my life."

I nodded, then got up from the couch and headed out the door.

As I suspected, Simon was standing not far away.

I stopped walking and we stared at each other. "Well," I said after a time. "Are you here to threaten me once more? Or kidnap me? Or in some other way attempt to make my life more difficult?"

"I am just here to remind you of what you've promised."

"A promise," I reminded him, "that was obtained through

trickery that you and Nuskin and who-knows-who-else con-ceived." I cocked my head slightly. "Do the other Shews know of your alignment with her? Do they know that you sneak into the palace and have your way with Nuskin?"

"Of course they do," he said quickly, but far too quickly for me to readily believe him. I kept my gaze fixed upon him and he veri-fied my suspicion by not being able to hold it, but instead dropping his eyes from mine.

"I doubt that," I said. "Furthermore, do I need to remind you that you are on my territory now. All I have to do is shout loudly that you are threatening me, and guards will show up to apprehend you. I could convince the Rama to have you executed immediately."

"Do it then," he said challengingly. "Do it and prove that your promises mean nothing."

"Oh, my promises mean a great deal. But I never promised to keep you alive."

He began to respond, but then stopped when he realized that I was absolutely right. Then he shrugged. "That is true. Very well. Summon the guards and have me killed. You will doubtless sleep well tonight."

"And I will simultaneously then deprive Nuskin of your pres-ence. You think I would do that to her?"

"I don't know what you would do, Apropos. I'm still waiting to see what steps you will take to keep your promise to us."

I glanced around to make certain that no one was listening, and then dropped my voice to a lower register. "What I have to," I said. "And I expect you to tell the others of your associates to trust me. I don't want to have to worry about being stolen away one night while I am attempting to do my best to free your people."

His jaw twitched slightly in irritation, and then he nodded. "As you wish."

I exhaled slowly. I was actually extremely relieved that Simon seemed to be content in acting in accord with my desires, whatever those might be. But I wasn't about to show it. I felt that that would indicate weakness, and in dealing consistently with Simon, I could only do so if he respected me and my efforts. "Good," I said, as Simon walked away from me without another word.

I sagged against the wall then, unsure of where to go or what to do. I could have returned to Nuskin's room, but I didn't feel as if there was anything else to say to her.

It was at that moment that Ahmway, with remarkable timing, found me in the corridor. "What do you need?" I said, anticipating his desire to bring me somewhere for some purpose.

"The Rama wishes to see you."

"Fabulous," I said. The Rama was absolutely the last person that I wanted to see right then, but I knew that I was not going to be given the option of turning down his invitation.

So I followed Ahmway as he guided me to the Rama's chamber. Moments later I was entering them, struck by the sheer size and majesty of it. I assumed that these were the traditional chambers of the Rama, and I had to say that they certainly had gone out of their way to make them appear as majestic as possible.

The Rama was seated on a smaller version of the throne that was situated in his main room. It was not quite as majestic as the main throne, but it was still sizable and impressive. I could not help but notice that it was sufficiently tall that the Rama's feet did not quite reach the floor. Instead they dangled comically several inches above, and he was swinging them loosely as if he were a child sitting in a chair designed for adults. Which, I supposed, to some degree he was. Mane was standing near him, watching me with what seemed great fascination.

"Apropos," the Rama declared, "thank you for coming. It is time to discuss when you will marry my sister."

"Whenever you wish, Excellency," I replied.

"I was thinking in perhaps a week. I wish to make a vast celebration of it." The Rama was leaning back in his throne, drumming his fingers absently. "The fact of the matter is that there are nearby nations with whom we are not on the best of relationships. I was thinking that it might be wise to use this opportunity to try and solidify relationships with our neighbors."

"That sounds like a plan. Are relationships dubious at the moment?"

"They are always dubious," Mane spoke up. "Rogypt is the mightiest empire in the east, and there are many who are jealous and suspicious of us. So it would benefit us tremendously if we could put an end to that. And we see this wedding as the ideal opportunity to do so."

"All right, then," I said, feeling agreeable. "Make the arrangements and Clea and I will be happy to marry each other and present a united front."

"That is excellent," said the Rama. Slowly he eased himself off the throne and walked carefully toward me. I remained where I was. Once he was within range of me, he made me feel most uncomfortable by throwing his arms around me and drawing me into a fervent embrace. "I am looking forward," he whispered, "to you being my older brother."

"I'm happy to accommodate you, Rama."

The young man smiled up at me, and for a moment I actually entertained the notion that all this might genuinely turn out for the best. If I could manipulate the Rama's obvious affection for me, I might well be able to accomplish the goals that had been set for me. It was entirely possible that I would be able to talk him into freeing the Shews after all. This insane plan might actually work.

Naturally it did not. Naturally it all fell horribly apart, as I should have known it would. I have to think that my advancing years was somehow diminishing my usual and typical sense of belief that the entirety of the world was out to make my life as miserable as possible.

I left the Rama then. Ahmway fell into step beside me and said, "Congratulations," in a low voice.

"Thank you," I said. I was going to ask him why he was congratulating me but then realized it was because I was supposed to be getting married. Foolish of me that I was not considering that something worth being congratulated for.

"The Rama's idea of having all the leaders of various countries here is a good one. The people continue to remain uneasy over our fractious relations with our neighbors. Perhaps he will be able to settle matters."

"That is certainly something to be hoped for."

"But I doubt it."

I frowned at Ahmway. "Why do you doubt it?"

"I just do," said Ahmway, shrugging slightly. "It is not my belief that the Rama is capable of dealing with the other leaders in anything remotely approaching a decent and reasonable fashion. That is my concern. But it is possible that I will be surprised. That we will all be surprised."

And we were. But not in any manner of a pleasant way.

I decided at that point to go to Clea's quarters, and Ahmway led me there. I was beginning to get the hang of where everything was laid out in the vast palace, but it was nice to have Ahmway along to guide me just in case I wound up becoming misplaced.

Moments later I was standing outside her quarters. I cleared my throat and rapped on the door. "Come in, Apropos," her voice floated to me. I cast a glance at Ahmway and then strode in while he remained outside.

She was inside, sitting at a desk, and she appeared to be rendering some sort of drawing upon parchment paper. I extended my neck to see it better and saw that she was making a sketch of me. It was of my head and upper shoulders, and it was not a bad likeness. I said as much.

"Thank you," she said. She placed down the feathered quill she was using to make the sketch and fastened her gaze upon me. "What can I do for you?"

"Your brother is planning our wedding. He wishes us to get married within a week. I was simply checking with you to see if that is satisfactory to you."

"Of course it is." She continued to stare at me for a time and then she interlaced her fingers and tucked them under her chin. "Ask what you want to ask."

"There's no point in doing so. You've already told me why you killed the slave."

"But you don't consider my excuse sufficient."

"And if I say I don't? Will you have me executed for finding fault with what you did?"

She appeared to be thinking about it, which certainly did not sit well with me. "I doubt that I would," she said finally. I took some relief in that, although not much. "I have to admit, I am disappointed. It's odd to feel disappointed. I don't really recall the last time I felt that way, if ever."

"Well then," I said, "perhaps in the future, you want to do whatever you can to avoid disappointing me."

"Either that or you decide that it is far better for you to approve of whatever I do." She gave that some further consideration. "Yes, I definitely think that would be preferable. Does that seem like a reasonable move to you?"

Not remotely.

"In retrospect, it may very well," I said.

She looked me up and down and then asked me the very last question that I wanted her to inquire: "Would you be interested in having sex with me?"

"Wh-what?" In retrospect, I should have been prepared for the question, but I admit that she caught me flat footed.

"Sex. Would you like to have sex? I watched what you did with the slave quite closely and I am reasonably certain that I can emulate her. Or is it too soon?"

That seemed as reasonable an explanation as any. "Yes. Much too soon. And...not only that. I would rather wait until we were married before engaging in that phase of our relationship."

"You would?" She was clearly startled by the decision. "I find that somewhat puzzling. I thought males were always happy and anxious to engage in the practice whenever the opportunity was presented to them."

"Young men, yes. That much is certainly accurate enough. But for someone older, like me...well, we tend to prefer to wait for the right opportunity where our ability to perform will not be in doubt."

"And because it is evening, you are worried?" she asked.

I shrugged. "Something like that."

"Well then," she said, and kissed me upon the cheek, "we can easily wait until some other time when it better suits your body."

"Yes, absolutely," I said, and I immediately knew when I would see her again. She would show up in my quarters in the morning, because the morning hours were when the slave had called upon me, and I had certainly had no difficulties suiting her needs.

So I knew without question that I'd best be somewhere else in the morning.

I had Ahmway wrest me from my slumber an hour earlier than I had awoken the previous day. I cast a quick, longing glance at the tub before deciding that the absolute worst thing I could do was to denude myself in the room. That would only lead to very negative consequences insofar as Clea was concerned.

I decided to go down and speak with the only individuals with whom I felt I had managed to establish a true and solid bond: the team of horses that we had taken to the pyramid. They were wandering around in their corral and seemed to greet me most courteously when I entered. I rubbed their noses and scratched the backs of their heads, mingled with all of them and told them how excellent they were in soft words. Once again it seemed that my affinity for the animals might serve me well. I started to think about ways I might be able to rid myself of Rogypt immediately if I chose to simply go back on my word (a concept I had no trouble conceiving at all) and envisioned myself on the back of one of the horses, galloping away as quickly as I could. I had never ridden the horses for pure speed, but they seemed quite strong and I was sure that if I was astride one of them, I could put this place far behind me most expeditiously. Granted, the Rama would send people in pursuit, but perhaps if I fled after dark I could put much distance between myself and this hell hole before any of them became aware of my departure.

Yes, that was starting to sound like a satisfactory plan.

Of course, that would once again send me directly into conflict with what that god had desired of me, and one did not directly trifle with gods without considerable risk. Which brought me back around to where I was.

"You seem to be enjoying my horses."

I was quite startled by the Rama's voice that drifted in from behind me. I turned and there he was, leaning against the fence. "I have been here for some minutes and you did not notice me. I have never seen anyone so engaged with the horses before."

"I tend to be focused," I said simply.

The Rama stared at me for a time and then said, "Hitch the horses up to the chariot. I want to take you somewhere."

I had no idea why, but one did not question the Rama when he issued an order. Quickly as I could, I attached the horses to the chariot and moments later we were riding away from the palace. I was apprehensive because this was a purely spontaneous action on the part of the Rama and so there were no soldiers in escort of us. If the people chose to assault us, I would be the sole means of defense between the Rama Lama and the people, and it was my intent—if it came to that—to get out of the way as quickly as possible.

Fortunately enough, no one bothered to impede our progress, and many bowed as we went past. Also fortunately, we did not go all that far. Within minutes the Rama had guided us to what seemed a large outdoor track of some sort. It seemed by my offhand estimation to be somewhere between four hundred and four hundred and fifty yards around. "What is this?" I asked.

"A practice track," replied the Rama, and he pointed to where he wanted me to guide the chariot. I did so and then Lama carefully stepped down out of the chariot. "Now," he said, "I want you to take them around the track as fast as you can."

"As fast...?"

"As you can, yes," said the Rama. "I want to see what happens when you open them up."

I shrugged but did as he instructed. I kept the horses paused for a moment and glanced down at the whip that was situated near my leg. I decided not to use it. I knew it was traditional, but I didn't understand how inflicting pain or threats of pain on the creatures was supposed to somehow generate obedience and good feelings. "Okay, boys," I said. "Let's work together and impress the Rama."

I snapped the reins and shouted, "Yaaahhh!" because I felt that to impel them to move quickly, I should certainly say *some*thing. The horses immediately understood my intention and leaped forward as one. They did it so violently and efficiently that I almost tumbled backward out of the chariot, but managed to hold on barely enough as the vehicle rumbled forward. I steadied myself, clutching onto the reins, and continued to snap them while bellowing encouragement.

The horses thundered forward, picking up speed with every passing moment. I was pleased to see the increase in their velocity and that I did not have to whip them to encourage it. Their hooves moved in amazing unison; it was as if they shared one mind and were capable of propelling themselves in perfect synchronicity. I was tempted to glance back at the Rama to see whether he approved or not, but I had to keep my attention fixed firmly on what was in front of me.

We covered half the track in what seemed barely more than an eyeblink and then I managed to keep them on course, clutching the reins tightly as they continued to pound their way around. As I approached the point where we had first started, I pulled back on the reins to slow the horses and they obeyed my direction as they gradually came to a halt. The Rama was standing there nodding with what I could only discern as approval. Once the horses had ceased their movement, I used my staff to clamber down from the chariot. First I went to the horses, patting them on the heads and making sure they were not too exhausted and then I made my way over to the Rama.

"That was excellent," he said. "You handled them perfectly. They seem to have bonded with you, Apropos."

Honestly, I thought he was overstating it, but I was not about to disagree with him.

"It is my intention," he continued, "to have a vast chariot race as part of the celebration of your wedding. My team is going to race, of course, and I would be most honored if you were willing to take the reins and ride as my representative."

"That sounds immensely interesting."

"And of course, if you win, I will grant you a reward."

"Really? What sort of reward?"

"Well, I would give you a ping pong. And you can use it to wish for something that I will grant you."

There it was, right there. My means for solving everything. The Rama seemed obsessive about remaining faithful to the spirit of the ridiculous ping pongs, and if he adhered to that, I had him. All I had to wish for was for him to grant freedom to the Shews. If he did that, it would solve the entire situation. His tendency to slaughter their first born sons would be completely moot if he gave them their freedom, because there was no doubt in my mind that once he did so, they would take the opportunity to put Rogypt to their backs as expeditiously as possible. That was the only option that made sense. Why on earth would they remain in Rogypt and wait for him to change his mind and re-enslave them once more? No, they would unquestionably be gone, of that I was certain.

How would the Rama react? Probably not especially well. He would certainly be wroth with me, perhaps even order me slain. That would be something that I would have to deal with, if and when it came. I had to admit, this philosophy struck me as odd. That I was placing the well-being of others over my own. It seemed that perhaps I was losing my touch as a selfish individual. Maybe I was getting too old. Honestly, I had never expected to survive as long as I had, so I supposed that anything was possible.

But he would accede to my request. I was certain of that. Mostly certain of that. Perhaps fifty percent convinced. Which was, granted, not perfect, but at least it was better than what I had at the moment.

"That sounds like an excellent deal, your highness."

"Good. You have two weeks to train the horses."

"I'm getting married in two weeks, then? Not one?"

He nodded. "Mane assures me that that is the fastest that the leaders of other nations can assemble. Messengers are currently heading in all directions with invitations. No one, of course, would dare to refuse being summoned to such a gala event."

"Well, good." Then I glanced right and left as if I was concerned that someone was listening in on our conversation and lowered my voice to emphasize the way that we were speaking in confidence. "You might be able to aid me in that regard, Rama."

"Aid you how?"

"Well, if I am going to be focusing on preparing the team, that is an all day endeavor. Every hour of every day. Even if I am not with the horses at the time, I must be focusing my energies and studying and preparing for the race. It is a very time consuming course of action."

"All right," and the Rama nodded. "I understand so far. How can I be of service, though?"

"Would you be so kind as to talk to your sister and command her to keep her distance from me during the intervening two weeks? She is, I must admit, somewhat enamored with the advent of our upcoming nuptials and is particularly interested in the impending sexual encounter. So she would like to pressure me into servicing her in advance of our marriage and such an assignation would be nothing but a distraction. And I cannot afford to be distracted."

I was pleased to see that the Rama's cheeks actually reddened. Clearly he was embarrassed discussing his sister's sex life. He cleared his throat and said, "I would be happy to give her that instruction."

"I doubt she will be thrilled to hear it."

His face hardened. "I do not care in the slightest whether she is happy to hear my orders or not. If I issue the edict, she has no choice but to follow it."

I was ecstatic to hear that because I had no desire to sleep with the murderous little bitch. I wasn't interested in telling the Rama that, of course, but he was hardly in a position to have to know.

I continued to ride the chariot around the track for a time while the Rama kept watching, and then eventually returned him

to the palace. I assured him that he would not have to accompany
me to future ridings, but he replied that there was nowhere that he
would rather be.

I could have timed down to the minute when he informed Clea
of the new restrictions, because she was banging on the door of my
chambers within seconds after hearing the edict. "Apropos!" she
shouted.

Ahmway was standing nearby the door and stared at me
questioningly. I nodded to him and he opened it. But when Clea
endeavored to stride in, he put out one of his large arms and prevented her from getting more than a foot into the room. She stared
at him with open incredulity. "Out of my way!" she instructed.

"I am under the Rama's orders," Ahmway said calmly.

Her hand flashed, but it was much too slow and Ahmway
was far too skilled a soldier. He intercepted her arm at the wrist,
snagged it, and twisted sharply. A knife slid out of her fingers and
clattered to the floor.

"That was not nice," I said.

Ahmway released her, allowing her to stumble back. She was
shocked that she had been so easily disposed of and dispensed with.
"You...*dare*...?"

"Dare what? Save myself for our wedding night? How is that
daring anything?"

"This is about her, isn't it. About the slave." It was a question
that was not a question, and she already knew the answer.

But I was not about to give her the satisfaction. "Not at all. I'm
sure the Rama told you the reason."

"Some nonsense about horse training."

"It's not nonsense. I have to concentrate, and I cannot have you
distracting me."

"You're lying."

"Believe of me what you wish," I said, "but the Rama's instructions could not have been more specific. I strongly advise you to
attend to them, because it will not end well for you if you refuse
to do so."

"What," and she laughed incredulously. "You think the Rama would discipline his own sister if she—"

"I absolutely believe he would," I told her in a flat voice. I had been lying on my bed but now I rolled off, my feet dropping to the floor. I strode over toward her, keeping my face impassive. "I believe that if you disobeyed him, he would not take it well at all. But we can find out, if you wish. Ahmway," and I nodded toward him, "stand aside. Let her enter. And once you do," I turned to her and continued speaking, "and endeavor to have your way with me, you'd be well advised to kill me. Because if you do not, then I will go directly to the Rama and inform him that his sister both ignored his ruling and may have endangered his desire to win the chariot race. So come if you wish, Clea. Perhaps you are right. Perhaps the Rama will do nothing. There is no way to find out but take the chance."

I folded my arms across my chest and waited for her to advance.

She did not. She stayed right where she was for a long moment, and then she nodded toward me. "As you wish, Apropos. I will keep my distance if it serves you."

"I think it serves both of us."

She spun on the ball of her foot and walked away. Ahmway watched her do so and then turned to me with open incredulity. "I have never seen anyone refuse that girl anything and manage to live."

"I have accomplished a surprising number of things in my lifetime, Ahmway," I said carelessly. "As achievements go, this is truly something of a minor one."

Except I knew that was not the case. For all I knew, on our wedding day, Clea might gut me in my sleep just to avenge herself for my having dismissed her so casually. I certainly would not put it past her.

Anything was possible when it came to my fiancée.

CHAPTER 11

A Bet's a Bet

THE DAYS PASSED BRISKLY AND SURPRISINGLY amicably. Of particular interest to me was the bond that I was beginning to form with the Rama.

The truth was that, insofar as depraved dictators went, the Rama Lama was not really all that bad. Once I was able to carve myself past the arrogant exterior and the sense that everything he said or did was superior to whatever anyone else might say or do, I found that he was actually somewhat easy to talk to. Yes, granted, he was the ruler and did not hesitate to remind anyone within hearing distance of his rank. But once I managed to get beyond that, the Rama was not difficult to be around. He had little pretentions beyond that of the average young teen boy; even less, since he had no dreams of what he would do once he grew up. His life's destiny was already determined by the circumstances of his birth.

It frankly irritated me that I found myself liking the boy. I had to ascribe it to the fact that I myself had never had any children, or at least certainly none that I knew of. So the entire business of father/son interaction was new to me. Many was the time that I had speculated as to what such a relationship would be akin to, and honestly I had never been able to come up with much of anything in terms of imagining it. Now that I was actually confronted with it, I had to admit that it was rather nice. Even pleasant.

Of course, all of that would very likely fly apart the moment I broached to the Rama the prospect of freeing the slaves. He would probably see it as a betrayal of the current relationship. But that could not be helped. I had both made a promise to the Shews and also been instructed to do so thanks to the burning shrubbery in the desert.

What I found interesting was that Mane seemed intent on watching all my interactions. He never once interfered. He was just always nearby somehow, keeping an eye on any time that I was with the Rama. I figured that he was simply being possessive of the boy. That he enjoyed being the main advisor and was not interested in seeing some stranger show up and insert his influence into the Rama's daily interactions. I supposed on some level I could not blame him. I certainly knew how I would react if I was in his position insofar as the Rama was concerned.

Matters shifted abruptly one evening, however, when Mane came to my quarters with a sizable jug of wine in his hand. "We need to get to know each other," Mane announced. Naturally I am always happy to get to know anyone bearing a jug of wine, and I graciously invited Mane to take a seat.

At this juncture the gathering for the wedding was a mere three days away. I was busy appraising all the ways that what I laughingly referred to as my plan could go horribly awry. The first and foremost of them was that I was unable to win the race. That was not an impossibility. I had taken a natural enjoyment and liking to maneuvering the team of horses, but certainly the leaders of the other countries would have their own expert charioteers in the race. Despite the fact that the Rama and I had been working on building a relationship with one another, I did not hesitate to consider the possibility that he would not take a loss well. He might choose to punish me if he felt that I had deliberately not done my best for some reason. That punishment could take the form of anything from cancelling the wedding to cutting my head off. Yes, I liked him well enough; but I was not sufficiently foolish to think that I was invulnerable from his wrath.

Secondly, I might win the race but he could take such offense at my wish that it would bring us right back to the various potential punishments.

So it occurred to me that having Mane on my side in my endeavors would not necessarily be a bad thing.

We drank from the wine, although I was cautious enough to have Mane drink first. I was no fool and was not about to fall prey to poisoned wine. Mane seemed friendly enough, but there were still reasons not to trust him although, as the night wore on, those reasons seemed to dissolve.

Mane seemed mostly interested to find out about my background. I told him as much as I felt comfortable with. I didn't think he was being especially nosy; just conversational. Plus, again, if I were going to be influencing the Rama, it made sense for him to determine as much as he reasonably could about me.

I naturally took the opportunity to find out as much about Mane as I could beyond what I already knew. Unfortunately there was not all that much to learn. Mane remained rather tight-lipped about his history before arriving in Rogypt. "I did much of which I am not proud," he admitted, "and see no reason to dwell on it." I hated to admit it, but I readily understood the attitude. Gods knew that on the ledger of my life, there was certainly an assortment of deeds that I took no pride in, and was disinclined to share my life's story with pretty much anyone.

So we continued to drink, continued to chat, and then he put down his goblet and stared intently at me. "Apropos," he said, "what is your true opinion of the Rama?"

I half-smiled at that. "You truly wish me to answer that? You are his chief advisor. If I say something negative, you will naturally report it directly to him in order to sour me in his opinion."

"You are very wrong, my friend. Completely wrong. You know nothing of me."

"True, although that is mostly because you have told me very little."

"That is correct. Very well," and he looped his hands around his knee. "I shall instead tell you my opinion of him."

"As you wish."

"I believe he is a tyrant."

I have to admit, I must have been visibly startled at the flat pronouncement. "Really?"

"He has an entire race of people as his prisoners. He has no true vision of his own for Rogypt, but instead simply tries to guess what his father would want him to do and then does that. One could argue that he should not be harshly judged because he is so young, but there are plenty of youthful rulers in the world who have far more going on in their heads than the Rama Lama. The longer he is allowed to rule, the more danger and destruction he is going to bring down upon Rogypt."

"How? I don't understand. How is he going to bring danger and destruction down on us?"

"This wedding…this," and he gestured widely as if to encompass the world, "gathering that is impending…it is simply an excuse to gather the leaders of all neighboring countries in one place. Do you not understand the significance of that?"

"Not really, no."

"He is going to kill them all."

I had been drinking a bit of wine when he said that, but it caught in my throat. I almost choked before I managed to recover myself. "Do you know that of a certainty?"

"Not definitively. He has discussed it with me in the abstract. Wondered aloud how simple it would be to just behead everyone who came here. To his mind, all the neighboring countries represent a potential threat to the future of Rogypt, and he reasons that if he simply disposes of them in one fell swoop, then he would effectively secure the future of our land. The alternative would be to execute half of them and keep the rest as hostages to avoid any potential assaults."

"Well, that would certainly be more judicious," I said, making no effort to keep the sarcasm from my tone. "He can't kill them. It would be a complete violation of the rules of hospitality."

"Are those rules written down anywhere? Are they laws of any sort? Is there any manner of punishment that is written down somewhere that would be inflicted on any violators of the law?"

Slowly I shook my head. "None of which I am aware."

"You see the problem then. He feels that the other countries represent a perpetual threat to Rogypt, and who knows? Perhaps he is right. By striking first, quickly and viciously, he undermines the threat."

"He can't be allowed to do that."

"I had the very same thought, but as long as he remains the Rama, the opportunity remains open that he might. Unless something is done about it."

My eyes narrowed in suspicion. "What exactly did you have in mind?"

He leaned forward, his gaze intent on mine. "For whatever reason, the Rama trusts you, Apropos. He believes in you. And he is convinced that you are going to win the chariot race."

"Yes. So?"

"So we can use that."

"Use that how?"

He glanced around as if to make certain that no one was listening in on us. It was a gesture that I had employed myself, usually for effect. But he seemed genuine in his caution. "You need to throw the race."

"You mean lose deliberately?"

"I do."

"But why? What possible reason is there for me to do less than my best?"

"The Rama's greatest weakness is greed. Promise him vast treasures and he will do almost anything to achieve them."

"Why? He has so much."

"There is nothing that attracts the interest of the greedy like more. He wants more, Apropos, and will do whatever he can to achieve it, particularly when it requires no risk for himself."

"What does my losing the race have to do with any of that?"

Mane smiled grimly. "Because he is going to place a bet with Lucy Anno."

"Who is Lucy Anno?"

"Lucy Anno is the ruler of Afrasia," Mane informed me. "She is one of the wisest and most beloved rulers of them all. I happen to know that she has long coveted this land, but she dislikes the concept of war and is disinclined to launch any sort of hostilities against us."

"However..." I prompted him.

"However, Lucy Anno is renowned as something of a bettor woman. Some consider it a weakness and others a strength. She is also known as Lucy Anno the Lucky because she has never lost a bet."

"Never?"

"None of any kind. It is believed that the gods adore her for some reason and always conspire fate to align in her favor. The fact that she is literally unbeatable only provokes people to make bigger and bigger bets with her."

I was beginning to see where the conversation was going. "You want to have the Rama make a bet with her."

"I do indeed," said Mane, bobbing his head in approval that I was ahead of him. "I am going to encourage the Rama to bet his kingdom."

"The entirety of Rogypt?" I was having trouble imagining it.

"His ruling of it. Against a massive fortune in gold and jewels."

"But I thought he already had a fortune in gold and jewels."

"Not as vast as he would like you to think," said Mane. "He lives quite the exorbitant lifestyle and always has. He does not have quite the fortune that he wants all to believe and a massive cash infusion would solve many of his problems. I think he will easily bet his kingship against the money that Lucy Anno has to provide."

"And he's going to make the bet that I will win the race."

Mane nodded. "That is absolutely correct."

"And you need me to lose."

"It does not have to be a huge loss," Mane assured me. "Nothing that will provoke the Rama to retaliate."

"Retaliate. You mean kill me in revenge."

"Well, yes," Mane admitted. "But I assure you it will not come to that."

"You assure me? I don't believe that when it comes to the Rama, there is anything of which you can assure me except that you cannot assure me of anything."

"There is some truth to that," Mane said. "But I can guarantee you that the Rama will make this bet. And if he loses the bet..."

"Then what? Then Lucy Anno becomes the new Rama?"

"Technically, yes. But she will not be inclined to leave Afrasia to take over. So she will place a regent here to run things in her stead."

"A regent." Then, of course, it immediately all made sense to me. "You. She's going to put you in charge."

Mane tilted his head slightly in acknowledgment. "There is no one more appropriate."

"Because you are working with Lucy Anno to establish that the Rama will make the bet. Of course. It's a brilliant scheme. And the only thing that you have no control over is whether I will cooperate or not."

"If you do, I will make it worth your while."

"How?" I said. I did not really care about the answer. The fact was that Mane had delivered himself into my hands. He was a traitor, pure and simple. All I had to do was go to the Rama, inform him of Mane's treachery, and the Rama would have him executed...

Or refuse to believe you.

My inner voice reminded me, much to my annoyance, that there was no predicting exactly how the Rama would react to my news. He might think that I was trying to tear down Mane because I was endeavoring to take his place. He had known Mane for far longer than he had known me, after all. There was no reason at all to assume that the Rama would believe whatever I told him. And Mane certainly knew that. I had no doubt that he would not hesitate to deny any charges that I made against him, and who knew who the Rama would believe?

"How would you want me to?" Mane asked me. I was so lost in my own thoughts that at first I nearly didn't hear him, but then the question caught my attention. "What would you want from me to make it worth your while?"

"Free the Shews," I said immediately. "All of them."

"Done," he said so quickly that at first I thought perhaps he had not actually listened to what I had said. His next words, though, made it clear that he had. "I was already thinking about that, truth to tell. Frankly, I have never been enamored of the situation with the enslaved Shews. Having that many people residing within our borders with enmity for the ruling class. That is simply a revolution waiting to happen. Far better to free them and let them lead their lives. The main activity in which they are engaged is building pyramids and tributes to us, and really, how many do we truly need? We have plenty of room in the existing tombs to lay out the bodies of the next hundred Ramas, so there is no point in keeping them here."

"What about the supposed curse?" I said, clearly suspicious.

He shrugged indifferently. "What do I care what some dying wizard swore? It is nonsense. Slaying harmless first born? Heightening the enmity of their parents as a result? No, to blazes with them. Let them go."

I was having trouble believing that Mane was being completely honest with me. He saw the look in my eyes and immediately discerned what was going through my mind. "You do not trust me."

"I am...skeptical."

"I cannot blame you. Trust me, do not trust me. Do as you see fit. But I know what you are planning to do; it is not all that difficult to figure out. You are assuming that if you win, you will be able to prevail upon the Rama to free the Shews. That will not happen, Apropos. Not ever. The Rama lives in fear to this day of the orders that his father placed upon him. He firmly believes that if the Shews are freed, it will mean the end of his kingdom. He will slay you before he frees them."

"Not if I do it publicly. If he promises publicly…"

"What happens publicly does not matter. The true events that impact on our realm happen in private, and I assure you that even if he promises to free the slaves, you will then be dead before that can happen. And as soon as you are dead, he will retract his promise because he will contend that a promise to a dead man does not have to be maintained."

I wanted to respond but no words came to mind. So I simply sat there and stared at nothing in particular.

To my surprise and mild discomfort, Mane reached over and took my hand. He squeezed it firmly and said, "Promise me, Apropos. Aid me in this endeavor. Free the Shews and rid Rogypt of the oppressive tyrant who rules over us."

"And what will happen to him if he has his throne taken from him?"

"He will retire," Mane said immediately. "He has a smaller home in one of the outlaying areas of Rogypt. He and Clea and, if you are welcome and so inclined, you, will go there and live out your lives in comfort." He paused and when I didn't respond, he said, "It is a good deal, Apropos. A great deal. All you have to do is not do your best, and everyone gets a happy ending."

Slowly I nodded. "It makes a good deal of sense, what you're saying. Of course, it would still mean disappointing the Rama…"

"He is a murderer, Apropos. A brutal murderer who happily enforces some law that results in infant boys being slaughtered. He is the very last person you should be concerned about disappointing."

In my heart, I knew he was right. Still, that image didn't jibe with the young man whom I had come to know over the recent days. But there was simply no denying his homicidal actions. Mane was right about that. There was no trusting the Rama to keep his promises or not kill me.

And would it really be so bad if he were driven out of power?

"What if he refuses to go?" I asked. "There is no guarantee that he will adhere to the terms of the bet."

"Yes, he will," Mane said firmly. "There are some lines that even the Rama will not cross. Because the bet will be made when the other rulers are there, at the grand feast to welcome them. He would not dare to back out of a bet under those circumstances. No one would ever believe anything else he ever said. His effectiveness as a ruler would be over."

It made sense. I considered the situation for a time. Mane said nothing as I just sat there and thought about all the ramifications.

The bottom line was that I was betting the future that I knew against the future that I did not know. Granted, there were unknowns in both realms, but the more I pondered the choice before me, the more that Mane's line of attack seemed to be the most reasonable.

Finally, I spoke.

"All right," I said. "I will do it."

A grin broke across Mane's face. It was doubtless aided by the fact that he was a bit inebriated, but that made it no less sincere. He stuck out his hand and I shook it firmly, and then—to my discomfort—he actually leaned over and embraced me. I patted his back awkwardly. For some bizarre reason it felt like the most natural thing in the world, to be hugging him.

He lingered for a time more, discussing in increasing details the changes he was planning to make to the land of Rogypt once he was effectively in charge. It all sounded rather convincing and I even found myself admiring his enthusiasm somewhat.

Yet I could not help but feel that I was betraying the Rama. Which made no real sense. I was not remotely obliged to be faithful to him, and yet somehow the way in which he had come to admire me and look up to me could not help but appeal to the non-existent father's heart that did not reside within my chest.

The grand dinner was the next evening. It was amazing to me how quickly the two weeks had sprinted past. Granted, one day was very much like the next for me in that my daylight hours were spent in the chariot and my evening hours were mostly occupied with Mane coming over and bringing bottles of wine. We talked long into the night and I found Mane to be continuously engaging and endlessly curious about the adventures that I had had in my life. Over the time we spent together I held nothing back. He seemed so intrigued by everything that I had undertaken that I must admit it was at that point in my life that I truly began to consider undertaking the task that I am now spending my twilight years engaging in: writing down my various adventures for the amusement and edification of future generations.

A solid dozen leaders had shown up over the two days previously. The leaders themselves were assigned luxurious rooms in the palace where they could rest themselves. Their escorts were monumental in number, and a variety of pavilions were set up in the vast flat area surrounding the palace. I would gaze out of the window in wonderment at the impressive number of visitors who had brought themselves to this place, all to witness my damned wedding.

Clea was deeply involved in the wedding plans and so, to my ever-lasting gratitude, had little to no time to come to me and demand that I engage her carnally or in some other method that I did not wish to undertake. Ahmway remained on guard through much of the time; his endurance was quite remarkable. I told him that he was welcome to take time off, but he did not attend my statements. Instead he stayed nearby. I could not help but notice that he seemed suspicious whenever Mane came by, and at one point I asked him about it. I did not tell him about the arrangement that Mane and I had come to in regards to the chariot race, but I probed him about this thoughts regarding Mane.

Ahmway shrugged in response. "I am suspicious of him. On the other hand, I am suspicious of everyone. So you really cannot look to me for a dispassionate assessment of Mane's state of mind."

"Is there anything specific that he has done to encourage the suspicion?"

"Well," he said thoughtfully, "he seemed most interested in ingratiating himself with the Rama once he arrived here. Then again, I suppose he cannot really be blamed for that."

"No, I guess not." I scratched my chin. "All right. Thank you, Ahmway."

He bowed slightly. "Happy to oblige, Prince Apropos."

I stared at him. "Prince?"

"That will be your title, yes? As the husband to the princess?"

It was not something to which I had given any thought at all. "I...suppose so. It sounds awkward."

"You will get used to it," he assured me.

I hoped he was right.

When it came time for the grand banquet itself, I was escorted to a large room that I had not seen before. I could not believe it when Ahmway brought me there; it was the single biggest room I had ever seen in my life, and that included the throne room of the dread Warlord Shank. Honestly, it seemed that in the unlikely event the outdoor festivities were cancelled because of rain, we could have the chariot race inside this room.

I had stopped walking and instead simply gazed ahead in stupefaction. Ahmway gently prodded me at the elbow, urging me to move forward. "Where to?" I asked.

"The head table, obviously," and he gestured toward the far end of the hallway.

We walked past large rows of table on either side. There was a vast assortment of all manners of food spread upon the tables, and people were already engaged in shoving it into their faces. There was lamb, beef, pork. There was what appeared to be pigeon stuffed with rice; lightly grilled stuffed eggplants festooned with onions and green peppers; a tray of baked squash, and at least half a dozen other dishes of which I could not discern the contents.

Not only that, but music was playing courtesy of men on some sort of horns combined with a harpist. And there were women dancing for entertainment. They were scantily clad and were making gyrations with their stomachs that I had no idea women were capable of performing. I felt a stirring in my loins that I promptly endeavored to squelch. This was most definitely not the time to allow any amorous thoughts to cloud my judgment.

The Rama, Clea, and a number of assumed royalty were at the front table. The Rama spotted me en route and gestured for me to come up and join them, and Clea indicated the empty chair next to her that was clearly waiting for me. I nodded and managed a smile and left Ahmway behind me as I made my way to the front. I walked around the back of the table and felt compelled to embrace Clea, who responded with a deep kiss that drew amused "aaaahs" from all around.

The Rama then proceeded to introduce me to the other rulers who were seated nearby. Each of them stood individually and bowed to me, not deeply but more in a matter of making acquaintance. The one who caught my attention, naturally, was the striking woman named Empress Lucy Anno. She was surprisingly tall, near to six feet, with dark skin and a wide smile. Her eyes were hazel and almond shaped, and most striking was her black hair, which hung long and straight, down to her buttocks. When she spoke, her voice was deep and throaty, so much so that for a heartbeat I wondered if she was actually a man in disguise. But her obvious cleavage in the skimpy gold outfit she was sporting, and her clear lack of Adam's Apple, quelled those concerns. "So you are the groom," she said.

"That would be me, yes."

"And may I ask as to how you managed to attain Clea's love," and she nodded toward the princess.

"I am honestly not sure," I admitted. "One day she detested me, and the next she had become enamored of me. I really am unable to explain it."

"My sister has always been someone of swiftly transitory moods," the Rama Lama spoke up. "Frankly, the reason I'm embracing this marriage is so that she will actually have a commitment to someone for once in her life. For all I know, a week from now she'll want out of the marriage, but that won't be so easy a goal for her to achieve. Right, Apropos?" He punched me lightly in the shoulder and laughed, and all the other rulers immediately joined in. I had no idea if they actually thought the comment was funny or if they were simply endeavoring to be polite. Either way, I was not exactly enamored of a round of merriment being directed at me and my future, but I managed to smile and nod and take it in stride.

The rest of the evening went relatively smoothly. Clea insisted upon keeping in physical contact with me the entire time, caressing my hand or resting her hand on my shoulder. The more she did it, though, the more I could not help but worry about what the Rama had said when I first arrived, about her mercurial attitude. I had certainly seen evidence of that myself, and I wondered how long it would require for that to shift to my detriment.

The more I thought about it, the more I became enamored of Mane's scheme to get the Rama out of power. Mane was seated at our table as well, but at the far end, away from most of the powerful people. Nevertheless I could not help but notice that his gaze kept wandering back to Empress Lucy Anno. She, by contrast, was not paying the slightest bit of attention to him, and I had no idea what to make of that. Was she deliberately ignoring him because she did not care about him? Or was it to prevent any possible rumor of there being some manner of alliance between the two that would be certain to warn the Rama? Unfortunately no answer provided itself.

I did my best to remain interested in the discussions as the evening progressed. For the most part I was silent, responding politely to questions that were tossed in my direction but otherwise keeping mostly to myself. Clea was sufficiently effusive for the both of us, reveling in the attention that was being paid her as the forthcoming bride. I suppose that should not have been surprising to me. She had spent much of her life feeling inferior to her brother, the ruler of Rogypt while she endeavored to find various means of keeping herself entertained. Unfortunately part of that pursuit to find endeavors included the slaying of the helpless slave. And that was just one instance that I had witnessed. Who knew what other travesties she had committed in the years leading up to that particular murder.

The more I thought about it, the more my head began to hurt. I could not recall a time where I had so felt myself being torn into so many directions at once. As my head throbbed, I quite legitimately excused myself as feeling a bit unwell. Clea did not even take notice; she was much too entranced with the attention being paid her by the other rulers. I returned to my quarters and excused Ahmway for the night. He wanted to remain there on guard, but I was beginning to feel guilty over the notion that I was taking up so much of his time.

I slumped back onto my bed and simply stared at the ceiling. The race was supposed to be tomorrow morning, and the wedding itself in the evening. So I was spending my last night as a single gentleman. In some societies, that alone would warrant some manner of party with my gentleman friends, but who in the world would I have invited to such a celebration? Ahmway? The Rama? Simon, for gods' sake? No, it was better this way, that I remained with myself and contemplated my intention to lose the race the next day and put an end to the Rama's reign.

Eventually I drifted to sleep, I know not for how long, because I was awakened by a pounding at the door. "Come," I said in a groggy voice.

The door was flung open and Clea ran in. Suddenly I was sorry that I had given Ahmway the night off. He would have managed to chase her away.

I was scarcely able to see her because the room was so dark, and for a heartbeat I was concerned that she could no longer wait for our wedding night and had come to accost me in my semi-slumber.

The moment I saw the agitation in her face, however, I knew that there was something else far more profound on her mind. I was lying naked in the bed and so kept the cover over myself as I frowned and demanded to know what in the world she was doing there.

"My brother is an idiot," she said.

"And you felt that this was the only time you could impart that bit of knowledge to me?"

She wasn't even looking at me. She was so agitated that her gaze was jumping all over the room. She sat on the edge of the bed clearly because she just felt the need to get off her feet. "He made a bet with Lucy Anno, the Empress of Afrasia."

Ah. Obviously Mane's reportage of the scheme had been one hundred percent accurate. But I was hardly in a position to inform her that I knew what had her so upset. So instead I simply shrugged and said, "So? People make bets all the time. It's hardly the sole occupation of fools."

"You don't understand. He bet his kingdom."

I did my best to sound surprised. "His kingdom? What did he bet it on?"

"The outcome of the race that is to be run tomorrow! The one that you are riding to represent him!"

I said nothing for a long moment, as if I was trying to process what she was telling me. "That's madness," I finally told her. "I mean, I will certainly do my best, but I cannot guarantee how the race will transpire. Something could easily go wrong. There is no assurance that I will win."

"Don't you think I know that!" she cried out. "And that does not even take into account the fact that Lucy Anno is notoriously lucky! It is said the gods favor her above all others! Personally," and her voice darkened, "it would not surprise me if she were a witch or sorceress or some sort of magic user."

For me, magic users were generally referred to as weavers since they were capable of manipulating the lay lines that ran invisibly through the world and crafting spells out of them. But I was not exactly in the mood to split hairs about the specifics of magic users with Clea at that moment. "Well, I assure you, Clea, that I will do my absolute best to try and win."

"Forget that! I want you to go to the Rama and talk him out of this foolishness! He will listen to you, Apropos, I swear that he will!"

"I think you are overestimating my influence on him…"

"No, I'm not. He sees you as the older brother he never had.

You can convince him."

I tried to insist that she was overestimating how much he would listen to me, but I was unable to convince her...which is, I suppose in retrospect, somewhat ironic. She wanted me to convince her brother of something and I wound up being unable to convince her that I should not. So ultimately I gave in and she led me over to the Rama's quarters. There were twin guards standing in front of the doors, holding their spears upright, but they did not strike a defensive posture as we approached. "Announce us," Clea said.

One of the guards nodded, turned to the door and opened it slightly. "The princess and her fiancé," he declared.

"Just him," said Clea, nodding toward me. "He wishes to speak privately with his future brother-in-law."

Which, of course, was the last thing I wanted to do, but this wasn't about me, it was about Clea. So I simply nodded and shrugged to the guard.

"Send him in," called the Rama.

I entered. The room was brightly lit; clearly the Rama, unlike me, had not sought the arms of Morpheus. Instead he was seated at a small table and he was drinking something from a goblet. "Apropos!" He waved me over. His voice sounded slightly slurred which indicated to me that he had definitely imbibed more than he should have. Which, considering his age, should have been nothing at all. "Join me!"

"I've really had a bit too much to drink already this even—"

"Join me," he repeated, and this time it was not a convivial invitation. It was clearly an order. I was not being given a choice.

"Of course," I said and walked across the chamber. I dropped into the seat opposite him and watched as he produced another goblet and proceeded to fill it. I had no clue what he was filling it with, but the odor of the grape wafted off it.

"I must be judicious in how much I drink," I reminded him. "I certainly do not wish to wake up tomorrow morning with a hangover."

"Oh, of course not. Of course not. Have to keep you sober. Just have the one," he said and gestured toward the goblet that he had poured for me.

I nodded politely and sipped from it. It burned as it ran down my throat. "So Clea informs me that you have made a bet with another ruler. That you have staked the entirety of your realm on the concept that I will win the race tomorrow."

"Not a concept. A reality. You will win. And I will benefit handsomely from it."

He was speaking with such confidence that it almost crushed me to consider the fact that I was going to lose. "You cannot know that," I said.

"Yes, I can. You are the man who defended Clea and me and saved our lives from whatever the curse was that someone laid upon my father. You can do anything."

"But we don't know that for sure," I said again. "Anything can happen. What if one of the horses injures itself while running? Or if one of the other charioteers slams into us?"

"Then you will handle it," the Rama said with conviction. "I believe in you, Apropos."

"That's very kind of you," I said, fighting to keep the exasperation out of my voice. "But I would like you to reconsider this bet you've made. Call it off."

He stared at me with an utter lack of comprehension. "Why in the world would I do that?"

"Because I may not win!"

"Yes, you will. I know that you will."

"How do you know?"

He pushed his goblet aside and leaned forward, staring at me with determination. "You did not arrive in Rogypt by accident, Apropos. That much has become clear to me. You are here for a reason. And I am positive that this is the reason."

"To win a bet?"

"Yes!"

I shook my head. "As destinies go, it seems rather pathetic, don't you think?"

"Not at all. It's for my benefit, so that automatically makes it wonderful."

It was hard for me to argue with such a fixed attitude, plus my heart wasn't really in it. Nevertheless, I felt obliged to do my best. "I beg you to think twice about this decision."

"Absolutely not," said the Rama. "The decision has already been made. All you have to do is win the race and I will make a fortune from it! If you'd like," and he lowered his voice, "I will even share it with you. Does twenty percent seem like a reasonable division?"

In point of fact, it didn't. I was the one who was doing all the work, after all. He was just going to sit there and watch the race. But I realized it was absurd to argue with him about it because I had no intention of winning. So I simply nodded and smiled.

We continued to chat for several minutes more and then I took my leave of him. Clea was standing outside the door and stared at me expectantly.

I shook my head. "He refuses to back down. He believes I'm going to win the race."

She stared at me for a time and somehow I felt as if she was peering right into my brain.

Then she simply said, "Then you'd better win." And she turned and walked away.

I did not like the implication of what might happen if I did not win. Then again, if she were stripped of her power, what real threat could she be to me?

Then I thought about what she had done to the slave and realized that I did not want to learn the answer to that question.

CHAPTER 12

Chariots on Fire

IT WAS A SURPRISINGLY GORGEOUS DAY in the land of Rogypt. The sun had crept up over the horizon but it was not as blazingly hot as it had been on previous days. The cloudless sky was a dazzling blue. It was almost as if the gods were pleased to see the day's festivities and were providing themselves as clear a view as possible.

I was out early, feeding the horses and interacting with them. They of course had no idea what was going to be asked of them this day, and honestly, neither did I. My mind was still whirling over what was expected of me. The bottom line was that I did not ultimately trust anyone who was asking things of me. Mane wanted me to throw the race, but I had no real reason to believe that he would free the Shews in response. The Rama wanted me to win and had made promises to me of vows that he would keep and money that he would reward me, but there was no way of knowing whether he would keep those vows. And Clea had simply sounded rather ominous in informing me that I would be well advised to triumph. So many people were expecting so many things of me, and ultimately I had no idea which way to turn. I was leaning toward keeping my agreement with Mane, but I could not say I was enamored of the potential outcome.

"So what are you going to do?"

I jumped slightly, the voice from behind me startling me. I turned and saw that Nuskin was standing there. I had no idea how she had managed to sneak up on me so completely, but I didn't dwell on it. I glanced pointedly behind her. "No sign of your boyfriend, I see."

"Do not change the subject," she said brusquely. She walked toward me, her sandaled feet kicking up small bits of dirt on the barren ground. "What are you going to do?"

"About what?"

"About this ridiculous bet."

"Ah. You know about that."

"Everyone knows about that," said Nuskin. There was clear worry in her face. "The Rama is betting his kingdom on your team winning the race."

"I'm very aware of that."

"Can you?" There was no hint of nonsense in her eyes. "Do not give me some easy answer steeped in your own sense of your masculinity. Answer me honestly. Can you win?"

"Honestly? I don't know." I patted the nearest horse affectionately on the nose. "These are good horses, strong and true. They move together well as a team. And I can keep control of them right enough. But I have no clue as to what I will be facing out there. Men of far more experience, most likely." I smiled. "Too bad I couldn't just drug them."

"Pardon?"

"Well, it was quite a few years ago, but I was once in a situation where there was a joust..."

"A what?" She frowned in confusion.

"A series of battles between kni...between warriors. And I wanted to make certain that the warrior that I was assisting would win. So I took the liberty of drugging the horses."

"You drugged them?" She appeared shocked. "You mean you cheated?"

"Well, if you're going to go with the obvious word for it, then yes. I suppose so."

"But how did you drug them?"

"I slipped alcohol into their feed. It was a rather clever strategy when you get down to it."

"But you cheated!"

"Yes, you keep saying that." I made no effort to hide my impatience.

"That was not an honorable thing to do."

"I did not care about honor," I said. "I still don't, particularly. All I cared about was winning, and that was the way to do it. And it worked. So I don't have any regrets on that score."

She was silent for a long moment and then she said, "So why aren't you doing that now?"

Because I'm planning to lose the race. That was the thought that went through my head, but naturally I didn't tell her. "Because those were the actions of my youth. As you say, it is cheating, and the older I've become, the more I've endeavored to turn my back on the habits of my past. So no," and I laughed at the idea, "I have no plans to drug the horses."

"That's very wise," Nuskin told me. "If you are going to win, then it is best that you do it on your own merits." She paused and then said, "I suppose you tried to talk the Rama out of this mad wager?"

"I did, but he wouldn't hear of it. I'm assuming you're opposed to it; have you tried? He might listen to you more readily."

She shook her head. "Believe me, as much influence as I may or may not have over Lama, I am quite aware of the way he thinks. It would never occur to him to walk away from any sort of wager. He would see it as an act of cowardice, and there is nothing more appalling to a teenaged boy than being considered a coward."

I was not entirely sure I agreed. When I was a teenaged boy, I was most certainly a coward and did not especially care who knew it or called me by such an appellation. Then again, I did come from a somewhat unique background. But I didn't feel that this was an argument that I wanted to have with Nuskin. So instead I simply nodded and said, "That is very true."

"Well...best of luck to you, then." She reached over then and patted me on the shoulder. Then she turned and walked away, and I gave her no more thought.

Eventually Ahmway came to me and informed me that it was time to prepare for the grand processional, in which all the riders would assemble at the great ring and engage in one lengthy parade around the track. I had to admit, I was somewhat interested in seeing what this vast track looked like; the Rama had never brought me over to it, preferring me to practice in the area set up behind the palace. I returned to my room and found to my surprise that there was lightweight armor lying on my bed, waiting for me to put it on. I was not sure why in the world I would require armor, but mentally I shrugged it off.

There was a leather breastplate that I assumed would afford me some protection, although I did not know from what, and gauntlets that, once on me, would cover the entirety of my forearms while leaving my hands exposed, the better to manipulate the reins. There was also a plumed silver helmet on the stand. It was long and would encompass the entirety of my head, and there was a purple feather in the top of it. It all seemed a bit ostentatious for my tastes, but when in Rogypt, do what the Rogyptians do.

Ahmway aided me in strapping the armor onto my chest. "I heard about the bet," he said in a low voice.

"Yes, it's becoming obvious that everyone has."

"Of course they have. The Rama told everyone who had a pair of ears."

I rolled my eyes. That was certainly damned typical of him. As if I didn't have enough on my mind, it was likely that every single person in the place knew what was at stake. "Fool," I muttered.

"Why? You're going to win," said Ahmway with confidence that I could only envy.

Once I was armored up, I returned to the horses and strapped them to the chariot. They did not fight me in the least, which I considered a good sign. Ahmway was there assisting me, and once they were harnessed to the chariot, I turned to him and said, "Where am I going now?"

"I'll show you," he said as he clambered up into the chariot. I climbed in after him, snapped the reins, and guided the horses out of the corral.

We made our way through the streets of the city. It was quite an easy endeavor because people scrambled to get out of my way. They undoubtedly recognized the imperial markings on the chariot and must have realized who was driving it.

As Ahmway quietly provided directions, I continued to watch the reactions of people around me. Most of them were Rogyptians, but some of them were Shews, and I could see the looks of hopelessness and despair in their faces. *Be strong. I'm doing all I can to set you free,* I told them silently. Naturally none of them heard me. I was sure I saw a few familiar faces in the crowd, some of Simon's men observing me, but none of them made a move against me. So that was a plus, I supposed.

We rode for about half an hour. Finally: "Up there," said Ahmway, pointing, and I saw what he was indicating. It was an impressive structure, all right. It was a vast, round ring, astoundingly tall, perhaps three stories. If that was all seating area, I was reasonably sure that it could accommodate every resident of Rogypt. People were already on line, crowding into the place. It was a most impressive turn out, although I supposed I should not have been surprised. After all, the leaders of a dozen countries were going to be there, as well as their own Rama, so naturally it made sense that they would turn out.

Some of them spotted me and started making a huge deal about it. The closer I drew, the more they shouted my name and pumped the air in a repeated chant. "A-Pro-Pos! A-Pro-Pos!" Over and over again, as if I were someone famous. As if I were a god.

I had to admit, it felt good.

I supposed that I had to credit the Rama for the spreading of my name and fame. That was certainly amusing, to hear those repeated chants as if I were someone of importance. But I imagined that to the Rama, that was exactly what I was. I was the father figure that he was missing, the elder brother that he never had.

And I was going to disappoint him this day. I was going to

lose and cost him his kingdom.

Ahmway directed me around the back to a separate entrance for the charioteers. I wheeled the vehicle in and the path took me to a set of underground stables. Apparently I was the last of the charioteers there, because the area was already quite crowded. They were all of them dressed similarly to me, in leather armor and helmets. There were great differences in the helmets that I could see; each one was customized, presumably to fit the head of the individual sporting it. None of them even glanced at me, nor at each other. There was no chitchat, no interplay between the charioteers. Each one was busy bonding with his horses, giving them last minute oats or some other means of sustenance. The silence in the room was almost deafening.

There was one who kept glancing over at me. Perhaps he couldn't help it; I certainly was distinctly different from the others since I was the only one walking with the aid of a staff. I nodded in greeting to him but he simply ignored me and turned away. I shrugged it off. There was no point in dwelling on it. I had much greater considerations to worry about.

I lost track of how long we remained in the waiting area. Ahmway had long departed at that point, not seeing that there was any way he could provide any manner of service to me in this place. I instead waited there patiently. The groomsman approached me with bags of feed for the horses and strapped them on so that the horses could enjoy themselves while they were waiting. It seemed a harmless enough endeavor.

Then the keeper of the area clapped his hands loudly, garnering our attention. "All right," he called out. "The procession is about to start. Once the music begins, we will lead you out one at a time until all of you are out and onto the track. Is that understood?" There were silent nods from all around. "Very well. Then let us do this for King, Queen, Rama and country!"

There were ragged if not outright laudatory cheers from all around and then music began to play, blown through what sounded like extended horns. Slowly, one by one, we were guided to the vast double doors that provided entrance to the coliseum.

As big as it had been on the outside, it seemed even larger on the inside. The stands were packed with thousands of people, cheering deliriously. The Rama himself was perfectly positioned in an imperial box that was dead center on the far side, situated right at the front. I would have thought he'd have wanted something higher up so that he could see the entirety of the ring, but no, there he was at the base. He spotted me, probably because he recognized the helmet, which was unique with its purple plume, and he waved at me enthusiastically. I tossed off a salute to him, not being certain what was the proper way to acknowledge a royal huzzah in the land of Rogypt.

Clea was seated next to him, and Lucy Anno was behind him, leaning forward and whispering in his ear. He smiled, clearly liking whatever it was that she was saying to him. Clea, as near as I could tell, did not. She would occasionally glance in annoyance and even borderline anger at Lucy Anno, and said and did nothing to interact with her. I supposed I could not blame her. She saw the woman as a threat, and indeed why should she not? Lucy Anno *was* a threat and Clea knew that all too well.

We slowly made our way around the arena, waving to the people as they howled our names in approval. I heard quite a few "Apropos!" shouts amidst the crowd, and I had to admit, it felt reasonably good. I was not exactly accustomed to having people bellow my name in approval. Usually when my name was being loudly declared, it was by someone who was angry with me for some reason or other. But here, now, people were cheering me. It was a most unusual sensation for me. I felt a swelling in my chest and realized that it was my heart. It was as if it was feeding on the acclaim.

My waves became more enthusiastic. Even the horses seemed to be enjoying themselves. I smiled broadly within my helmet and nodded to people as if I could see them or discern them individually.

I couldn't help but notice the driver who had been glancing at me earlier. He was easy to spot because unlike the other drivers, his armor was dyed bright red, and his helmet matched. The man in red kept his attention squarely on me, and I could not for the life of me understand why. Perhaps he had heard something, perhaps he suspected something. Was he in league with Mane, maybe? That would answer the question. I did everything I could to ignore him because my concentration had to be focused elsewhere.

Finally we made it all the way around the vast ring, having effectively greeted everyone who was there. The starting line was demarcated at one end, and it would also serve as the finish line. We were slated to traverse the ring ten times, and the first one over the finish was the winner. It was fairly straightforward.

From my position, I could see the Rama watching me, waving at me. He was smiling broadly. He had every confidence that I was going to win, and no clue that it was my intention to betray him.

The horses knew that a race was about to start. They were anxious to break into a gallop; they certainly had a sense of competition honed into them. Most of the other horses, save for the red man's, seemed indifferent, even lackadaisical. I did not chalk that up to anything in particular; I had every confidence that once the race began, they would get up to full speed quite quickly.

I became more and more aware of the Rama's attention upon me. And the more I thought about it, the more I considered it...

The more I came to the realization that I couldn't do it.

You have to. You HAVE to. My mind was shouting at me, trying to get me to cooperate with the promise that I had made Mane, and yet somehow I could not bring myself to commit to what I had promised.

Part of it, I suppose, was the way that the Rama kept looking at me in such expectation, certain that I would not let him down. But I had to admit that there was something else involved as well, and that was Lucy Anno, herself. The famed, Lucky Lucy Anno, who was so beloved of the gods that she never lost a bet.

I found that extremely irritating. The notion that the gods felt such a need to insert themselves into our daily existence that they favored this woman so that she was perpetually fortunate? It was bad enough that some god or other had felt the need to address me from a burning bush. But they also felt compelled to always support this particular woman whenever she decided to undertake a bet? That was just exceptionally annoying.

How wonderful would it be if I were able to win this race, and thus effectively spit into the faces of the gods? Would that not be worth it?

And perhaps I could convince the Rama to release the slaves. Anything was possible.

The horses were now all lined up at the finish line. It was everything I could do to keep my team stable; they were so anxious to start running. Their spirits lifted mine. The more eager they were to go, the better it made me feel. "Steady," I called to them. "Steady." There was a whip hanging on a hook to my right, but I left it there. I simply wasn't going to beat the poor creatures to get them to go faster.

The red rider was half a dozen chariots over, but he was still glancing my way. I had no idea why he seemed so fascinated with me, and no answer readily suggested itself.

The Rama stood then and the entirety of the cheering coliseum dwindled to total quiet. The Rama was holding a white handkerchief over his head and the silence seemed to extend for an insanely long time.

And then the handkerchief fell from his fingers.

The horses barreled forward.

I snapped the reins as hard as I could as the horses charged into the race. I suppose I should have developed some sort of plan about how to handle the horses. Perhaps start them at a moderate pace, allow them to conserve their strength, and then have them cut loose toward the end. But my mind was not working that way. All I could think about was to go as fast as I could for as long as I could, and let all of the rest of it play out however it did.

We hurtled around the track as quickly as possible, and as I snapped the reins and urged more speed out of the animals, I started to notice something about the chariots nearest me. The horses were not running in unison. Some of them actually seemed to be staggering, and then to my shock two of the chariots began to skew toward each other. The drivers were visibly yanking on their reins, desperately trying to get the horses back on track, but were unable to do so. Seconds later the two teams collided with each other, the chariots slamming together, the wheels breaking as they crushed together. The horses kept trying to run but instead their legs became entangled with each other and the poor animals collapsed into a massive pile of horse flesh.

I couldn't believe it. I had no idea what in the world had happened.

And then I did.

Instantly.

The horses had been drugged.

It was Nuskin. I had told her what I had done at the joust and she decided to do the same thing to the horses in this race.

Part of me was furious with her for interfering. The rest of me was exceedingly grateful. As the years had passed, I had never accrued any sense of fair play and never hesitated to cheat when and if it could benefit me. Obviously Nuskin felt the same way, and had thus taken it upon herself to assure that the chances of my winning had leapt exceptionally high.

The only problem was that when I had drugged the horses at the joust, it had simply given the knight I was supporting something of an advantage. He still had to disarm and/or dismount the various knights that he had fought. And it had happened over a period of time, so the spectators had assumed that my knight had simply developed impressive powers of combat rather than that all of the opposing horses were off their game. That was not the situation that we had here. All of the horses were running simultaneously, and as near as I could discern, Nuskin had overestimated how much to drug them. Horses were staggering all over the course, stumbling into each other, crashing hither and yon. The entire thing was rapidly devolving into some ludicrous show of who-could-remain-moving-the-longest, and it was becoming clear that the winner of that particular endeavor was clearly going to be me.

Helpers came running in from the sides as the horses continued to bang into one another, dragging the teams by their bridles to the side to clear them from the track. I had already circled the track twice and was embarking on my third go around, and of course my horses were in perfectly fine fettle. Nuskin had clearly bypassed my horses, or perhaps some agent whom she had hired or convinced to do her dirty work had taken that precaution. It certainly became easier for me to make my way around as fewer and fewer other teams took up space.

What the hell are you going to do? That was the question that kept pounding through my mind. As benevolent and well-intended as Nuskin's plan had been, it was insanely unlikely that this mass, staggering mess of horses was not going to garner commentary from the onlookers. Anyone with even half a brain in his head was going to be able to discern that something illicit had been done. And considering that I was the one who was benefiting from it, it would be painfully obvious—at least to them—who was responsible. Which, technically speaking, I was, even though I had done nothing to incite any of this. If an investigation was held, I had to pray that it would not wind up pointing to me. If the suspicion fell upon Nuskin, I would be fine with that. The fool had done nothing to consult with me and so I would not hesitate to throw her in front of her potential accusers and leave them to punish her however they saw fit.

That was when I noticed something that surprised me: the red rider's horses were doing just fine. There was no hint of anything the slightest bit the matter with them. They were pounding around the track as fast as they could and were gaining on me very rapidly.

I snapped the reins, trying to drive the horses faster. But I was unable to shake the red rider, and the closer his chariot drew, the more clearly I was able to discern the markings. The face of Lucy Anno was etched in gold on the front; obviously he was her rider.

And he was shouting at me.

It was nearly impossible for me to make out anything he was saying, but the closer he drew, the more clearly I was able to discern his words. He must have been shouting at the top of his lungs for his voice to carry over the pounding of the horses' hooves.

"I knew you would do this!"

I stared at him, not understanding. My puzzlement must have been evident on my face.

"Don't pretend! You did this! Just like you did before!"

As I did before? *Bloody hell. He knows what I did during Runcible's joust. How in the name of all the gods on Earth could he possibly know that?*

We kept circling the ring. Four times, then five. I could see that the other rulers were angrily arguing with each other, clearly upset that their riders had fallen out of the race altogether. But the Rama and Lucy Anno were both continuing to shout and cheer, the Rama gesturing for me to hurry up.

The red rider was starting to fall behind me, which was good news as far as I was concerned. Apparently the Rama's horses really were the fastest. But then the red rider, who had been following at a relatively safe distance, endeavored to close the gap in what I could only say was a most dangerous fashion. He was drawing nearer, nearer, until he was almost beside me. I continued to snap the horses' reins, trying to urge even more speed out of them. My staff rattled around in the holder strap that I had fashioned in the chariot, keeping it stable. I did not expect to have to use it for anything. At that point in my life, I kept it with me as much as a good luck charm as anything else.

The chariot driven by the red rider hurtled directly toward me. I was horrified to see that he was setting it in a direct collision course. I did the only thing I could think of, which was to yank back on the reins, slowing the horses down. His chariot shot in front of me and quickly I guided the horses to the right, trying to jockey my way around him. But he cut hard back and seconds later our chariots had collided. The horses were running neck and neck, each trying to bypass the other, as our chariots locked, the wheels spinning against each other.

"*Are you out of your mind?!*" I shouted.

"*You're supposed to lose!*" he howled back, and that was when I realized who it was. It was Mane. Mane was driving the official chariot of Lucy Anno. This had gone beyond him endeavoring to foster some sort of bet that would cost the Rama his kingdom. Mane was a full on traitor to his country.

Except it wasn't really his country, was it.

That was when it all became abundantly clear to me. Mane was secretly Afrasian. He must have come to Rogypt at Lucy Anno's behest and had willfully maneuvered the Rama in ways that would serve the interests of Afrasia, up to and including this ultimate plan of causing the Rama to lose his status.

Was the Rama aware that Mane was driving the horses of his arch nemesis? The chances were that he was not. If he were, that would certainly not sit very well with him. On the other hand, if Mane won, then how it sat with the Rama would not matter in the least.

He was doubtlessly expecting me to cut my speed and so disengage us. Instead I did the opposite, snapping the reins in order to get more speed out of my team. He endeavored to do the same thing, using his whip to hammer away at the poor creatures. Our wheels continued to bang up against each other.

And suddenly he turned and swung the whip at me.

It lashed across my chest and I let out a startled cry of pain. Again and again he brought it down on me and I had no choice, I had to yank back on the reins to slow my horses. Our wheels disengaged and he took the lead, and I started snapping the reins again. Gods only knew what the horses thought as I kept sending them mixed messages, ordering them to slow down and then speed up, but I had no choice.

We completed our sixth revolution and I was coming up on him again. He glanced over his shoulder, saw my approach, and cut left to block off my progress. I cut right and so did he, doing everything he could to hold me back. I did the only thing I could think of, which was to tilt my body to the left as if I were going to guide the horses in that way. But at the same time I yanked hard with my right arm, keeping them on their course. My body language fooled him and Mane cut left as my horses galloped to the right. It brought us alongside again and we were pounding around the track as fast as we could muster our animals.

And once again I felt the lash of his whip against my shoulders. Infuriated, I grabbed my staff out from the place where it was attached to my chariot and as he brought his lash around, it wrapped around the upper half, including the head. I pushed the hidden button and the dragon's metal tongue snapped out. I twisted the staff and the knife sliced through the lash, cutting it loose from the handle. Infuriated, he threw the handle at me but I batted it aside.

He angled his chariot toward me once more and he was shouting, *"I was never going to free the slaves, you idiot! I can't believe that you believed me!"*

"I should have known!" I bellowed back at him.

Once more he tried to swing his chariot into mine, but now I had the advantage. My horses picked up speed and I started to pull ahead of him. Within moments I was going to leave him behind.

And to my utter shock, he suddenly looped his reins around the upper part of his chariot and vaulted the distance into my chariot.

He had a dagger in his hand and he attempted to drive it straight into my chest.

Immediately I brought up the staff to block the downward thrust. There was no question in my mind that he was stronger than me, and only the angle of the staff was preventing the blade from striking home. I was pushing back with all my strength. I released my hold on the reins, but fortunately my horses didn't need my guidance to keep running in the same direction.

"You are going to die now," he snarled. "You've had this coming for years."

I was hardly in a position to dispute him, but I certainly didn't have to cooperate with him. Using what little strength I had left, I swung my left foot and knocked him slightly off balance. He stumbled slightly and I was able to actually lift him up and throw him back toward his chariot. He landed in it and his horses swerved from the impact.

The chariots slammed together once more, and while he was scrambling to his feet, I saw my chance. I swung my staff toward him and the metal tongue of the dragon sliced right through the reins. They fell away and he no longer had control of his horses.

My chariot barreled forward as I clutched onto my staff and suddenly I hit something. I never knew what it was, exactly: a rock or perhaps some manner of hole in the path. Either way, the abrupt jolt slammed me to one side and I lost control of my staff.

The metal tongue slammed forward and into the eye of the foremost horse of Mane's team.

The horse screamed. I had never heard an animal scream in such a manner and hope never to do so again.

The horse veered wildly, and the other horses had no choice but to follow it. Mane, no longer having reins to control it, was helpless to do anything except hold on for dear life.

I yanked back on my reins and slowed my horses as Mane's chariot hurtled right past me. The lead horse was out of its mind with pain and it was charging desperately across the track, bringing the others along with it.

I saw where they were heading and watched in horror, unable to do anything except look on.

They were barreling straight toward the seating area where the Rama and his guests were.

Clea and Lucy Anno saw it coming and backpedalled as fast as they could. But the Rama was in his chair toward the front, and his lame leg prevented him from moving quickly. His guards were not near him; instead they were positioned at the back of the box, toward the entrance, presumably to prevent attackers from entering the box and coming at the Rama. So they were caught completely flatfooted.

To the likely astonishment of the horses, I yanked hard on the reins and sent them galloping toward the box, but it was far too late for me to do anything to prevent the impending disaster. At the last second Mane leaped off the chariot and fell to the ground, rolling across the hard ground of the track and narrowly avoiding being trampled to death by the horses of my own team.

The Rama was unable to dodge that fate. The berserk horse team of Mane's chariot crashed through the front of the viewing stand and I saw the Rama's terrified face before it disappeared under the horses' hooves. The horses kept going, stumbling over the Rama and the furniture in there before grinding to a halt because there was nowhere else for them to go. The injured horse was still whinnying terribly and it reared up and slammed down again and again. I saw that its hooves were becoming covered with red and I knew where it was coming from.

I yanked my horses to a halt, grabbed my staff and ran as fast as I could to the seating area. Onlookers from all sides were screaming, shielding their faces so that they could not see what was transpiring, although others were gazing raptly. No one, I noticed, was endeavoring to help him.

I snapped out the blade of my staff and started hacking away at the harnesses that bound the horses together. It took long seconds but eventually I managed to cut the injured horse loose from its mates. It twisted around and I was able to dodge back just in time as it trampled its way through the debris and stampeded out into the track. The other horses, now separated from their mate, seemed to calm down and simply stood there as if waiting instructions.

I clambered over the destruction and found the Rama. His poor body had obviously been crushed and yet, to my utter astonishment, he was still conscious. He wasn't looking at anything in particular; instead his eyes were staring blankly upward. I wasn't even sure he understood what had just happened. He was doubtlessly in shock.

I dropped to my knees next to him and cradled his upper body. He stared up at me and his gaze focused on me. When he spoke, blood welled up from between his lips and his voice came out as thick and hoarse.

"*Did you win?*" That was all he said.

"Yes, Rama. I won. You beat Lucy Anno the Lucky. She has to pay you a fortune."

"*I knew you would,*" he managed to tell me. There were tears in his eyes and they dribbled down his face.

He was a murderer. There was no question of that. He had thoughtlessly applied laws that slaughtered who-knew-how-many innocent children, and he had thought nothing of it. He was, at his heart, a creature with no conscience whatsoever. And yet I could not help but feel sorry for him as his soul slipped away from him and escaped his body. The boy died in my arms and I did not sob over his passing, but I mourned it nonetheless, for all that he might have been able to accomplish if he had only been allowed to survive.

And then the fury within me began to build.

It was Mane's fault. All his fault.

Slowly I lowered the Rama's dead body to the ground and then stood. I scanned the track and saw that Mane was right where he had leapt out of the back of his chariot. I immediately saw the problem: he had broken his leg in the fall. It was sticking at an odd angle. Two doctors had come running out to him and were tending to him.

I clambered out of the box and started toward him, running as best I could. There was fury on my face and the doctors saw it as I approached. Apparently it was intimidating enough that they stepped back, clearing a path to what was my obvious focus.

The crowd had fallen eerily silent. They must have known that the Rama had died. Perhaps they were too stunned to believe it. Or maybe too joyful or unsure of how they should react lest angry guards wind up striking down anyone who celebrated.

The doctors came toward me, trying to stop me in my tracks. They had no success. As lame as I was, my pure anger overcame any hesitation that my body might have instilled, and I shoved them aside. Mane saw me coming. He had removed his helmet, or perhaps the doctors had removed it, and when he perceived my approach he tried to reach for it, presumably so he could slap it back on his head to afford him some protection. That was not an option I provided him as I swung the bottom of my staff and knocked the helmet away from him.

I had retracted the dragon's tongue back into the head of my staff, but that did not make the staff any less lethal if it was employed with striking force. That was exactly what I did as I swung it down and around and struck Mane in the side of the head just as he was starting to sit up. The impact was a most pleasant loud "thunk" as it impacted with his right temple and knocked him backward. Blood and skin flew and now there was a large gouge in the right side of his head. Head wounds tend to bleed very easily and this was no exception as the red fluid cascaded down the front of his face. He tried to wipe it from his eye and was only partly success-ful. "Wait," he tried to say.

He was once again trying to sit up. I shoved the bottom of my staff forward into his chest. The impact was more than enough to knock him back. He cried out and I was sure I heard a rib break from the blow. He sobbed. I loved the sound of him suffering.

The doctors tried to approach me but I froze them with a look and they quickly backed off. They were healers, not fighters, and neither of them was remotely interested in taking me on at that moment. That was very likely a wise move on their part.

"You killed him," I whispered. "You killed the Rama. That was your plan all along, wasn't it."

"Are you out of your mind?" Mane managed to ask. He winced as he spoke, his drawing in breath causing great pain in his chest. I hoped one of his broken ribs was stabbing him in the lung. "You're the one who caused me to lose control of the chariot!"

"After you tried to kill me!"

"It was the race! I did what I had to do!"

"And now I'm doing what I have to do." I slammed my staff down upon his chest again and he shrieked. I could not begin to imagine the amount of pain that he was in. Actually I was beginning to worry that he was in so much agony that his brain might overload and not allow him to feel any. But his moans dampened that concern, at least for the time being.

"You coward," snarled Mane. He spat out a glob of blood. "You couldn't even race me fairly! You had to drug the other horses!"

He was wrong about that, but I was not about to finger Nuskin for what she had done. "What are you talking about? Your horses were fine!"

"Of course they were. I knew what you were likely to do and made sure to monitor everything they ate! I fed them myself from my own private stock of feed that you could never get to!"

"What made you think I would do such a thing?"

"Because you did it before! At a joust!"

There was no way he could have known unless Nuskin told him. But why would she do that if she were going to embark on the course she undertook? This was making less and less sense. "Who told you that?" I demanded.

His eyes narrowed and his voice choked. "My mother."

"Your *mother?*" I could not believe the words that were coming out of his mouth. Was Nuskin his mother? That would explain everything. "Who in the hell is your mother?"

He grinned. He actually grinned.

"The Princess Entipy," he snarled through gritted teeth. "And you're my gods damned father."

CHAPTER 13

Father Disfigure

I ROCKED BACK ON MY HEELS, stunned at what he was saying. I stared at him, at first completely disbelieving his claim, but the longer I looked at him, the more I saw Entipy in his face. Yes, there was always the chance that he was lying, but that seemed insanely unlikely. He knew Entipy. He knew about the joust. How was that possible?

She had told him. That was it. She had told him because I had told her. During our long winter together I had told her about many of the stunts that I had pulled in my life, and the joust had definitely been one of them. And if I had told her, then she very easily could have told him while she was raising him.

Raising him.

My gods. I have a son?

I knew when he had been conceived, of course. It had been the one night that Entipy and I had been together. The night when we had blended our bodies and then, come the harsh rays of the morning light, I had spotted the birthmark she bore that was identical to the mark I myself carried. The unique family crest that indicated we had the same father. We were half-siblings, but that relationship had been sufficient for me to end our union...and wound up getting myself tossed into prison for my efforts.

But that was all a long time ago. A lifetime ago.

My mind snapped back and reminded me where I was: in the

middle of a vast track where everyone around me had gone mad. People were moaning and wailing from the stands, horrified at the horrendous turn of events that they had just witnessed. Guards had swept in and were carrying the corpse of the Rama out of the place. Doctors were speaking to me and I was not fully registering their words because my attention was so thoroughly scattered.

"Get him out," I said abruptly to the doctors, gesturing vaguely in his direction. "Get him out of here." I then moved away from him and toward the seating booth where the royals and their guests had been seated. I watched mutely as the Rama was hauled away. He seemed so little at that point. He had never been especially imposing even when he was in his prime. But now, with the life stripped from him, he looked vulnerable and helpless. Well, yes, of course helpless. He was dead. One really isn't more helpless than when one is dead.

"Apropos!" An alarmed female voice sounded from across the way. I turned and saw Clea coming toward me. She was bleeding from a couple of superficial cuts on her forehead, but otherwise she seemed unharmed. The arrogant and self-absorbed teenager whom I had met some time ago was gone. Instead she was a terrified young woman whose entire world had just been turned on its ear. "Apropos!" she called again, and her arms were flopping about as if she were a recently landed fish.

Having no idea what else to do, I took the hysterical young girl in my arms and held her tightly. "I don't believe it. I don't believe it. Lama is dead. He's dead!"

"I know," I said as softly as I could. "It's all going to be all right..."

"All right? *All right?!*"

And then she started to laugh. I pulled my head back and looked at her in surprise. There was no bereavement in her voice, no sadness. Her face was twisted in delight. "It's more than all right! I'm in bloody charge, Apropos! I'm the ruler of Rogypt now! The reign of my idiot brother is finally at its end!"

I could not believe the words that were coming out of her

mouth. I stepped back and stared at her with open incredulity. "You're…happy about this? He was your brother!"

"He was an idiot," she replied brusquely, dismissing any compassionate thought about him. "He was foolish enough to bet the entirety of his kingdom on a horse race. I have no idea what happened out here today, nor do I care. All I know is that fortune has favored us by ridding us of that fool."

Never in my life have I hit a woman. And never in my life have I been as sorely tempted to violate all those years of practice and belt one right in the face. Indeed, my hand curled into a fist and trembled with the desire to drive straight into her nose and shatter it. I envisioned her blood spilling out and even if she then ordered the guards to cut me down, it would be worth it for that one brief moment of satisfaction.

But then I mentally pictured the guards slicing me to bits and, as was always the case, my interest in my self-preservation reined in anything monumentally stupid that I might do or say.

"Of course," I said and patted her shoulder. "Yes. Of course."

Then she took me by the shoulders and spoke to me in a low, intense voice, "I must have you. Right now. I am the Rama and my word now commands all. Even you."

"I live to serve," I said tonelessly. I did not sound defeated, although gods knew that I was.

She smiled broadly and draped an arm around my waist. The groomsmen had emerged and were rounding up my animals to bring the poor, confused beasts back to their stables.

Clea went with me back to my room and I simply stood there as she removed my clothes. I forced a smile and stared down at her, but there was no joy in my eyes, no pleasure in my face. Fortunately for me, she wasn't remotely engaged with my face.

I took her then. I did so without a shred of enjoyment or caring about whatever pleasure she might have derived, and as I thrust into her, I imagined that I was slamming a dagger into her, skewering her as if she were some manner of wild beast that I had confronted. She certainly seemed to enjoy it, crying out in something that was a combination of pain and joy. I said nothing. I did my business in silence, and when we were done, she lay there with an idiotic smile on her face.

"I need to go out," I said in a low voice.

She gestured lamely. "Go ahead."

I dressed myself quickly and headed out of the room. Ahmway was standing guard as per usual, and yet oddly I could not even look him in the eyes. Instead I turned away as if I had something to be ashamed of, which I knew was not the case and yet I felt as if it were.

"If someone were injured, where would they be taken?" I asked.

Ahmway quickly guided me through the vast hallways to what I only assumed was some manner of medical wing. That was definitely the case because Mane was lying there on a cot. His right leg had apparently been reset and it was propped up in some manner of bandage that hung from above. The wounds he had sustained in falling had been attended to, although I saw that his left eye was swelling. That brought me some degree of pleasure, but not much.

A doctor was hovering near him but Mane waved him away. The doctor bowed to him; obviously Mane still maintained a measure of respect in the palace. The doctor hastened out of the room and I strode up to Mane. For a long moment I simply stood there, staring at him.

"My full name is Germane," he finally said. "Since my father's name is Apropos, my mother thought it an appropriate moniker."

"Germane." I said it slowly, allowing it to roll off my tongue. "Fitting."

"I'm relieved you approve." There was no sarcasm in his voice but I sensed that he was being sarcastic nevertheless.

"What did your mother tell you about me?"

"Everything. About how you bedded her. About how you left her. You broke her heart. And you left her pregnant with me."

"Yes, obviously."

He continued to stare at me, almost as if he were seeing me for the first time. "If you had known what you had done, would you have left her anyway?"

I had been thinking about that very topic ever since he had first revealed his identity to me. "I don't know. It would have been a very hard decision for me. I might likely have encouraged her to ingest some medication that would have served to terminate the pregnancy."

"Why?" When he spoke his voice was barely above a whisper, and I was reminded of just how youthful he truly was. "Why would you do that to me? Why did you do it to her? How could you have—?"

"She was my sister."

That caught him off guard. Of all the excuses that he could possibly have come up with for why I did what I did, I was reasonably sure that explanation had never occurred to him. "Ex...excuse me?"

"My sister. Well, half-sister, if we're going to be wholly accurate. We have the same father."

He stared at me, not fully comprehending what I was telling him. "That...that isn't possible. The king would never have cheated on his wife!"

"That's very true. Unfortunately the same cannot be said the other way around."

"You lie!" He spoke with such violence that he nearly managed to yank his leg clear of the bandage suspending it and knock himself clean out of his bed. As it was, the cot tipped precipitously and it was only by my placing my foot against it and pushing it back into place that it didn't topple over completely. But he was still clearly having difficulty processing what I had told him.

"Happily and often," I replied. "But not about this. Your mother has a birthmark on her...body. I have the same one. Apparently it's family lineage. I spotted it the morning after we had our assignation that resulted in you nine months later. Upon seeing that revelation, I then understood who and what she was." I leaned on my staff, my shoulders feeling heavy from the weight of reflecting upon moments long lost to me. It had been many years since I had dwelt on that morning, which was conceivably the worst morning of my life that was quickly followed by the worst entire day of my life. Typically I didn't dwell on such things, but my face to face with Germane made it impossible to avoid. "That is the truth of why I left. You can believe it or not believe it as you see fit, but that is entirely your decision."

He was silent. I could see by his expression that he was still uncertain of what to think. Gods knew he had spent the entirety of his life forming his opinion based upon whatever the hell Entipy had told him…

Entipy…

"How fares your mother?" I asked.

"Do you care?"

"Of course I care. I've often wondered what became of her. Is her father—?"

"Dead. My grandfather died some years back." Then he paused. "Except he was not truly her father, was he. You just said…" I shook my head and he continued, "So who was? Do you know?"

"Odclay."

It took him a moment to place the name and then his jaw dropped. "The jester? The *jester?*"

"That's correct."

"You're lying!"

"Oh, I wish I were," I sighed. "I wish that I were spewing calumnies to you right now, but I am most definitely not. My mother was a tavern wench, you see, who was raped by a group of knights out and about to enjoy themselves. Odclay was amongst their group and was compelled to join in their merriment. For a man who became acquainted with my mother through assaulting her, he was actually a rather reasonable fellow."

Germane was clearly having difficulty processing what I was telling him. Small wonder, that.

"So my mother," he said slowly, "is not actually descended from the king. Which means when she took over the throne, she did not have the right to do so."

"Well, her mother *is* the queen, at least to the best of my knowledge. But technically, if she is ruling now—which I assume she is—then she is doing so illicitly, yes. The throne should go to her mother, I suppose. Or perhaps the men would come together and simply choose a new ruler. Or fight over who gets to rule. That is a popular pastime, so I'm told." I cocked my head slightly, curious. "How is she as a ruler? I'm curious considering that during the time I knew her, she was somewhat…unstable."

"She is an excellent ruler," Germane said fiercely. "Her subjects adore her. She is a superb adjudicator. And on the occasions when she has had to employ force, she has done so with ingenuity and cunning."

"You must love her deeply."

"I do."

I leaned forward. "Then what the hell are you doing out here?"

He was about to give a quick answer, but then his jaw clicked shut without providing a response. He sat there silently for a time, and I could see that he was endeavoring to decide whether he should be honest with me or not.

"I left," he said finally, "because there was no place for me in her kingdom."

"As I recall, the kingdom was rather spacious. Hard to believe that you could not find somewhere to fit in."

"That's not what I mean. People knew who my father was," he said, making no effort to keep the bitterness from his voice. "Her father advocated exposing me at birth. Leaving me to die on a hillside somewhere."

"Runcible wanted that?" I could scarcely believe it. Runcible had always treated me well, up until he decided to throw me into prison when I had rejected his daughter. A move that, ultimately, I could not really blame him for. Were I in his position, I likely would have done the same thing. But I wasn't about to tell Germane that.

"He did indeed," said Germane. "I was somewhat young, so naturally I don't recall it. But my mother was strident that I be

allowed to live. She supposedly threatened to depart the court for-
evermore if her father's suggestion were carried through. And so I
was permitted to stay. But I was never given the respect and courtesy that should have been accorded a prince, because I wasn't one.
I was just a royal bastard and was treated like one. Even the lowest
stable boy had a higher standing than I did, and no one ever let me
forget the circumstances of my birth. I had no friends, nor did I
ever have a lover.

"And so I left. At the age of thirteen, I fled the palace because
I had had enough. I left the city, left the country, put it all behind
me, determined to do two things: make my own way in the world,
and find you so that I could kill you."

"You would certainly not be the first who desired my death," I
informed him. "If you lay them end to end, you could likely cover
the length of Isteria."

"I've no doubt." Then he was silent for a time, considering.
"Although now that I know why you departed, I suppose—as
much as I despise admitting it—that it is understandable."

"It's a rare event for anyone to be understanding of me."

"I would not go that far."

"Well, thank you for clarifying that."

"So anyway," Germane continued, "I made my way across
various countries, and eventually the ocean, until I wound up in
Afrasia. There, in what I assumed was the random garden of some
rich individual, I encountered Lucy Anno. It was shortly before she
ascended to ruling the land, and she found me extremely interesting. One thing led to another and eventually we became lovers. We
could never be more than that because I was an outsider and they
have laws against marriage with foreigners."

"How extremely generous of them," I said sarcastically. "But
how did you wind up here in Rogypt?"

"Because Lucy Anno had wanted to conquer this land ever
since she came to visit as a child. But she was loath to declare war,
especially when there was no provocation. So she sent me here,
instructing me to endeavor to become close to the Rama and

develop a means of unseating him peaceably."

"And you conceived the notion of betting on the race."

"That's correct."

"And let me guess: you were Lucy Anno's horse master. So you knew that you would be driving her team. But why did you try to convince me not to win?"

"I didn't trust you, obviously," he said in annoyance. "And clearly for good reason since you drugged the horses."

"No, I didn't."

"Don't lie to me..."

"I'm not lying. It wasn't me. My best guess is that it was Nuskin..." My voice trailed off as I thought of her for the first time. How devastated must she have been? She had looked upon the Rama as if he were her own blood. Her "son" had just died horribly. She was, to put it mildly, likely not in the best of moods. After I was done with Germane, I would have to seek her out and see how she was holding up.

"Nuskin?" He stared at me disbelievingly. "How would you know that? How would it even have occurred to her?"

"I, uh...I may have mentioned to her that it was something I had done."

"Hah!" said Germane. "Then it was your responsibility!"

"I imagine that it somewhat was," I had to admit. "I didn't encourage her to do it, but she likely got the notion from me. So to that degree, yes, it was my responsibility. Satisfied?"

"Yes," he said. He shifted in his cot, clearly trying to make himself more comfortable, which was problematic considering that his foot was elevated. "Yes, I am. I don't know why I am, but I am."

"I can tell you why," I told him with grim confidence. "It's because you've spent the entirety of your existence blaming everything that's gone wrong on me. So being able to blame me for this," and I gestured toward his leg, "and everything else that happened simply tracks with the way you've lived your life. So congratulations. You've achieved your goal."

His expression soured. He clearly didn't like what I was saying, but he had no way in which to refute it. So he simply nodded and then angled his head so that he was staring upward. Then, very softly, he said, "I imagined this moment for so long. But of all the ways in which I thought it would go, somehow this was never one of them."

"You will find that's generally the case when it comes to life."

Then we sat there for a time, no words passing between us.

"You should tell her," he said abruptly.

"Tell who what?"

He turned his gaze back upon me. "You should return home and tell Entipy why you left her."

"Tell her she's my sister?" I laughed at that. "Why in the world would I tell her that?"

"Because she might be able to start living again."

"I don't understand what you're talking about."

He stared at me for a moment, looking surprised that I wasn't following what he was saying. "There was never anyone else after you. Gods know people tried. She had plenty of suitors. Most of them, I imagine, simply wanted to share in the power she wielded. Some saw marrying her as a way to tighten allegiances. Who knows, perhaps one or two even loved her as much as they could. But she was never interested in any of them."

"Why not? Did she ever tell you?"

"One night, when she was in her cups, yes. She was convinced that whomever she chose to wed would eventually betray her, as you had done. As she believed you had done," he quickly amended. "So she shut down her heart and refused anyone who endeavored to claim it."

"I...am sorry to hear that." And I truly was. I had lived the entirety of my life without ever truly knowing love or finding an individual whom I could have considered my soul mate. But it was not a conscious decision on my part. It was simply the way things had turned out for me. I had never determined to avoid love. It had simply managed to avoid me.

"If you ask me," he continued, "she never wanted to take the chance of causing someone else to walk out on her. She simply believed that she was not deserving of love."

I hung my head. Never in my life had I ever felt so ashamed. Entipy may have been relatively insane, but I had come to believe that inwardly she was a good person. Or at least my memory of twenty years had softened my recollections of her to the point where I was willing to give her the benefit of the doubt. Whatever the reason, I felt it was an appalling way in which to live her life. To some degree, it was as if I had died and she swore to remain a widow the rest of her life for fear of losing a second husband. That was no way to live, and yet it was the fate for herself that she had chosen.

"I didn't tell her for the right reasons," I said softly, as much to convince myself as Germane. "For her to learn that she was not truly a princess. To learn that her mother had been unfaithful to her father. It would have destroyed them in front of the entire court. Runcible might well have killed himself upon learning the news. Or he might have had Queen Bea executed. Hell, he might have killed her and then himself. Leaving Entipy with what? No status? No court? No friends? To live the rest of her life as a royal bastard?"

"Which is how I lived the entirety of my life," he pointed out, and I had to admit that that was true enough. "I survived it. I'm sure she would have been able to as well."

"What do you want of me?" I said in exasperation. "Go back in time and do things differently? Find a weaver who can change the past in order to effect the future?"

He sat up and looked surprised. "Are there such individuals?"

"*No!*" I rolled my eyes. "That is an impossibility. And even if I could do it, I doubt that I would. I made the right decision with all of the information I had at my disposal and if I had the opportunity to repeat it, I would do it again."

"Except it would cost you nothing to return and tell her the truth now. Her father is dead. She rules and if she knew the truth, I very much doubt that she would feel compelled to turn her back on her kingdom. She would keep it a secret, and at least she would be able to put her loss behind herself and live something approaching a normal life."

I had no idea what to say or what to do, so I put up my hands in a manner evocative of surrender and said, "I will consider it. All right? But I'm not going to do a damned thing until you have managed to recover and we have freed the Shews."

"Clea won't do it," he said firmly.

"How do you know?"

"Because she has never done anything for anybody. She is an extremely non-generous person and the notion that she would make such a grand gesture is unthinkable."

"Well, I have to make sure that she does it."

"Good luck with that."

I studied him for a time and then said, "Why didn't you identify yourself to me immediately. You recognized my name, you knew who I was. Why did you wait until you did?"

"Because I figured that I could manipulate you more adroitly if you had no idea of my true identity."

I considered that and then nodded. "That is true, I suppose. Good thinking."

"Thank you."

I got to my feet. "I should go talk to Nuskin. See how she is holding up."

He stared at me, seemingly surprised. "You really do care about others, don't you."

"Of course I do. What sort of monster would I be if I did not?"

"I have spent the entirety of my life wondering what sort of monster you were, Apropos. And after years of pondering, I am interested to see that I still have absolutely no idea."

Having no clue how to react to that statement, I simply nodded, turned and walked away from him.

I made my way quickly to Nuskin's quarters and knocked gently. When I received no response, I opened the door slightly to glance in, unsure of what I would see.

Nuskin was inside, all right. She was seated on the edge of her bed and staring out at nothing. I whispered her name softly and at first she did not respond. I said it a second time, somewhat louder than before, and this time she tilted her head slightly and focused on me.

"Nuskin?" I said. "I assume you've heard?"

She managed a single nod. That was all.

I started to walk toward her but she held up a hand, stopping me in my place. I stood there and stared at her questioningly.

"We're all going to die," she said. "Soon."

"What? Why?"

She didn't reply. Instead she just shook her head. I queried her again as to what she was talking about, not having the slightest clue why she was under the impression that we were going to die, but she didn't respond. It was as if her mind had departed her body. I tried to bring her back down to reality but was unable to garner any further response from her other than her initial and frankly discouraging warning that our destruction was imminent.

I sat there for some minutes but finally gave up. I had no idea what she was referring to, and it was clear that she was not intending to provide any further hint. I squeezed her hand once but she did nothing to return it, and then I got up and left her room.

The Rama Lama's body was quickly mummified. At Clea's declaration, no formal funeral service was held for him. Her assertion was that he had explicitly told her that he did not desire any. I very much doubted that. When one is a teenage boy, one's own death is something that is never discussed or even considered, because one firmly believes in the reality of one's own immortality. So I was skeptical that it had ever come up in conversation between Lama and Clea. Her declaration, however, did not forestall the palace holy men from having prayer convocations where they prayed for the gods to look well upon Lama and welcome him into their world. I did not participate in any of these because they were not designed for outsiders, but nevertheless I could not help but send my wishes along for Lama's safe transition to the netherworld.

There was also a great deal of concern over placing the Rama into the main pyramid into which his father was entombed. I could not blame any of the soldiers for having no desire to set foot in that place. There was a smaller tomb that had been erected for people of lower value in the vast Rogyptian escutcheon, and it had been there that the Rama Lama's remains had been dispatched. Clea offered no objections, and that was not surprising. She had as vivid a memory of what had transpired as anyone else and was not especially enamored of having to return to that pyramid, ever.

So it was that the Rama Lama was laid to rest. The population did its best to try and shed its collective tears, but no one mourned his loss. No one gave a damn.

No one except me.

How the hell had I fallen this far? To care about some teenaged punkish dictator? It was almost embarrassing.

I sat sullenly in my room. Ahmway entered and saw the way that I was sitting there, uninvolved with the world. He asked me what was bothering me and at first I considered shrugging or perhaps just lying to him. But instead, much to my surprise, I was honest with him. I told him what was going through my mind, and how I was actually mourning the loss of the little rat.

"Easy answer," said Ahmway immediately. "You mourn him because you don't have your own son to mourn. So he stepped in and filled that emptiness in your life. So it makes sense that you would feel his loss."

Except of course I did have a son, but I wasn't about to tell Ahmway that.

"Yes, I suppose you are right," was all I said in response. Then I gazed toward the door. "I'm surprised that Clea hasn't come in and arranged for our immediate marriage."

"She cannot," Ahmway told me. "It is tradition that no member of the royal family can engage in any manner of happy ceremony for a week after the death of a Rama. As Clea is the succeeding Rama, she would be more than aware of that."

"Ah. That was something I was unaware of. So where is she now?"

"This evening is her crowning as the new Rama. She is doubtless preparing for that. And she has quite an audience. All the leaders of the foreign lands are still here. They are probably going to remain here for a week until the wedding ceremony can be held. And wait until you see the crown. It's very impressive. It has a—"

"There isn't going to be a wedding ceremony," I informed him. He blinked in surprise. "There...there isn't?"

"I very much suspect there won't be. Not after this evening. Because I am going to mortally embarrass my future wife in front of all those leaders."

"Why on Earth would you do something like that?"

"Because I don't like her very much," I said grimly. "And I think it's about time that she knew it."

Chapter 14

Pestilence, Famine and Breath

It was difficult to believe that the leader of Rogypt had been so brutally killed considering that the great hall was filled with laughter.

I knew that Clea was expected to be brought forward from a back room. The high priest was at the front of the hall, speaking with an assistant over some matter or another. He caught a glimpse of me from the corner of his eye, turned and nodded in acknowledgment of my presence. I tilted my head slightly in response and moved toward the front. I was amused as people saw me coming and stepped out of my way. A number of them even bowed to me, which I considered to be wholly excessive, but I did not bother to correct anyone.

I saw Nuskin seated over to the side, and to my surprise, Simon was with her. Certainly his bravery was growing, that he allowed himself to be seen beside her, clearly accompanying her. He was clutching her hand and she still appeared as distant and disconnected as she had been when I'd last seen her. Simon and I locked eyes, but he said nothing; simply gazed at me. I wondered what his reaction would be when he saw what I was about to do.

People continued to gesture to me in greeting, and I nodded to everyone. I took a seat that was off by itself and whenever anyone tried to engage me in conversation I would politely nod but otherwise ignore them. Soon apparently word got around and people stopped coming over to me. That was fine with me. I was hardly in a social mood.

What I could not understand was why the air was feeling different to me. It seemed thicker somehow. I could not determine why that was. Perhaps there was some manner of storm rolling in. I wondered if anyone else sensed it.

Eventually the high priest spread his arms wide and began to chant. Others joined in for what were clearly a series of prayers with which they were all familiar. Since I did not know any of them, I simply kept my silence.

Finally he said, " I now bring forth the next Rama." From behind a huge, elaborate curtain that was hanging at the back, Clea emerged. She was smiling broadly; much too broadly, as far as I was concerned, for someone who had just lost her brother. But obviously she was not especially worried about that. She was looking resolutely ahead: not at me, not at the high priest. There was no telling what thoughts were going through her head, but I suspected that if I knew, I wouldn't be all that thrilled about it.

The High Priest then engaged in a string of prayers to their gods, asking for their aid in guiding the newly established Rama in her path to rule. Clea listened impassively, and on occasion muttered some manner of reiteration over what he said. I assumed it was all part of the ceremony.

Then another courtier came from behind the curtain. He was carrying a sizable crown, one that I had never seen Lama wear. It was obviously the one that Ahmway had mentioned. I assumed that it was something purely reserved for ceremonies. Clea dropped down to one knee as the courtier handed the crown to the High Priest. "Crown" was not truly the best word for it. It was a towering piece of headwear, glittering in gold, so much so that I could not begin to imagine how much the damned thing weighed. It was at least a foot tall and there was a red gem glittering in the middle of it that reflected the rays of the sun filtering through a skylight.

It was the gem that most caught my interest. I had never seen anything quite like it. As insane as it may sound, it almost seemed… there was no other way to say it…alive.

"That gem," I whispered to Ahmway, who was seated right behind me. "Whence came it?"

"That is the gem of Moomy," he replied. "Or so the legend says. It used to be a headpiece in a staff that he carried. Upon his death, the Rama became so enamored of it that he added it to the crown."

"He added the gem of a supposed wizard that hated him to the crown? Why on Earth would he do that?"

Ahmway shrugged. "To prove that he wasn't afraid, I suppose."

Slowly the High Priest placed the crown atop her skull. It encircled her head and I could see that she was moving very carefully so as not to dislodge it as she rose to her feet. Then the High Priest turned to the crowd and said sonorously, "I am honored to introduce you all to the Rama Clea."

A resounding round of applause burst from the populace. I glanced briefly at Lucy Anno's face. She was managing to keep herself composed rather admirably, considering the circumstances. The race could not have ended worse for her: her man had clearly lost since he had never completed the race, although I heard she was contending there was trickery and therefore she did not owe any money. She was as suspicious as everyone else was regarding all the collapsing horses, but could not prove anything, of course. Obviously Germane had not brought her current with my identity. There were some things that he wished to keep to himself.

When the applause faded, Clea took her place in the grand throne that was erected on a podium in the front. There was another, smaller throne next to her and she extended a hand to me. "Come to me, my future husband," she called out. "And someone bring me some water, for my throat is quite parched."

A servant hastened to fetch her water as I slowly approached her. I did not, however, take my seat. Instead I simply stood there, staring at her.

She smiled smugly down upon me. She had everything in the world that she desired, and as I stared up at her, I could not recall more fervently hating someone in my life than I despised her at that moment.

I only had one thing going for me: she had no idea what I was going to say.

"I request a boon, my Rama," I said to her.

I was speaking so softly that it was obviously difficult for her to hear me. She leaned forward, clearly a bit confused, uncertain what I might be asking her for. But she kept her face gamely smiling, as if anxious to accommodate me in whatever I desired. "Of course, my future husband. Anything you desire."

I took a deep breath and let it out. "Let the Shews go."

"Go where?" Obviously she did not understand my request.

"Away from Rogypt," I said. "Free the slaves."

There were scattered gasps from around the room. Clearly no one could quite believe that I had the temerity to make such a request.

The servant brought the mug of water to Clea. She took it without even looking at him. Instead all her attention was upon me. "Have you lost your mind?"

"I am reasonably certain that I have not."

"Why in the name of all that's holy should I free the slaves?"

"Because it's the right thing to do."

"I," and she raised her voice, "am the only one in the position to declare what is the right thing to do when it comes to the slaves! Not you; not anyone else in this place. The slaves are going nowhere!"

"That is a mistake," I said, gripping tightly onto my staff. I tried to sound as threatening as I could. I imagined that the god who had addressed me through the bush had inhabited me and was speaking His will through me. "For your safety, and the safety of all others, let the people go."

"For our *safety?!*" Clea roared with laughter at the notion that I was lecturing her on how to keep the people of Rogypt safe. "Is this some manner of joke, Apropos? Because if it is," and her voice dropped to a deadly tone, "I do not find it the least bit funny."

"Nor am I amused by how you've treated your slaves. The

execution of their first-born. The endless construction projects; the brutal manner in which you treat them. You have abrogated all responsibility in terms of treating them like human beings…"

"They are not human beings! They are property! They are *our* property," she informed me, and I could not determine at that moment if she was referring to the whole of Rogypt or herself in the royal "we." She had now risen to her feet and her hand was trembling with rage. Perhaps she felt betrayed by the fact that her future husband was challenging her in front of everyone of importance. "I will not release them! But if you wish, I will release you from your vow to wed me!"

"That would be fine with me," I said.

There was a rush of hushed whispers amongst everyone observing. It was rare that they had the opportunity to witness a relationship dissolving before their eyes. Such things typically occurred behind closed doors.

"Then," she said in full fury, "you have removed any reason I would have not to kill you!" She pointed at me and was clearly about to order her people to dispatch me.

Ahmway was directly behind me. He had pulled his sword from his scabbard and to my astonishment he said in a low voice, "Get behind me. I'll protect you."

I could not believe it. This man, this murderer of infants, was prepared to walk directly into his own slaughter in order to try and guard me. Either the overwhelming number of guards would kill him, or if he managed to survive somehow, Clea would have him executed for flying in the face of her commands.

And that was when Clea screamed.

No one had any idea why she was screaming, but she sounded terrified. The glass that she was holding slipped from her hand and the contents spilled in front of her. It was a thick red liquid and at first I thought it was some manner of wine rather than water, but then I realized what it was.

It was blood. Thick and oozing down the steps that led up to her.

She glanced at the servant, but the shock on his face spoke volumes. He had handed her water and was as dumbfounded as anyone else that somehow it had changed into blood.

And right in the middle of all this, a servant burst in through the back doors, and he was screaming, "Rama! Rama! The river has turned into blood!"

I had, of course, no clue why in the world it was happening. But I did not hesitate to take advantage of it. I stepped forward and pointed as majestically as I could at Clea. I could see that her legs were trembling; she was having trouble remaining standing. "That is but the first of the plagues that will fall upon you! And they will continue until you let the slaves go!"

"Kill him!" shouted Clea. "Kill him and this will stop!"

To my astonishment, it was Lucy Anno who stepped forward and spoke up before any of the guards could follow Clea's order. "You do not know that! Perhaps he is the only one who can stop it! If you kill him, you could be condemning the entirety of your country to who knows what?"

"You don't know that," said Clea, but she sounded uncertain.

"All I know is that as long as I'm here, and my followers are here, we're as threatened as you are! And I think that gives me some say in the matter!"

Clea could see that not only was Lucy Anno not backing down, but the other leaders were starting to nod as well. Her hands were clenched into fists and she said tightly, "Fine. Return him to his quarters and make certain he doesn't go anywhere!"

Ahmway grabbed me by one arm and another guard came up beside me. But before they could drag me out of there, the air started to become filled with a distant noise that slowly rose, louder and louder as it drew nearer to us. It was like nothing that I had ever heard before. A steady strumming, like a million strings being caressed simultaneously.

Clea's eyes were darting left and right, as if she could perceive the invisible source of the noise. Everyone else seemed confused; everyone save for Lucy Anno as recognition blossomed upon her face.

"Locusts!" she cried out, right before they erupted into the room. They dove in through the open skylight above, and there were thousands, millions of the creatures. They were hurtling all over, clearly not having expected to wind up inside an enclosure, desperately looking for a way out.

I threw my arms up to shield my face and dove for the floor, taking refuge under a nearby bench. People were running, screaming, desperate to get away from the creatures. It wasn't as if they stung or even bit, but the sheer volume of them was nearly suffocating.

The servants threw open the wide doors at the end of the room and the locusts blew through them. The downside was that put them in every corner of the palace, but at least it substantially lessened their number in the great hall.

Clea was on the floor, gasping for air. Her normally bronzed skin had gone ashen, so overwhelmed was she by the assault of the locusts.

I did not hesitate. I clambered to my feet, brushing away the remains of the creatures, and I shouted, "There's going to be more, Clea! More plagues are going to be visited upon you, unless you—!"

"Go! Go!" Clea was screaming, clearly horrified by the supernatural might that she had just seen unleashed. "Take the Shews and go! Get them out of here! Take them and be damned!"

I couldn't believe it. I had a feeling that if the Rama Lama had still been in charge, he would have indeed taken his chances with executing me. He certainly would never have been pressured into freeing the Shews thanks to insects and some manner of trickery with water into blood. But I was not about to shrug it off. Instead I bowed and said, "As you wish."

Simon had emerged from his seat. It hadn't been difficult because others who had been sitting near him had fled when the locust had assaulted them. He ran up to me and there was pure, unbelieving joy in his face. "I will tell the others," he said. "We will be ready to depart by sundown." He clapped a hand on my shoulder. "You will lead us?"

"Of course," I said immediately. I had no idea why, but as far as I was concerned, I was along for this ride whether I wanted to go or not.

"Good." He glanced back toward Nuskin, but she was exactly where she had been before, unresponsive to everything. His brow creased in concern and he started toward her, but I grabbed him by the arm.

"Go," I said. "I will attend to her."

He nodded, gave her one final glance and then headed out. He had a good deal of company because the room was emptying out rapidly. Clea had vanished behind the great curtain from which she had emerged, the High Priest had likewise taken off, and the leaders of the various countries had also fled. It was obvious to me what was going on. They were faced with something that was clearly supernatural in origin, and none of them had the stomach to deal with it. They wanted to be as far away from all of it as possible.

I slid into the seat next to Nuskin and touched her shoulder. "Nuskin? You need to listen to me…"

"It's not you," she said.

"Yes. Yes, it is me."

She turned and focused her face upon me. "No, you don't understand. The blood. The locusts. That isn't you. You have nothing to do with it."

I glanced around to make sure there was no one near enough to be listening and then I said in a low voice, "I'm reasonably sure you're right, but what does it matter if it gets the Shews freed?"

"It's the curse," she said.

"Curse?"

"The curse of Moomy."

"Don't be ridiculous," I said dismissively. "That's about the first born son of a Shew. That has nothing at all to do with—"

And the next words she spoke struck a cold chill in my spine:

"He was my son."

I stared at her, uncomprehending. "Who was?"

"The Rama. He was mine."

"No." Slowly I shook my head. "No, that's...that's impossible."

She continued to speak. It was as if I was no longer there. As if she were instead speaking to herself, reliving moments in her life from the past. "I was pregnant at the same time as the wife of the Rama. The Rama was quite virile, you see. Such virility could not be restrained to one woman. He had had his way with me and impregnated me the same time as he did so with his wife. The result of one drunken night of assignation that he likely did not even remember after it transpired. But he would have had to execute my child because I am a Shew. It would have meant nothing to him, even though he was the father, for the prophecy still resounded within his head as much as any of his predecessors.

"The Rama's wife felt sympathy for me. I had long been one of her most faithful retainers and so she decided to help me as much as she could in concealing the existence of my child. I dressed in loose fitting clothing to conceal the expansion of my belly. Fortunately Lama was quite small, and the swelling was scarcely noticeable.

"And because the gods have a sense of humor, and because prophecies have a knack for causing odd things to happen, the Rama's wife and I went into labor at the same time. The Rama himself was not present, of course, but his orders were quite specific. I will never forget that moment, when he stood before me and the other retainers. I had to stand there, covering the fact that I was in labor, forcing a smile upon my lips. And the Rama said to us, 'Deliver my child safely, or else you will surely die.' We were to be executed if the Rama's child was deceased.

"Which is, of course, exactly what happened. The delivery went as disastrously as it could have. Not only was the infant stillborn, but his mother died in childbirth. It could not have been a greater calamity.

"And all the women wailed, because they knew their time was done, and then I was fallen as my own child decided it was time to present itself to the world. It did not take long, for he was clearly anxious to make himself known. So it was that right there, on the floor, lying upon some blankets that were tossed under me to give me some minimal comfort, I gave birth to my son.

"At which point the answer to our situation readily presented itself: Give my son to the Rama. Admit that his wife died in childbirth, and there was no help for that. But he had specified that he was concerned only about the birth of his child, and ideally he would not dispose of us in the wake of his wife's death. It seemed unlikely. He had no idea how to tend to children and would require our aid. The infant was presented to him, and he expressed little to no concern over the demise of his wife. Instead as he cradled the child, he declared it to be his heir, which naturally endeared the child immensely to his older sister, who would have inherited the title had a son not been born. Indeed, several times in his first months, Clea endeavored to kill him but was thwarted by the women. Finally we managed to convince her that if she succeeded in her endeavor, her father would doubtless end her life as vengeance for her deed, and that brought her in hand.

"So I raised my son to manhood while convincing his father that he was the son of his own loins...which he was. But he was not born of wife; he was born of me. And I am a Shew. And according to Shewish law, the nature of a child is determined by the mother. Because he was mine, that made him Shewish, despite the fact that his father was not.

"The rest of the women did not know my origins. They had no idea of my Shewishness because I had always kept that part of my life to myself. If they had known, perhaps they would have warned the Rama, but they did not.

"So the Rama raised the child that the Moomy had warned everyone would destroy the entirety of Rogypt as his heir and never had the slightest idea of what he was doing. But I always knew. And I prayed that the Moomy's curse was just the stuff of legends. But it's not. The plagues you've seen," and her voice rose in its urgency, "they're just the beginning. Lama has become a mummy, but he is not just any such corpse. He is alive. He has powers. He is doing all this!"

I took her by the shoulders and nearly shook her. "You're imagining it, Nuskin! Dead is dead!"

"You fought an undead mummy! You cannot know! You—!"

That was when we heard distant screaming from outside. Immediately I sprang to my feet and made my way as quickly out of the room as I could. Nuskin followed me, doubtless because she had nowhere else to go.

I sprinted across the hallway toward a vast window that overlooked the streets below. I stopped at the window and stared out, unable to believe what I was seeing. Nuskin came in behind me, as did Ahmway and others who resided within the palace. No one said anything; we collectively just looked down at the chaos that had descended below.

The sky was black as night, which was interesting considering it was early in the morning. People were running in all directions as thousands of frogs leaped everywhere. The streets were flooded with them. They were bouncing all over the place, croaking incessantly. You couldn't walk two paces in any direction without stepping on them.

"This is madness," I said in a low voice.

Nuskin shook her head. "This is Lama. He is doing this…"

"I don't believe it," I told her fervently, except deep down I suspected it was entirely possible. I had witnessed far too many things in my life that any sane person would dismiss out of hand, and so was hardly in a position to do that in this instance. I decided the best thing to do was move forward with the evacuation of the Shews. "Go to your people. Go to Simon. Assemble everyone so that we can get the hell out of here. Do you understand me?" When she didn't respond, I grabbed her by the shoulders and shook her fiercely. *"Do you understand me?"*

It was as if I was snapping her out of her walking dead state. She blinked several times and managed a nod. "Good. Then why are you standing here listening to me?"

She turned and ran off.

At that moment, for some reason, all I could think of was

Germane. If I was going to lead the Shews out of Rogypt, I knew I wanted him by my side. There was only one way I was going to be able to accomplish that: by harnessing the chariot to the horses and enabling him to drive himself out of there. It was going to be hell helping him to his feet, but I had no choice. "Ahmway, with me," I said briskly. I started down the hallway and Ahmway fell in beside me as we left the rest of the servants and onlookers to stare out at the insanity that had befallen the streets.

"Where are we going?" he asked.

"To get to..." I almost called him "Germane" but caught myself. I wasn't interested in explaining who Mane truly was at that moment. "To get to Mane. We're bringing him with us."

"We are? Do you think he'll want to go?"

"Yes, I do."

"Why?" Ahmway's eyebrows knit together in confusion. He couldn't fathom why in the world Mane would want to join us, and I was not about to go into detail.

"Just a feeling I have."

Ahmway shrugged. Obviously he didn't feel it necessary to probe too deeply, and that was probably wise on his part.

And then, just before we got to Germane's room, I heard a terrified shriek that will stay within my mind for the rest of my life.

I sped up, the lameness of my leg forgotten, but Ahmway was ahead of me. He slammed his shoulder into the door and it exploded open, and when I saw what was inside, I screamed. I actually screamed.

Lama was in the room.

He was not as I remembered him. His body was clothed in the wrappings of the mummified, although pieces of it had been torn from his face so that he could see. His eyes were wide open and there was a cold fire burning in them. He was slowly approaching Germane, reaching out toward him. Germane was trying to throw himself from his bed but was unable to do so because his foot was still lashed up.

"*No! Get back!*" I howled at the thing that had been Lama,

and for a moment he looked at me. He barely seemed interested in my presence. He glanced at me up and down and then turned his attention back to Germane.

I should have run toward him. I should have yanked out my bastard sword, or attacked with my staff, or done something, anything to defend him.

Instead I stood there.

I like to look back at that moment and think that at least I didn't run away. Once upon a time, that is exactly what I would have done. I would have turned and fled. Without so much as a look behind, I would have been out of there and not given the slightest of damns what happened to Germane. Instead I remained rooted to the spot and I stood and I stared as Lama grabbed Germane by the face.

Lama roared at him then, and his breath, my gods, it was awful. It was a poisonous, gaseous thing, exactly what you would expect to come rolling off a corpse. Even though I was standing some feet away, I still wound up inhaling a sizable portion of it and violently wretched upon doing so.

Ahmway was no longer there. He had fled from behind me. So it turned out that he was a coward in the end. He had departed the room to leave me to my fate. Part of me respected that. Obviously he had his priorities in order, and his own wellbeing transcended any care for mine. It was inconvenient but understandable.

I tried to stride forward toward Lama and Germane. The creature's breath was far too overwhelming. I lost my grip on my staff and collapsed.

And I watched in horror as Lama's grip tightened on Germane's face, and Germane's face began to dissolve. It rotted away within seconds, transforming from its normal skin tone to blackened, deteriorating flesh. The rest of his body followed suit, although his vocal cords remained intact for somewhat longer since his shrieking continued. His eyes also stayed for a time, and they were riveted upon me, looking to me for help, for some manner of succor. I had none to give him. The son I never knew I had, the son who had hated me, despised me, and now had come to think of me as some-one who might perhaps, just perhaps, be worth loving, was being taken from me and I was helpless to do anything to help him.

Then his eyes crumbled away and seconds later, so did the entirety of his body.

I had stopped screaming. Something within me died at the same time as he had passed. I lay upon the floor, helpless, and a deep sobbing rose from within my chest.

Lama stood upright and stared down at me. Then, slowly, he started toward me, his hand outstretched.

All I could think was, *Take me. I don't care anymore. Just take me.*

That was when a flaming arrow thudded into Lama's chest.

Lama staggered back, clearly astounded, and then a second arrow landed just to the right of the first.

I turned and looked in astonishment. Ahmway was there, a bow in his hand, standing next to the flaming brazier that was illuminating the room. He had a quiver of arrows slung over his shoulder and was shoving the arrow tips into the flames. He was drawing back his third arrow and let fly within seconds of the first two.

The third arrow thudded into Lama's head.

Lama staggered and from somewhere within the depths of the creature that he had been transformed into, there came a swell of fury. The flames quickly consumed him, or at least seemed to, except it seemed more as if he were absorbing them into his physicality. I shielded my eyes as he erupted into a miniature tornado in the room. Wind blew everywhere, as did the flames, leaping onto nearby curtains and carpets.

Ahmway grabbed me by the arm and hauled me to my feet. *"Come on!"* he shouted. I grabbed my staff and ran out of the room as the massive winds blew directly past us, knocking us over once more. Fire continued to roar within the room and Ahmway slammed shut the door in order to contain it.

"Now what?" he managed to gasp out.

My head was whirling. I had just witnessed the death of the

son that I had not known that I had. Our entire life together that
would never be flashed before my eyes and something deep within
me wanted to sag to my knees and start sobbing piteously. But
there was no time for that. I managed to focus on the situation at
hand and something within warned me where I had to go next.
"Clea," I said. "He's going to go after her next, if he hasn't already."

"Clea? Why?"

"Because he's destroying all connections to his old life. He
killed Ger...Mane because Mane was responsible for his death.
And he'll blame Clea for the fact that she never truly loved him.
Which is hardly her fault, since I think she is incapable of loving
anyone."

"And you?"

"He'll probably come up with something."

We sprinted toward Clea's door and as we approached we saw
what I knew we were going to see. The permanent guards who had
been posted outside Clea's doors were lying dead. They were nothing but skeletons, and I noticed a couple of stray cats were already
licking at their bones. Marvelous.

I was moving so quickly that I actually vaulted over the nearer
of the skeletons and burst into Clea's room. I saw exactly what I
thought I was going to see. Clea was in her chambers, backing up,
a look of pure terror on her face. Lama was approaching her, and
he seemed none the worse for wear insofar as having been punc-
tured by flaming arrows. I suspected that he was busily learning
the parameters of his abilities and had been more startled than
anything by the flaming missiles that Ahmway had sent flying into
him. Now he was coming nearer and nearer his sister, staggering
and lurching but inevitable.

Desperate, horrified, Clea did the only thing that she could
think of. She was standing near a pedestal upon which the crown
had been set. Now she reached out, grabbed it and swung it desperately at him.

It should have presented no threat to him at all.

Instead, to my astonishment, he backed up. He looked far more wary than he had when he had first approached her, and I couldn't fathom why. What threat could a crown pose to him?

Clea didn't notice his reaction. She was just swinging the crown desperately, as if it were a mace. Lama dodged right and left, and then timed it correctly and swung his arm. It knocked the crown out of her hands and sent it rolling across the floor. Lama paid it no mind but instead remained focused on his sister.

The crown rolled up to my feet and came to a halt. I stared down at it, trying to figure out what to do.

The large red gem glittered back at me.

The gem of Moomy.

That was when a desperate thought occurred to me. I grabbed up the crown, gripped the gem tightly and yanked it out of the setting. Something within it seemed to hum the moment it came into contact with my skin. I began to suspect I knew what was going on, although I had no way of knowing for sure. But there was certainly one way to find out.

"*Lama!*" I bellowed and held up the gem. Lama's hand was outstretched, ready to envelop his screaming sister's face, but he stopped and turned and stared at me in confusion. When he saw what I was holding, he roared in wordless outrage, as if I had no right to possess it. His attention on Clea lost, he instead lurched toward me, flinging his arms about.

"By all means," I snarled at him, "bring it here! Bring it to me!" I advanced on him and within an instant Lama realized that he was in trouble, just as I'd hoped he would. He stumbled backwards, and there was no fear on his face because he was likely incapable of feeling such an emotion. But he was doing his best to avoid the gem, which was exactly what I had anticipated he would do.

I strode toward him and his foul breath rolled over me as he roared, but I was holding my own breath so as to avoid inhaling it. And at the best possible moment, he tripped over a short stool and stumbled backwards, falling to the floor. At that moment he did not appear like a monster, but more like an innocent teen who had dressed himself as a mummy in order to scare the hell out of some people. Yet the expression on his face remained one of inarticulate rage.

I did the only thing I could think of: I shoved the gem directly into the remains of his face. His bloodshot eyes opened wide in shock and his body began to tremble violently. He tried to bring his hands up to grab my face, but I batted his hands aside and kept pushing the gem harder and harder into him.

The shaking of his body increased more and more and then he let out the most horrific roar I have ever heard made by anything living or undead. It sounded as if it was originating from the pits of hell. He vibrated so aggressively that it was getting harder for me to keep my gaze fixed upon him.

He threw his arms wide and let out one final shriek and then transformed entirely into a massive gust of wind. I was blown backwards, hit the ground, but kept my grip upon the gem like a thing of iron. I watched, amazed, as Lama's body dissolved into what seemed a tightly contained tornado and was drawn into the gem. It shook as if it had a life of its own, trying to twist itself out of my hand, but I kept it tightly in place as if my life were on the line, which I was pretty sure it was.

Then there was a loud popping sound and just like that, Lama was gone. The gem's red color sparkled even more brightly and I could tell that it was keeping the mummy's spirit contained.

Clea was on the floor, looking up with astonishment. "What... what did you do? How did you do it?"

"This is the Moomy's gem. Obviously either it was the source of his power or else he invested a deal of his power in it. Either way, it's obviously a puissant gem. I think I'll keep it with me."

"Yes, yes!" Clea said urgently, waving it away. "Take it! Take it and get it as far away from me as you can! Was that Lama? Was that really—?"

"Yes, it was," I told her. "And I strongly advise you not dwell on him overlong. You'll only give yourself a headache." I nodded toward Ahmway. "Let's get out of here."

"Apropos, wait!" said Clea.

I turned and stared at her, and there was something in her eyes, something that made me nervous. She was gazing at the gem and then she said slowly, "Was...was Lama causing the things that happened? The blood, the locust—?"

"No. That was God. My God. And he'll do way worse to you," I said, but I was speaking far too quickly, as if I were covering up something. I was ashamed to admit that for the first time in my life, my lies were not coming trippingly off my tongue. Worse, I suspected that Clea was aware of it, but my hope was that it would not prompt her to take any action against the Shews as a result of her suspicions.

As it turned out, as with all things in this matter, I was wrong.

CHAPTER 15

Up the Sea Without a Paddle

IT WAS NOT DIFFICULT TO DISCERN where the Shews was gathering. The section of the city where they resided had never been more alive. They were massing in the streets, their belongings hastily packed into knapsacks or whatever they wound up being able to get their hands on.

Ahmway, somewhat to my surprise, was accompanying me. "You don't have to," I reminded him. "I'm departing the palace, and I'll be surrounded by people. Your duty to me is over."

In response, Ahmway shrugged. "I've become accustomed to you. And I will never forget the mercy you showed me," and his voice dropped, "when I did not deserve it. So I find the prospect of turning my back on you to be anathema."

I had no response to that. Instead I glanced at the bow that he had slung over his shoulders. "Just how good are you with that thing?"

"I'm the best marksman in the army," he said with a touch of pride.

I had no idea of just how formidable the archery skills of the rest of the army was and so had nothing on which to base any assessment. So I simply nodded and then waded my way through the Shews as they hastened together.

I heard a startled gasp from the side and turned to see the origin. It was Rebeka. She had been moving past with her husband,

Tommen, at her side. Apparently he had forgiven her for her attempt to save their child's life. She had a bundle of her possessions slung over her shoulder, but now her attention was focused entirely on Ahmway. I immediately knew what the problem was: she recognized him. I had no doubt that she did. His features were likely etched into her brain. She would never forget him.

Slowly she raised her trembling hand and pointed at Ahmway. It was certainly easy to single him out since he was still clad in the gear of a palace guard. Tommen looked in confusion from Ahmway to his wife, and, sensing an impending disaster, I stepped forward quickly. "Rebeka, I know what you're thinking..." I began.

She didn't let me continue. "You're allied with him?" she said incredulously. "You're allied with..." She turned to her husband. "This is the man who killed our son."

The blood drained from Tommen's face. Surprisingly, he took a step back. That movement spoke volumes to me. If Tommen were going to be moved to outrage, as I would have assumed, he would have stepped forward and there would have been fury in his eyes. Instead he slightly retreated as if concerned that Ahmway might launch an attack on him next. So at heart, it seemed that Tommen was something of a coward. That might be something that I could use to our advantage.

That was when Ahmway drew his sword from his scabbard.

Tommen actually let out a quick, alarmed shriek. Rebeka stood her ground, glowering at Ahmway, looking as if she were ready to make a grab for the sword and try to use it against him.

The, to my utter shock, Ahmway reversed the sword so that he was presenting the hilt to Rebeka. She stared at it, not understanding what he was doing.

"I killed your son, yes," Ahmway said. He was not looking at her; instead his gaze was fixed upon the ground. He had dropped to one knee and was offering her his weapon as if she were a queen. "Had I not done so, my partner would have executed him...and then me as well for failing to follow the law. I killed him because I was a coward and chose to live. And if you wish to execute me now, here is my sword. I will not offer any resistance. Do it."

She stood there, continuing to gaze at him as if he were some manner of freakish animal that had just dropped from the heavens.

"Do it," he said again, his voice flat and even.

Rebeka took the sword from his hand then, and I was positive that she was going to use it to kill him. I doubted she had the muscular strength to cut his head off, but she could certainly slay him if she drove the sword right through his back.

I started to say something, started to defend him, but quickly realized there was no point. This was happening because Ahmway wanted it to happen, and it was not my place to intercede.

For a moment I thought Rebeka might turn the sword over to her husband and allow him to dispose of Ahmway, although I very much suspected that his temperament would not permit him to take any sort of action. In that regard I was apparently right because he was just staring at the entire event and not doing anything to take a hand in it.

She drew her arm back and she seemed about to drive the blade downward.

And then she asked the last question I would have expected: "Are you married?"

He looked up at her, surprised. "No," he said, his tone of voice clearly indicating that he had no idea why she had asked.

Slowly she lowered the sword. "Find a woman. Get married. Have a child. And when you do, I will find you and execute the child." She dropped the sword on the ground. "Then we will be even."

She turned on her heel and strode away. Tommen looked at Ahmway, then after his wife and quickly hurried away after her.

"I doubt she'll do that," I said.

Ahmway picked up his sword, stared at it as if contemplating driving it into his own chest, and then sheathed it. "It would not surprise me if she did."

Truthfully, it would not surprise me, either. I never did find out if she wound up effecting her threat, but if she had, it would certainly not have been unexpected.

There was a large main square in the Shewish section where the people were massing. I could see that Simon had taken the lead in gathering people. He was shouting orders, getting everyone together, and detailing the path that the Shews were going to be taking to get out of Rogypt. Apparently he had the entire route mapped out. The Shews were going to be heading for a region called Samdonia, a forty day's march through the desert, so everyone had to make sure to have as much as they could carry with them in terms of supplies. Burros were being hooked up to carts that were laden with all manner of dried meats and fruits. The bakers, having no time to leaven their bread, were rushing dozens of pieces of unleavened bread into boxes. I couldn't imagine who in the world would eat unleavened bread, but it wasn't my concern.

Then Simon noticed me in the crowd. "Apropos!" he shouted to me as if greeting an old friend. Ahmway and I made our way over to him as he stepped down from the box that he was standing on. To my astonishment, he embraced me. "You did it," he said. "You got her to free us. I still can't believe it."

"I would not keep believing it," Ahmway spoke up. "Believe me when I tell you that she is not only more than capable of changing her mind, but she likely will do so. The sooner you get out of here, the better."

"We shall," said Simon.

And he was as good as his word. As the sun slowly descended toward the horizon, the Shews began to move out.

I moved my way through the crowd to get to the front. People saw me coming and whispered to each other and stepped aside. Clearly I was known and recognized as their savior, and that was perfectly fine with me. If nothing else, by putting myself at the front, I could set the pace since moving over long distances at great speeds was not one of my assets. I drew next to Simon and noticed that there was no sign of Nuskin. "Where is she?" I asked, glancing around.

"She chose not to come," Simon said. He was clearly not pleased with the decision.

"Why not?"

"Because she said she had nothing to live for." He shook his head. "I know she raised the boy, but it wasn't as if she was his mother. Sometimes I do not understand women."

"Yes, they can be hard to fathom," I agreed, not bothering to explain to him what was actually going on in Nuskin's head. It was not my place to tell the story.

We walked through the night since evening was generally the best time to travel through the desert. Initially there was much animated discussion, talk of what would happen with the Shews once the destination was reached, and hopes that they would be able to establish a homeland of their own. There was laughter, there was singing. The children particularly seemed to consider the entire thing a vast adventure.

As time wore on, the voices began to die down as people focused purely on the sheer act of walking and walking.

In the distance, the sun was beginning to crawl into the sky. The sun did not give a damn that the Shews were embarking on a vast exodus from Rogypt. It just knew that it had its own job and it was about time that it attended to it. It continued to climb and provide us a better view of where we were.

To our right stretched a vast body of water that I was told was called the Dread Sea. I had no idea why it had acquired such a fearsome sounding name, and when I inquired, was informed that some noted judge had named it after himself. That certainly seemed reasonable. The sea, as it turned out, was to be our guide to Samdonia. The sea stretched the entire distance and emptied into Samdonia's port, so all we had to do was walk its distance and we would arrive at our destination.

As the sun continued to crawl higher, Simon called a halt, believing that it was time for us to cease in our perambulation. Tents were quickly pitched and the Shews went about settling in for a lengthy slumber until the evening hours when we would be able to proceed once more.

That was when I heard something.

Not heard actually. More like felt. It seemed as if the ground was vibrating. At first I thought it was the initial effects of some manner of earthquake, but I quickly realized there was a steadiness to it. It was being caused by the pounding of horses' hooves. Hundreds of horses.

"Something's wrong," I said.

Simon heard me, turned toward me with a questioning look. But as it happened, he did not have to ask about specifics, because at that moment several youths came running to the front of the assemblage and there was panic in their eyes. "They're coming!" the lads shouted. "From behind! The entire Rogyptian army! They're coming after us!"

"And the queen is in the lead!" said another of them. "In a chariot!"

"She changed her mind," Ahmway said. "That has to be it. She's coming to drag you all back."

There were murmurs of rapidly rising panic among the Shews. Above that, Simon shouted, "We will never return! We will fight them!"

"Fight them?" It was Tommen. "They're armed soldiers! They'll kill us all! The women, the children—!"

"Better to die free than live slaves!"

The Shews began arguing. I couldn't believe it. With the Rogyptian army bearing down on them, now was the time for a concerted plan, and instead they were bickering over what to do.

My mind raced desperately. I glanced toward the vast Dread Sea. If there were some way to cross it, then we could get ourselves safely to the other side and have the waters keeping us separated from the Rogyptians. Unfortunately there was no means of creating a division.

And then a completely insane idea came to mind.

I reached into my satchel and extracted the glittering red orb of Moomy. The spirit of Lama was trapped within, and since it was intrinsically a mystic orb, perhaps that meant the power could be wielded. The problem was that I was no weaver, by any means. I knew no spells, could not manipulate powers along the ley lines. The only thing I had going for me was my will power, which was second to none when I was in the right mood. Considering that there were hundreds of Rogyptian soldiers bearing down upon us, I didn't see how the mood could get more right than that.

What I remembered most were the massive winds that Lama had been able to generate. It was those winds that I decided to try and utilize now.

I shouted above the bickering Shews. *"We're going to flee through the sea! Get everyone ready!"*

They stopped arguing, thank the gods, and turned to stare at me in confusion. "We're going to what?" said Simon.

I did not answer, but instead went straight to the shoreline. I held the gem out in front of me. The brilliant sunlight reflected off it so intensely that it nearly blinded me. I stretched out my arm and whispered to the gem, "Come on, Lama. Do this for me. I saved your life, and it wasn't for all that long a time, but I did it anyway. Plus right now both of us wants nothing more than to anger your sister, and just imagine what this will wind up doing to her if we all escape."

For a moment there was no reaction, and inwardly I mourned my failure because the Rogyptians were going to catch up with us and drag the Shews back into slavery, and likely execute me, and there was nothing that I could do about it.

Then I began to feel it. The power started to generate in my hand, shaking so violently that it was all I could do to hold onto it. And then a massive gust of wind ripped out from within the gem, slamming forward in a gigantic spiral that hammered through the sea's waves as if they weren't there.

Slowly, miraculously, a gargantuan wedge was driven straight through the waters of the Dread Sea. The further and more spread out it became, the less violent it was, but it was unquestionably working. Within seconds the Dread Sea had split, the waters surging on either side but a vast passageway down the middle being maintained through the power of the winds.

The Shews gasped collectively, which I must admit is quite a sound, hearing hundreds of people gasp simultaneously. We did not, however, have the time to dwell on it. "Go!" I shouted to Simon. "Take them through!"

"What about you?"

His concern about my welfare was touching if ill-timed. "Don't worry about me! I'll be fine! Just get everyone across!"

He needed no further urging. Within seconds the Shews were pouring forward through the gap. There was nothing orderly about it; they were running as fast as they could. I couldn't blame them, I suppose. They had no way of knowing when or if the sea would wind up crashing back together, and no one wanted to be there if it did.

Ahmway waited with me. I had to admit I was beginning to admire his loyalty. "Is this going to work?" he asked.

"I certainly hope so or we're going to have a lot of drowned Shews."

As the Shews spilled into the Dread Sea, I was able to see more clearly the advancing Rogyptians. They were coming in fast and would likely have caught up within minutes. Even though they were still a distance away, I could discern Clea rightly enough. She was driving a chariot and even from this distance I knew it was the chariot that had belonged to her brother. I recognized the powerful horses that were pulling it.

"Time to go," said Ahmway nervously, and I could see that he was right. The last of the Shews had entered the vast watery separation; some had even already made it across and were clambering up the other side.

"Let's," I replied, and that was all the incentive we needed. We scampered down the side of the bank and moments later were in the sea bed.

Getting across was not easy. It was all mud and sodden dirt, and I was not at my most mobile even on my best day. Ahmway saw my difficulty and grabbed my arm, giving me additional balance and helping to pull me along.

Not only that, but the gem was continuing to shake in my hand even more ferociously, as if it were trying to break away from me. My hand trembled as I gripped it and I could feel the buffeting of the wind increasing.

And then, as we neared the other side, I tripped and, even with Ahmway trying to support me, I was not able to keep my footing. I fell, stumbling forward, and I lost my grip on the gem. It tumbled away from me and rolled some feet away.

That's it. We're dead, I thought with surprising calm. Surprising because once upon a time, the prospect of an imminent death would have sent me hurrying in the opposite direction from whatever was about to kill me. But this time, just for a moment, I found myself willing to accept it.

Why the hell not? My son was dead. Everyone I had ever loved was dead, with the single exception of Entipy, who would go to her death never knowing what had happened to her own child. Perhaps it was time to leave the mortal coil behind, because there was certainly nothing happening that held any true appeal for me.

That was when the decision was taken out of my hands, because Ahmway grabbed me from behind and shouted, *"Move! Hurry!"*

I obeyed him. Clutching my staff tightly, I made my way up the far bank, wondering distantly why it was possible. Why had the sea walls not crashed down upon me? I was no longer holding the gem, no longer channeling the power. I could not fathom what was keeping everything in place.

I glanced back behind me. The gem was lying there on the ground, still shaking, and the wind whipping out of it was vicious but also funneled. It was continuing to keep the water at bay. The only explanation I could come up with was that it was functioning using the final command of the person who had been holding it.

Which meant that it would continue to keep the Dread Sea separated when the Rogyptians came riding up. They would follow right after us and overtake us, and it would all have been for nothing.

And indeed, here came the Rogyptians. With Clea in the lead, they barreled into the ocean bed on their mighty horses, thundering down and into the separation. The muddy ground did nothing to slow them as they pounded through, drawing closer and closer with each passing second.

Ahmway and I achieved the upper bank and then turned and stood there, watching as the Rogyptian soldiers drew nearer. There was not a damned thing I could do to stop them.

Then I glanced at Ahmway's weapons and a desperate idea occurred to me. "Can you hit the gem?" I demanded.

"What?" He looked confused.

"The gem! The one down there! Can you hit it with an arrow?"

His eyes widened and a wide smile broke across his face. "Absolutely," he said and yanked an arrow out of his quiver. He nocked the arrow, took careful aim and let fly.

The arrow thudded into the ground a good five feet away from the gem.

"I thought you could aim that thing!"

"There's a lot of wind," he protested even as he put another arrow into place and fired again. The previous one had struck to the right of the gem; this one hit to the left. "Shite," he muttered.

"Don't give up!"

He did not. He kept firing and each time his arrow hit to the right, the left, above and below, but never did he strike the gem.

The Rogyptians were perhaps five hundred feet away when he pulled the last arrow out of his quiver. He glanced at it expectantly as if he thought it might have something to say about the matter. Then without a word he nocked the arrow, drew back, muttered a prayer that I could not quite discern and let fly.

It struck the gem squarely and the gem shattered into red fragments, not ten feet away from the rapidly approaching Clea.

With a roar of fury, Lama exploded from the gem.

Clea let out a terrified scream and yanked back on the reins. The horses were similarly panicked as Lama lunged forward, his arms extended, his hands clutching spasmodically.

And the howling winds that had kept the Dread Sea separated promptly vanished.

The two sides of the sea slammed toward each other. The terrified soldiers tried to whip their horses around to flee in the other direction, or perhaps accelerate to reach safety on our side. Neither attempt accomplished anything. The mighty waves crashed together, hundreds, perhaps thousands of tons of water slamming down on anything and everything in its path. Clea's scream was truncated as the water hammered down on her and she disappeared beneath it, as did the horses, which to this day I feel guilty about because the horses hadn't done a damned thing wrong and they had been magnificent race animals.

Howls of anguish tore through the morning sky but were quickly extinguished by the crashing waters. As the waters came together, not only did Clea and her soldiers vanish beneath it, but so did Lama. The weight was so overwhelming that I saw Lama's body literally crunched together and collapse from the impact before it vanished beneath the waves. Seconds later the sea water roiled together, bubbled furiously and then finally all of the storming of the waters came to an end. The Dread Sea was a single body of water again, and the entirety of the Rogyptian army, or at least the ones who had been pursing us, were gone.

For a time, Ahmway and I just stood there, staring downward. Then I turned to Ahmway and said, "Nice shot."

"I aimed three feet to the right of it," Ahmway replied. "Since I wasn't hitting it while aiming at it, I stopped aiming and it hit just fine."

"Good thinking," was all I said.

CHAPTER 16

Where now?

THE TRIP TO SAMDONIA, MERCIFULLY, WENT without incident.

Was it an easy trip? It most certainly was not. Forty days of walking through the desert. That was not a fun endeavor for anyone involved. Eventually, though, the Shews developed a sort of internal rhythm so that the traveling during the night time hours was a period of interaction and socialization as they made their way along the Dread Sea. There was playfulness, there was laughter. The children in particular seemed quite happy, because naturally they were moving and children typically like to move. More games of tag were played around me than I could possibly count. On occasion they tried to drag me into them, but I typically managed to avoid being pulled into them.

It was astounding how the people revered me. By that point everyone knew that the limping stranger with the formidable staff was the one responsible for having freed them. They also knew that Ahmway's bow and arrow had shattered the gem that kept the sea parted and enabled everyone to not only escape the Rogyptians but witness their collective death. So we were constantly being feted or engaged in all manner of discussion.

Even Rebeka seemed to be calming somewhat in her hatred for Ahmway and her lack of trust for me. It may well have been difficult for her to maintain her hostility in the face of such uniform acceptance. I could certainly see the problems involved in that.

By day we sought shelter beneath the tents and talked quietly or slept, saving ourselves and our energy for the nightly excursion. I would like to say I slept well, but I most definitely did not. Day after day for long hours I would lie there and stare up at the top of tent. All I could think about was Germane.

I had had a son.

For all I knew, I had many children. I had certainly not led a life of chasteness. Plus there was that time that I had wound up with a magic ring upon my member and wound up bedding more women than I could possibly count. For all I knew, I had a battalion of bastards running around somewhere. But Germane was the only one that I knew of for a fact. He had spent the entirety of his existence despising me and had even tried to kill me. Yet when we had finally spoken face to face, we had actually seemed to be making a connection. And then, just like that, he had been taken from me by a vengeful spirit, a monster made by a man who had died generations earlier.

And his mother would never know.

The more I dwelt upon it, the more convinced I became that that was simply not right. Entipy should know her son's fate. It would bring closure to that aspect of her life. Not positive closure, gods knew, but at least it would be something.

Could I get a message to her? I had no real means of doing so. Here in the far flung land of Rogypt, there were no commweavers who could send a mystical message to the state of Isteria. They were, in fact, somewhat hard to come by even in my homeland. So that left me with no options. Entipy would simply never know what had transpired with her son.

Except the more that I dwelt upon that concept, the less enamored I was of it.

Entipy should know. She should know.

And I was the only one who could tell her.

But that was very likely a death sentence. She had spent two decades stewing upon my abandonment of her, and doubtless had had much time to conceive of the various punishments that she

would inflict upon me if she were ever unfortunate enough to see
me again. If I returned to Isteria, I was doubtlessly inflicting a
death sentence upon myself.

There was no reason at all for me to return.

Except…

Except…

I was tired.

I was simply tired.

I had lived over forty years; I was practically a senior citizen.
Considering the situations into which I had fallen throughout my
life, it was nothing short of astounding that I was still breathing.

I had seen everything, done everything that any reasoned and
reasonable person would possibly want to do. I had just freed an
entire race of people at the behest of a burning bush. A god himself had chosen me for a task and I had accomplished it. Certainly
it could be considered the high point of my life, if I was wont to
consider carrying out deified orders as some manner of validation.

So if I returned to Isteria, into the arms of Entipy, and she
executed me for my trouble…

…would it really be so bad?

All the adventures I had had in life. Perhaps the only adventure
waiting for me was the cessation of it.

I waited for my inner voice to speak up. To lambaste me for
even entertaining the notion. My inner voice, after all, was my survival mechanism, and whenever I even contemplated doing anything that could end my life, it was always very quick to chime in.

Instead there was nothing but silence. I was astounded. Where
was my famed instinct for self-preservation when I was considering
embarking upon a mission that would lead to my certain death?

You've already made up your mind, it informed me. I actually
imagined I heard a weary sigh. *You're not really interested in anything I have to say. So why should I bother to speak up?*

I was lying on the floor of my tent, my fingers interlaced behind
my head. "No," I said, "really. What do you think?"

It didn't reply.

It was as if my self-preservation instinct had, itself, died.

I, who had spent so many years of his life in total solitude, was actually, genuinely alone for the first time in the entirety of his existence.

And it actually didn't feel so bad.

For the first time in a long time, I drifted to sleep and stayed asleep for a number of hours. When I awoke, I actually felt refreshed.

We undertook the rest of the journey.

Admittedly, some things happened along the way that I don't want to bore you with. A stop on a mountain and an acquiring of some commandments. Which took longer than anticipated, so the Shews for some reason built a golden representation of the back part of the lower leg, a golden calf, and worshipped it. That angered Bob and He wanted to have them wander in the desert for forty years, but I put my foot down and after an hour of back and forth, He gave in and let us go on our way. All things considered, Bob could be a rather reasonable deity when He put His mind to it, although I still think He should consider doing something about His name because, really, what the hell kind of name is that?

So eventually we arrived in Samdonia.

I was bracing myself for the Shews to receive some sort of vicious pushback from the Samdonians who would not welcome hundreds of fugitives arriving in their back yard.

Instead they received the opposite reaction. Simon and I were brought before the ruler of Samdonia who extended warm welcomes to the people. Apparently there had been no love lost between the ruler of Samdonia, who had been in attendance in Rogypt only days ago and had witnessed the Rama's death, and the land of Rogypt itself. So on that basis, he was more than happy to accept the Shews into Samdonia's territory. He informed us that we were welcome to build residences for ourselves and we would be supplied with building materials and such.

How the Shews would dovetail into the Samdonian economy was anyone's guess. Simon's supposition was that the Shews would wind up creating a makeshift marketplace within the heart of their residences. They were extremely talented at providing things to sell, and that would doubtless give them the funds that would enable them to expand and survive.

That evening I sat down with Simon, Ahmway and several other Shews. We were in Simon's tent eating a light supper, relaxing and basking in the Shewish freedom. "I'm going to be taking my leave of you," I said.

Everyone seemed surprised. "Are you sure?" said Simon. "You know you have a place with us always, Apropos."

For now. But sooner or later, I will do something to upset you and you'll want to get rid of me. Or kill me.

How wonderful that my inner voice had decided to return to life specifically so it could come up with things that would depress the hell out of me.

"Yes, I am sure," I said firmly. "There are other places I must go, and other things I have to accomplish."

"Shall I accompany you?" asked Ahmway.

I shook my head and actually smiled. Considering the circumstances under which I had first encountered the man, it was astounding for me to see that I had actually become somewhat fond of him, or at least of his dedication to me. For a moment I considered telling him yes. I had a long trip to make back to Isteria and there would doubtless be dangers along the way. Having a powerful sword or a bow and arrow backing me up seemed a rather attractive notion.

But as quickly as I considered the idea, I then dismissed it. Ahmway deserved the opportunity to lead his own life, not follow me around as I tried to lead, and probably end, mine. Slowly I shook my head. "This is something I feel I have to do alone, Ahmway. Stay here. Stay with the Shews, or perhaps become a Samdonian. Hell, if you want, return to Rogypt. I have no idea what it would be like back there, but it would certainly be interesting. A smart man could easily set himself up with a stimulating existence."

"I think I won't be doing that," he said with an easy smile. "There is nothing for me in Rogypt anymore."

"There is for me," Simon said softly.

Immediately I knew what he was referring to. He was thinking of Nuskin, who had remained behind, buried in her grief. I empathized and when he looked in my eyes, I could tell that he knew that I was aware what was going through his mind. "I may go back for her," he said.

"That would probably be a good idea. I might wait a time, but yes, I think you should return to her. She deserves to have someone at her side."

And so it was that the next morning I boarded a vessel that I hoped would take me in the general direction of Isteria. I had spent the entirety of my life wandering as far from Isteria as I could, and yet now here I was, turning my back at a potentially peaceful life with the Shews in order to embrace likely death at the hands of Entipy.

Was I truly suicidal? Was the thought of continuing to live really so appalling to me?

Yet again my inner voice kept to itself. So I was forced to decide that no, I was not suicidal.

I was just tired.

For the whole of my existence, I had been running. Running from danger. Running from commitment. Hell, running from my sister, or at least half-sister.

My legs were exhausted. My spirit was exhausted. Exercising aggressively for an hour can be tiring. I had been doing it for forty years. I had nothing more to give.

It was time to just put an end to it.

Was I convinced that Entipy would have me executed? Absolutely. But I was no longer afraid of death. Some aspect of me welcomed it.

And I am sure I am not spoiling anything for you when I inform you that I did not, in fact, die. You, you poor benighted fool who has been reading my adventures for some time, and are aware that I am writing them now at an advanced age, must be fully aware of the fact that I obviously did not meet my end at

Entipy's hands. I am hoping that you are wondering how I managed to survive. Are you suspecting, for example, that I never actually returned home? That I thought about it and considered it and ultimately decided that it was a truly horrific idea and if I had an ounce of sanity I would continue to put Isteria behind me for the rest of my existence?

No. That did not happen. I did indeed embark on a lengthy journey to return home and I did indeed confront Entipy. She did not have me executed (again, obviously) but I can assure you that the outcome of our face to face was not remotely what I expected.

It took me the better part of six months to make the journey.

Things happened en route.

Again, I could tell you of what I encountered. I could tell you of my unexpected and extremely undesired detour through the Flaming Nether Regions. I could tell you of my experience with the Crossed Swords of Inbaq, the dreaded Man-Eating Shrimp of Outbaq, and the formidable schemes of Monsieur Peebody of Waybaq. Perhaps I shall do so at some later point in time.

But the fact of the matter is that I am getting old. Far too old.

It is taking me longer and longer to write the details of my adventures. My mind tends to wander and I discover that time has passed by while I sit here in my study. Also it is harder for me to hold a quill pen for extended periods of time. And sometimes if I sit for too long, I begin to lose any sense of sensation in my one good leg, so every so often I must get up and wander around a bit just to restore circulation.

In short, I am aging, and aging is not a generous experience to go through. The world slows down and it takes far longer to accomplish that which you once were able to handle with no problem.

I have to admit that in some ways I regret that Entipy did not choose to have me executed. Just think: if she had done so, I would have wound up missing out on all of my body's slow deterioration. Yet she decided that I should live.

Now you will learn why.

CHAPTER 17

Home Again

As I made my way through the streets of Isteria, I could not help but observe how much had remained the same. The marketplace was much as I remembered it. The small children who had run about in the streets so many years ago were now grown and running the very shops and booths that their parents had previously tended to. One had to admire that degree of consistency and perhaps even commitment.

Of the knights who wandered past me, paying me no mind, I did not recognize a single one. Then again, I had been gone for twenty years. Two decades is a host of lifetimes for the average knight. It is very rare that knights wind up dying from old age. It is a discipline that typically comes with an early date of termination. Had I wound up allowing myself to become a knight, concluding the career that began when I was a squire, I doubtlessly would have been long moldering in the grave by now.

Slowly I made my way to the guard post at the great gates that allowed people within to the central area, where stood the castle. From outside I could see that more ivy had grown on the exterior, but otherwise it was exactly the same as I remembered it. Which of course made sense. What were they going to have done in my absence? Paint it?

The two guards were not standing at attention. Instead they seemed quite relaxed, chatting with each other about inconsequential matters. They barely afforded me a glance until I drew sufficiently near that they became aware that my intention was to try and enter. They turned to face me, standing shoulder to shoulder, obviously waiting for me to say something.

"Good morrow," I said with a cheerfulness that I did not feel.

"Good morrow," said the one on the left. The one on the right simply grunted which, I suspected, was the extent of his vocabulary. "Can we help you with something?"

"Is the queen here?" I asked.

"Yes," said the guard.

"Good. I wish to see her."

This prompted an exchange of amusement between the two of them. When he had sufficiently regained control of himself, the guard said, "Should I just tell her that, then?"

"I would like you to do so, yes."

"And who shall I tell her is calling?" He was speaking in a mocking tone.

"Apropos."

"Apropos?" He seemed to be about to launch into another round of laughter. "What sort of name is Apro...?" Then his voice trailed off, because he was looking in confusion at his partner. The face of the guard on the right had gone deathly pale as if some oversized insect had descended and drained all his blood. His eyes widened and I saw his hand reflexively start to go for his sword. The guard on the left was clearly bewildered, unable to understand the other guard's reaction.

"Yes," I said, answering the unspoken question that was going through his mind. "*That* Apropos."

The guard on the right quickly stepped over to the guard on the left and whispered softly in his ear for a few seconds. And now the guard on the left was looking quite disconcerted as well. Evidently I had something of a reputation for those people who were interested in ancient history. Once he had imparted some information, he then spun on his heel and hastened toward the castle.

I studied the guard who was standing there, and I was amazed to see that there was actually some trembling in his knees. He was afraid of me. He was physically afraid of an elder with a lame right leg. It was most amusing and I made no effort to keep the smile off my face.

"Are you quite all right?" I asked.

He managed a nod.

I took a casual step toward him and noted that he actually took a reflexive step backward in order to maintain the distance between us. I stopped walking and cocked my head slightly. "What did he tell you? The fellow who just left?"

"He said…" He hesitated, as if fearful that whatever he said next would result in some extreme manner of retribution on my part, or perhaps a lightning bolt from on high. "He said you broke the heart of the queen. And sired the bastard prince."

"Yes. I did both of those things. May I ask why that makes you afraid of me?"

"Because…" Once more he paused and then managed to soldier forward. "Because you're a legend."

"A legend? I find that difficult to believe. I introduced myself and you didn't recognize my name."

"Because no one ever calls you that."

"Really? What, then, do they call me?"

"The Anti-Savior."

This was becoming more incredible by the moment. "The Anti-Savior? Why in the name of all the gods would they call me that?"

His voice dropped to scarcely above a whisper. "Because of the tapestry."

"Ahhh." Now I knew what he was talking about. "The tapestry rendered by a farweaver, depicting a man riding a phoenix. The man who was supposed to be the savior of the state of Isteria."

His head bobbed up and down so furiously that I thought it might end up toppling off. "That's right. And the tapestry hangs to this day. But you walked away from the prophecy. No one ever walks away from a prophecy."

The fact of the matter was that I knew perfectly well the

prophecy was incorrect. That another had been destined to be the savior of Isteria, and I had actually witnessed his death. So much for that. But I certainly wasn't about to tell this poor knight that little fact.

"I suppose I did walk away at that," I said. "I was never much for doing what other people told me to do."

That was when I heard the rushing of feet. I glanced toward the origins of the noise and my heart sank when I saw who was leading the half dozen or so knights who were running toward me.

It was Mace Morningstar.

Morningstar had been a frequent tormentor of mine since I first became a squire. He and his associates had tried to beat me down on any number of occasions. I remember that one of the main thrills I had when Entipy became enamored of me was that it made me virtually invulnerable to Mace's continued harassment. I was so looking forward to perpetually tormenting him, especially when Entipy became the queen and I ruled at her side. Unfortunately I had tossed that bit of joy aside when I had walked out from—or technically escaped from—my intended matrimonial celebrations.

Yet now he was here and the boot was once again on the other foot. And in this instance, there was no doubt in my mind that that foot would wind up repeatedly burying itself in my ass.

He looked much more massive than when I had last seen him. For one thing, he had put on a considerable amount of weight, at least fifty pounds. Except I had no idea if it was fat or if it was muscle. Might be a combination of both.

"I don't believe it," he growled, and he came right at me.

Idiot.

He clearly had me confused with the physically hapless young man whom he had known in his youth. My fighting skills had increased to a huge degree in the intervening years, and I was no longer concerned in the slightest of suffering a physical beating at Mace's hands.

He did not pull his sword, which I had assumed would be the case. He doubtless knew that the queen herself would want to dispose of me, but he likewise reasoned that if he produced me with a few bumps and bruises and perhaps a broken arm, the queen would certainly not be upset about that.

Instead he came at me with his fists.

That was a mistake.

He swung his right fist at me and I simply sidestepped him. Then his left, then his right again. All three times I was able to avoid contact by simply bending my body out of his way.

Then he swung left again even more forcefully, so much so that he threw himself slightly off balance and overextended himself. Not only did I step out of his way, but I brought the dragon head of my staff slamming down upon the back of his head. It struck with such force that everyone heard the sound of the impact; it sounded like I had bounced a rock off the side of a barn. Mace went down and with a touch of the release trigger I snapped out the blade from the dragon's mouth and brought it slamming down toward his unprotected throat.

It had all happened so quickly that every knight watching audibly gasped. Mace gasped the loudest and his eyes widened in clear terror as he suddenly realized that the seemingly easy target he had looked forward to demolishing had him at his mercy.

For a moment no one said anything. Casual citizens who were witnessing the battle had stopped in their tracks and were watching with amazed eyes how this lame fellow had just easily bested one of the knights.

"Here is what is going to happen," I said calmly, as if we were chatting over a pint in a local pub. "You are going to pledge your word of honor, in front of your fellow knights and these good people," and I tilted my head slightly toward the civilian onlookers, "that I will be brought straightaway and unharmed to the queen. In exchange for this, I will let you live and not, instead, stab you through the throat. I'm going to give you five seconds to make your decision. One, t—"

"Fine," snarled Morningstar.

"Are you sure?" I sounded most solicitous. "Don't want to

take a few moments to think about it? Make the countdown more dramatic?"

"Remove your blade. I give you my word of honor that you will be brought unharmed to the queen." Every word out of his mouth was laced with fury, but there was nothing he could do.

It was rather amusing to consider. Decades ago, I had wound up earning my status as a squire with the same weapon pointed at a knight—the long deceased Sir Justus—except it had been a somewhat lower section of his anatomy.

I retracted the blade into the dragon's mouth and stepped back. Slowly Morningstar got to his feet. One of the knights put out a hand to help him up, but Mace waved him away. Once he was standing, he looked me up and down and then, much to my surprise, he actually smiled. There was no sarcasm in it; it appeared genuine. "You've become quite the combatant since you took leave of us." There was almost a touch of admiration in his tone.

"Well, when every tenth person you meet wants to kill you, that's inevitable."

He barked out a coarse laugh. "Very true. This way, then," and he nodded toward the castle.

I did not trust him overmuch. I thought him perfectly capable of going back on his word and trying to slay me should I present my back to him for even a moment. But he was doing a convincing job of putting forward a wholly different attitude than the one he had displayed just moments before.

Word was apparently quickly spreading throughout the castle because people were emerging from it, gathering together, to watch my approach. I suppose on some level I should have been flattered. When I had first come to the castle, it was as a poor, lame bastard seeking aid from the king to help catch the individual who had killed my mother. Everyone who looked upon me back then did so with disdain. Not this time. I saw expressions that ranged from fear to reverence. Which was interesting considering that when I had refused to marry Entipy, I had been seen as a fool and traitor. Apparently there was nothing quite like the passage of time to bolster one's reputation.

I nodded to people as I approached, acknowledging them. Some bobbed their heads back in response. Several of them actually bowed. Of all the receptions I had expected to receive, this was certainly not remotely one.

They escorted me through the great halls of the castle. I had been in grand residences since my departure, but it was still an impressive place, although positively modest in comparison to the palace of the Rogyptians. There was little to no gold, for one thing. I realized belatedly that I should have absconded with some gold from the palace when I had made my departure, but I had been too preoccupied to worry about such things. Fascinating how my priorities had shifted. Once upon a time my emphasis would have been to find some way to enrich myself, preferably while risking my well-being in as minimal a fashion as possible. Yet now I had given riches no thought and had been mostly concerned with freeing the Shews...well, that and put myself as far away from my insane fiancée as I possibly could.

What in the world had happened to me? Had the years I survived really changed me so much? Was I truly developing into what could actually be called a hero? It was not a position in life that I readily embraced, but I supposed that anything was possible.

I was escorted to the throne room. Knights were entering from everywhere, dressed in a variety of ensembles. Apparently word had spread quickly enough that everyone had taken the time to show up, no matter what manner of task they were engaged in. Some had clearly been sparring, others had been dressed casually and doubtless drinking. One of them actually had dirt on his hands and knees, which indicated he had been gardening. It seemed that no matter what they were up to, they had taken the time to set it aside and see what in the world that idiot Apropos had gotten himself into.

Entipy was not on her throne. Obviously someone had gone off to get her.

Mace led me to the center of the room and stood by me, the

other knights falling back. He spoke to me then in a low voice. "You know," he said softly, "I always liked you more than you thought I did."

I tried not to laugh at that and only partly succeeded. "Are you out of your mind? You never liked me in the least."

"I didn't respect you," he replied. "You were a lowborn peasant who was placed with us as if we were equals. You couldn't fight. And you cheated in the joust, don't even bother to deny it."

"So what changed your mind?"

"You had the nerve to walk out on Entipy." His face soured. "I've never liked that bitch. Not in the least. Obviously you shared my antipathy, but it took a huge amount of guts to refuse her love. I doubt," he added reluctantly, "that I would have had the nerve to do that."

I wasn't entirely sure how to react to that. All of the aggravation and bullying that Morningstar had put me through was still fresh to me, and this new attitude of respect and even deference was catching me off guard. But he seemed sincere. "Well, I doubt it will come up," I said. "But I appreciate the admission."

"Not a problem, especially since the queen will doubtless have me execute you, so it won't be as if you would wind up telling a lot of people."

"That's very considerate."

Then the door at the far end of the throne room opened and Entipy strode in. There were two handmaidens on either side of her following along.

Once upon a time, her face had had merely a sort of vague prettiness, but that time was long gone.

I gasped, which I suppose I should not have done. I could not help myself, however. When I had first known her, she was barely out of adolescence. Now, though, she was twenty years older and in every aspect a lovely, grown woman. Her hair, the color of which she was constantly changing, was black today. Her formerly round face now had high cheekbones and her piercing eyes studied me as if I were some manner of animal that a scientist was looking over. More than that, though. They were eyes that had seen many things, endured much. They knew love, loss, triumph and defeat.

I glanced around and realized there was no sign of the jester, Odclay. I wondered what had happened to him. For all I knew, Entipy had had him executed because she didn't like a joke he'd made. How wonderfully ironic that would have been considering he was her father. Would he tell her that in order to save his own life? Doubtful. She likely wouldn't believe him anyway.

Everyone around me bowed to her. I remained upright. Morningstar swatted me in the back of the head to encourage me to bend at the waist, although I had no idea if he genuinely meant it or was just trying to anticipate what she would do for my failing to display proper courtesy. With an annoyed sigh I bent at the waist.

She did not go to her throne. Instead she strode across the room toward me. She was wearing a full green dress that seemed to be silk with velvet red trim. Entipy drew to within a couple of feet of me and then stood there, just continuing to stare. I was now standing upright.

"Apropos," she said. Her voice had deepened a bit. There was a neutrality to her tone, as if we were just being introduced. "Of all the ways I imagined this day was going to go, this was certainly not one of them."

"Highness," I replied. "I am sorry to learn of your father's passing."

"And my mother. Three years ago."

"I hadn't heard. Again, I'm sorry." I wanted to ask about Odclay, but this was obviously not the time, although I had no idea if I was going to have any more time beyond this moment. She could have me executed with a word.

She was continuing to regard me closely, as if dissecting me with her gaze. "You look handsome enough. What happened to your ear?"

I touched the side of my head. "Lost it in a game of poker."

Entipy actually smiled at that. "Knowing you, I almost believe it. May I ask what in the world you're doing here? For all you know,

I'm going to have you executed for escaping my father's justice."

I had actually more or less assumed that was going to happen. "I have some news for you."

"And you believed that the only way to convey it was to come in person?"

"Yes."

"What would it be?"

I lowered my voice so that she would be the only one capable of hearing me, since Mace had taken a few steps back as she approached.

"It's about our son."

Her eyes widened for half a heartbeat and then she immediately managed to compose herself. She spun on her heel, the green dress sweeping along the floor, and said, "Follow me."

There were confused looks from the knights. Doubtless they had expected that she would order me killed on the spot, not taken into the back for some private conference. But she was the queen and her wishes were to be obeyed, so I fell into pace behind her and we departed the throne room.

We entered a private study that was attached to the throne room. The handmaidens followed us in, but Entipy turned to them and said, "Leave us." Naturally they did as ordered, leaving the two of us to ourselves.

"What is his name?" she said.

She was challenging me. Perhaps she thought that I was lying for some reason.

"Germane. An appropriate one considering his father was Apropos."

"Is he..." She hesitated a moment, gathering herself. "Is he here? Is he with you? Has he finally returned to me?"

"I'm afraid not."

"Then what—?"

I took in a deep breath and let it out slowly. "He is dead."

She said nothing at first. If I thought that she was going to burst into tears, I was completely incorrect. Instead she just sat there with level gaze and then asked me a most unexpected question:

"Did you kill him?"

"What? No!" I couldn't quite believe that she even had to ask. "Why in gods' name would you think that?"

"Because I have no idea if you would or not. I don't know you, Apropos. I thought I did, but you fled into the woods rather than marry me. You gave me a host of reasons why, none of which, as I recall, made the slightest degree of sense."

"Well, the last thing you said to me was that you found me dull, so..."

"I would have said anything to hurt you, because you hurt me."

"Telling me I was dull was the worst thing you could think of to say to me?"

"At that moment, yes." Her gaze dropped toward the floor and she stared fixedly at my boots, but she was not really looking at me. "How did he die?"

I had had plenty of time to think of exactly what to say, and had still not come up with anything better than the simple truth. "He was slain by a monster. It happened very quickly and I was unable to save him."

"Where? Where did this happen?"

It was at that point that I filled her in, as briskly and without emotion as I could, how I had first encountered Germane in Rogypt. There were some aspects of the narrative that I omitted, such as that we had competed in the chariot race and that he had tried to kill me. The omission of this particular fact actually attracted her attention. "He despised you," she said. "If he'd met you, I'd have thought he would have kept his identity a secret and tried to slay you when you didn't expect it."

She really did know him quite well. "Well, he didn't. Instead he confronted me. And we managed to...to work things out."

"Work things out?" She sounded incredulous. "How in the world did you do that? You ran away rather than marry me. You reduced him to the status of royal bastard. What in the world could you possibly have said that would have eased his mind?"

Do I tell her? Do I let her know that she shares the exact same status as her son: a royal bastard? Do I tell her she's my sister?

It had been a question that I had wrestled with for the entirety of my trip to Isteria, and until this moment, I still had not come up with an answer that satisfied me. But at this instant, I knew that I couldn't tell her. I had just taken away from her all hope of her son returning. Was I also to rob her of her throne? The one thing of any importance left to her in the world?

"I told him I was a coward."

She looked astounded. "You told him what?"

"I told him the truth, Entipy. I told him I was simply too cowardly, too gutless, to take on the responsibilities that being your mate would have required."

"Because you told me that it was because you were worried that I would become bored with you. You said…"

"I said a lot of stupid things to cover my own lack of resolve. That's the truth of it, Entipy. I just didn't have the nerve. It was entirely my fault."

"Damned right it was your fault."

Her voice trailed off and then, very softly, she asked, " The monster…did you kill it?"

Technically Ahmway and several hundred tons of water had done it, but I was never loath to take credit. "Yes."

"And did Germane die well?"

He died screaming and begging for his life.

"Fighting until the end."

And now it came. The tears started running down her face and she began to sob. For a moment I had no idea what to do, and then I gave in to the obvious course. I rose from my chair, crossed to her, crouched next to her and embraced her.

Entipy, the girl whom I had perceived as some sort of complete devious lunatic so many years ago, emptied all of her emotions onto my shoulder. The tears flowed and kept flowing, I have no idea for how long. In a way, I was relieved. It showed that she was indeed capable of displaying normal emotions like a human being.

She was a grieving mother and I was there to comfort her in the best way that I was able. I patted her on the back, I said soothing and meaningless things to her. I did all that I could to help her deal with her grief and eventually, after a seemingly interminable amount of time, she managed to calm herself.

"I always feared that he would die violently," she whispered to me. "When he ran away, I was sure of it. I wanted to help him. I did. But I wasn't good enough."

"Yes, you were," I assured you. "Don't blame yourself for his desire to flee."

"Thank you." She was sitting up and wiping the last of her tears from her face. It was as if the regal persona that she bore reinhabited her body after departing for a few minutes to allow her to grieve. "Thank you for saying that. Thank you for everything. And I want you to know…"

"Know what?" I said when her voice trailed off and she didn't continue.

She reached over and took my hand in hers. Her hands were surprisingly cold, but I didn't withdraw mine from hers. She gazed at me, her eyes filled with sincerity.

"I've never stopped loving you."

Oh God…

"I've never stopped," she continued, "and I've never ceased imagining what our lives could be like together. I've forgiven you decades ago for walking out. Hell, I forgave you almost from the moment you did it. Not a day has not gone by where I've contemplated what I could have said that would cause you to remain here with me. I've come up with thousands of different things I could have said. And now you're here. You've come back to me."

"I came back to tell you what happened to our son, Entipy. That was the only reason…"

"No," she said firmly. "I don't believe that. Even you don't believe that. You could have found other ways to get the news to me. You wanted to come back to me. You wanted to give me life again."

"Life again?" I shook my head. "I don't understand..."

She released my hand and sat back in her chair. She was no longer looking at me, but to my right, as if addressing...I don't know...the spirit of our son. "Being queen has been a wonderful experience. You remember what I was like as a teenager. There is no other way to put it: I was a bitch."

"No," I said immediately, which we both knew was a lie. *Bitch* was actually one of the more restrained words that I could have used.

"Yes," she insisted. "I was, and you know I was. No matter what you tell me now, I know that it was my attitude, my beliefs, everything about me, that drove you away. If you aren't willing to admit that that was the entire reason for your departure, at least admit that it was a partial cause."

I shrugged. I didn't trust myself to speak.

"But I am no longer that girl, Apropos," she continued. "I have grown up."

"Yes, I can see that."

"The kingdom is peaceful. We are involved in no wars. Life here is idyllic. It's everything that any reasonable person could possibly want to undertake. Yet to me, it is empty. I have no husband, no son. I have no one to rule after me, or with me. I need you, Apropos. I need you by my side. I need you..."

Then, to my astonishment, she dropped to one knee and took my hand once more. She gazed at me with more love than anyone ever had in the entirety of my existence.

"Apropos of Nothing...will you marry me?"

I stared into her eyes. Into the eyes of my half sister.

A girl who had effectively stopped living her life when I had walked out on her two decades earlier.

A girl who had lost her father, her mother. Who had no family, but instead resided in a castle full of knights and servants.

A girl who had just learned that she had lost her son and felt as if she had no future left to her. How long had she hoped that eventually Germane would return to her? What dreams had I just crushed by telling her that her son would never be coming home?

She was a girl who had everything and yet had nothing.

And she wanted me to fill that gap in her life.

But she was my sister.

A fact that was known by exactly one person in the entirety of the world.

Four astounded words etched themselves in my brain:

Who would it harm?

I couldn't believe the thought had even occurred to me, and yet there it was, rolling around in my head, refusing to go away.

One of the most noble—indeed, one of the only noble—things that I had done in my life was to walk out on Entipy all those years ago, sacrificing my well-being in the spirit of morality.

And look at what the result had been. She had created a high tower around her heart and never let anyone in, and had raised a son on her own who was condemned to live his life as a royal bastard rather than a prince and future king. What had been the purpose of my departure, really? It wasn't in her interest, but only in my own comfort level. I had ruined her life in order to distance myself from her, and I had told myself that I was doing it for her own good.

I had abandoned her and yes, she was a queen and, by all accounts, a good one, but her inner life was pure emptiness.

Really...what would be the harm?

She was of sufficient age that I likely didn't have to worry that we would produce more offspring, so I did not have to worry about possible deformities resulting from the closeness of our relation. For that matter, the child we had produced hadn't seemed especially deformed. So even in the unlikely event that we did spawn another child, he or she might be perfectly healthy.

And the fact of the matter was, I actually felt closer to Entipy than anyone else in the world I had ever met. The truth was that all through the years, my thoughts had often returned to her and I had always wondered what had happened to her in the intervening time. Curiously, it had never occurred to me that our one night of passion might have resulted in a child, but that was entirely due to the limits of my imagination.

We had spent months together, on the run from enemies, doing everything we could to survive. During that time we had grown very close, even though we had done our best to deny it. Yes, we shared the same blood, but that wasn't actually all that unusual. I had wandered through kingdoms where cousins, and even siblings, had wound up marrying or at the very least had indiscreet affairs. These actions were accepted as the norm.

The long and short of it was that a union that had seemed anathema to me at a young age now, in my advanced years, did not come across as that much of a problem.

Did I love her? I wasn't sure that I was capable of love the way that other men were. But if I was, then certainly Entipy was the one individual in all the world that I could indeed feel that emotion for.

"Yes," I said.

With a joyous gasp, she practically threw herself on me, kissing me passionately. Something within me flinched at first, but then I blocked my knowledge from my mind and allowed myself to give in to the wonderful feeling of her flesh against mine. Her tongue darted forward into my open mouth and danced across mine, and she even giggled slightly like a child as she did so.

Our mouths parted and I found myself willing myself to put aside my knowledge of who she was to me. What had been something of vast importance in the past now seemed beside the point. I was indifferent to it.

Why? Why the change in my attitude?

In reflecting upon it now, I have to believe that my exposure to Germane, however brief, had awakened something within me. I had spent more or less the entirety of my life believing that isolation and aimless wandering was what the rest of my existence was going to consist of. Yet my time with Germane had led my imagination wandering down the path of speculation. I had wondered, in the entirety of my six month voyage home, what my life would have been like if I had actually had a family. If I had had a wife to love me. If I had lived the life that most men live. Yes, I had had many adventures, many exciting experiences. But I had far fewer days ahead of me than behind me, and in the end, is not a man judged not by the things he accomplishes, but what he leaves behind? None of us are immortal. The things that we do with others, the lives we build and the remnants of what exists after we are gone...that is the closest that any of us will come to living forever.

I had left nothing. Everyone to whom I had ever felt close was dead. For the most part, I was responsible for their deaths. Entipy was the last one remaining, the last person whom I had ever felt anything approaching love to still be breathing. And she clearly loved me, and had done so for twenty years. Twenty years.

"I suppose you're right," I said when I came up for air. "I suppose I have loved you all this time. I just never realized it until now."

"Of course I'm right. I am the queen. I'm always right," she said, for a moment sounding like her old imperious self. "We will arrange the wedding immediately. And tonight will be your wedding night. The most memorable wedding night anyone could have."

And she was correct.

Chapter 18

Flushed Down the Throne

I was only watching Mace Morningstar's face when Entipy announced to the assembled court that we were to be married immediately. I have to admit, he reacted with far greater equanimity than I would have thought possible. The Mace Morningstar of my youth: his jaw would have dropped, his utter astonishment would have been unmistakable. Instead Mace kept his face impassive and even joined in with the collective applause.

"I have already sent a messenger to bring the Arch Mage here immediately," she said, sitting in a relaxed manner upon her throne. I was standing next to her; since we were not yet married, it was not my place to sit on any throne. "Furthermore, I officially designate Apropos to be my heir. Should anything happen to me, he is to be your next king. All hail Apropos!"

"All hail Apropos!" they dutifully chorused.

I had no idea how they truly felt about me. My arrival had resulted in mixed reactions of fear and confusion. Now it seemed as if they were unanimously endeavoring to embrace me in the same way that the queen had done. If any of the knights who had despised me in my youth had been there, it might have gone somewhat differently, but they were all either dead or retired, and the new crop appeared to be taking their cues from Mace. And Mace's impassive expression was all the cue they required to maintain their decorum.

I was led to another room where I was bathed and presented with a brand new set of clothing to don for the wedding. It consisted of purple leggings and an absolutely gorgeous purple tunic with red trim. There was also a splendid cape accompanying it. The cape was solid red, which went nicely with the trim. Purple made sense, of course, because it was the color of royalty. As I adjusted the cape, I heard a knock at the door. "Come," I called.

The door swung open and Mace Morningstar filled the opening with his bulk. He stepped into the room and swung the door shut behind him. He stood there for a moment, staring at me.

"Are you out of your mind?" he asked.

I was sitting on a bench and pulling on a boot. "I don't believe so."

"Entipy is insane."

I stared at him. "That is hardly an appropriate opinion to have of your queen."

"It's the opinion everyone has of her!" He strode toward me and there was genuine urgency on his face. "Don't you understand? This is some manner of trick!"

"She's tricking me into marrying her? Doesn't that sound odd to you? And what do you mean everyone thinks she's crazy? She's beloved…"

"Who told you that?"

My son had. My son and hers. But I wasn't about to tell him that. "I heard it around."

"Don't you understand?" He pulled another stool up and sat down opposite me. It seemed hard to believe that there was genuine concern for me on his face, considering how terrible he had been to me in my youth, but there it was. "Everyone is afraid to speak of how much she terrifies them, because she has ears everywhere. If someone besmirches her, they are risking their lives."

"Isn't that what you're doing here? With impunity?"

"I'm trying to do you a favor."

"I don't need your favors, thanks."

"Yes, you do. You just don't seem to understand that." He

lowered his voice, and then said, "I've seen her make decisions that would leave you stunned. I've seen her embark on random wars for no reason. I've seen her advocate building a wall along the borders of our neighboring countries to keep them out. I've seen her proclaim that eighty percent of all white people are slain by Moors, which is patently untrue. I've seen her take action after action that is for the benefit of no one, just to amuse herself. The bottom line is that she is dangerous, Apropos. Very dangerous."

"I'm amazed no one has slain her," I said drily.

"That's because she pays well and has superb guardians on staff. She never departs the castle. She sits and stews and thinks about ways to cause trouble, and sometimes she embarks upon them and sometimes she doesn't. Why do you think her son fled when he was a teenager?"

"Because he was regarded as a royal bastard."

"Because he was afraid of her!"

Now I knew that he was lying. Germane had had nothing but affection for his mother. He had told me so himself and had no reason to lie...

Unless he was setting you up. Unless he was trying to trick you into coming here, knowing that his crazed mother would do something terrible to you...

Like marry me? Does that make any sense?

At that moment the door swung open and one of Entipy's handmaidens was standing there. "It's time," she said softly, indicating with a gesture of her hand that I should follow her.

I glanced one more time at Mace, who shook his head very slightly to indicate that I should not go. I ignored him, of course. I had no idea what had motivated him to come in there and "warn" me about Entipy. Perhaps he himself was enamored of her and hoped that, should I pull out again, he might have the opportunity to press some manner of suit. Whatever his reason was, I had no interest in indulging him.

I then turned my back to Mace Morningstar and followed her out.

I strode into the throne room and saw that everyone in the castle had gathered. My attention flickered to the large tapestry on the far wall, the one of their messiah, riding on the back of a phoenix. The one that some nameless farweaver had created to predict the coming of their savior. Well, here he was. He had taken something of a long time to get here, but now he had arrived and however things currently were, they would only improve with my presence.

The Arch Mage was standing at the far end and indicated that I should join him. He was quite a wizened individual, barely over five feet tall, with a long white beard, no hair on the top of his head, but the most insanely long eyebrows I had ever seen. I just wanted to take a pair of scissors and trim them down, but I restrained my sartorial instincts.

There was a gentleman with a violin nearby the throne, and when the door near the throne opened, he launched into some manner of tune with which I was not familiar. In retrospect I suppose it did not matter. Queen Entipy entered then, and she was magnificent. How in the hell she had managed to produce a white bridal dress in such a short period of time, I could not even begin to imagine, but she had done so. Her black hair was elaborately styled. I was grateful that she had not allowed it to return to its natural red color, since that would have matched mine and might have proven a bit much for me to handle.

She was smiling so broadly. It was as if all the years of mourning that she had carried with her had dissolved.

The warnings of Mace Morningstar continued to rattle in my head, but I brushed them aside. I knew without a doubt that I was doing the right thing. It was going to make her happy. And it wasn't as if we were brother and sister who had grown up together and developed a forbidden and incestuous relationship. When we had first encountered each other we were strangers, and the bonds that had developed between us were genuine. So what if we were somewhat related, if we shared a father? There was so much more to life than obsessing about who came from whose body. Our sires were long departed, although I had not yet found out what happened to the jester. I had to remember to ask her about that. But that was not going to worry me overmuch.

She walked in a slow rhythm to my side and took my hand, gazing up at me. For half a heartbeat I was startled because I thought I saw something else in her eyes—a brief look of, I don't know. Rage. Fury. Stark hatred. But then, as quickly as I thought I saw it, it was gone. I concluded that Mace's words to me had put my mind into something of a turmoil. Obviously I had imagined it.

Still, part of me was uncertain enough that I kept waiting for her to do something. To suddenly reveal that this was all some manner of grand jest and she was going to trot out an executioner to relieve me of my head. Which, I must admit, if she had done so, then good for her. It would have been quite the joke and would have caught me off guard.

But no such moment happened. The Arch Mage conducted the ceremony quite well, with no deviations from the norm, and within fifteen minutes, Entipy and I were married. The Arch Mage invited me to kiss the bride, and I did so with relish. As our lips came together, there was a unanimous roar of approval from everybody there. We held the kiss for a bit longer than I was comfortable considering the number of onlookers, but it seemed to make Entipy happy, so that was fine with me.

A great feast followed the wedding, and I have to say that I had never had such a delicious meal. Beef, lamb, freshly picked potatoes, carrots, and sumptuous fruits. All of it was laid out and the knights and lords and ladies lay into it with delight. Hard to believe that only six months earlier, I had been faced with a wedding to a teenager whom I did not remotely love. Now here I was, married to the one woman in the world whom I should not be with but nevertheless was.

And why the hell not, really? Had I not lived the entirety of my life doing exactly and precisely what I should avoid? Had I not taken the destiny of my former best friend, Tacit, for myself? Had I not absconded with his phoenix and set myself off on a long, tenuous course of adventures that had inevitably led me here? If I had limited myself to doing what I should have done, I'd likely have spent the entirety of my existence as a wandering beggar since I didn't really have any worthwhile skills save for the ability to say alive in various dangerous circumstances. So wasn't marrying my half-sister, something that I was the only person who knew that I was doing it, astoundingly consistent with the rest of how I'd lived my life?

Thank the gods that Odclay was gone, because he certainly could well and truly have buggered the entire thing.

Which reminded me...

I leaned over to Entipy as she was busy devouring a loin of pork and tried to sound as casual as I could as I asked, "By the way: where is Odclay the jester?"

"Is this entertainment insufficient for you?" She gestured toward the troop of jugglers who were busily tossing colorful balls to each other in a truly dazzling display.

"Oh no, not at all. I was just wondering..."

"He fled. Several years ago."

"Fled?" I frowned. "Why?"

"Because he thought I was going to execute him."

"What? Why?"

"Because I said I was going to execute him."

That froze me for a moment. I had been devouring a turkey leg but now I slowly lowered it back to the plate. "Why..." My voice caught and then I managed to speak. "Why did you say that?"

"He cried at my mother's funeral." There was a look of pure disdain upon her face. "Can you imagine? A jester. Crying. If you can't count on a jester to always find the humor in a situation, who can you count on?"

Of course he had cried at the funeral. He had loved her. He had sired a child with her.

"So anyway," she continued, oblivious of the thoughts going through my head, "at the end of the funeral I told him to get his affairs in order because I was going to order him executed. He nodded and said, 'Thank you,' and then he walked away and apparently kept walking. I've no idea where he went."

"And..." I hesitated. "Would you have actually done it? Had him executed?"

"Oh, I doubt it. I was in a bad mood. My mother had just died, after all."

I let out a low sigh of relief. She looked at me with a raised eyebrow. "Why?" she asked. "Of what interest is it to you?"

"No interest at all," I assured her. "I was just curious about his absence, that's all."

"Ah." She nodded, apparently satisfied with my slapdash explanation. "Well, he is long gone. Perhaps he will come back some day. Or perhaps he is dead. I suppose we'll never know."

"I guess not."

She took my chin in her hand, drew my lips to hers and kissed me soundly. "Don't worry about him. You have things of far greater interest to worry about."

"Absolutely," I said readily.

Eventually the banquet concluded.

Evening settled upon the castle.

I was led into Entipy's bedroom. I have to admit, my mind was whirling a bit since I had imbibed quite a bit during the festival and so was flying rather high. She was waiting for me, and she was still wearing her wedding dress. She had been sitting on the edge of the bed, and now she rose and walked toward me. She was smiling broadly. It was not remotely a regal smile, but instead as genuine and wide as that of an extraordinarily pleased child. She stood slightly on her toes and kissed me. "Get undressed," she whispered to me. "I just have to go into my changing room. I'll only need a few minutes."

"All right," I replied.

I removed my clothes as she went into the adjoining room and moments later was naked in the bed. As beds went, it was exceptionally comfortable. Possibly the most comfortable bed that I had ever been in.

I lay back, interlacing my fingers and resting my head on my hands.

So I had married my half-sister.

I knew that the first thing I had to do was stop thinking of her in that respect. She was my wife. That was all. My wife, and my queen. Those were the sole terms in which I should think of her. It might take me a while...even years perhaps...to adjust to that, but I was certain that I could do so.

Because she deserved happiness. And damn it, so did I.

It was honestly something of a new thought to me, to think that I was entitled to a life with genuine happiness in it. And why not? Why did I have to spend the rest of my existence as Apropos of Nothing?

I would finally be Apropos of Something.

Then I heard a thunk.

I was unsure of what it was. It had come from the queen's changing room, and it sounded as if a piece of furniture had fallen over. A chair or perhaps a stool.

Slowly I rose from the bed. "Entipy?" I called. "Are you all right?"

She did not reply. That concerned me. Perhaps she had tripped over a stool and had struck her head on the floor.

That was when I heard a slow, steady creaking.

Quickly I grabbed a sheet and threw it around myself to hide my nudity as I ran, as fast as I could, to the adjoining room. I banged open the door and stood frozen in the doorway.

Entipy was hanging from an overhead beam. She was naked, her clothing lying on a pile on the floor. There was a noose drawn tightly around her neck and she was slowly swinging back and forth. Her head was at a horrific angle. Her lips were blue and were twisted into the most demented smile I had ever seen. Her eyes were wide, empty and lifeless.

I screamed. I screamed and kept screaming. Curiously I did not cry for help. Instead what emerged from my lips was pure, inarticulate hysteria. I stumbled back, banging into the wall, unable to do anything except shriek.

People must have shown up. I was unaware of what was happening around me. I was too busy reacting in complete horror. I had no idea what had transpired. It was as if my mind had simply evacuated my head because I was unable to think. *Murder! Someone murdered her and left it looking as if she had killed herself!* Even as I thought that, though, I knew that was impossible. There was only one entrance to the room, through the bedroom. She had unquestionably done this to herself.

I suppose it was possible that, if anyone was of a suspicious frame of mind, they might have suspected that I myself had done it and tried to make it look like suicide. But I doubt that thought occurred to anyone, because I was so insanely, out of my head hysterical that no one would have thought it possible that I could be that good an actor. Plus if you were going to kill someone, hanging them was certainly an insane and relatively impossible means in which to go about it.

I have no idea when I finally managed to regain control of myself. All I knew, all I remember, is that one minute I was screaming insanely in the room, and the next I was sitting on the edge of my bed, staring at nothing. One of Entipy's handmaidens had brought me a drink and I was holding it in my trembling hand. I watched as Entipy's corpse was being removed from the room, covered head to toe in a blanket. Mace Morningstar was standing in front of me, his face impassive. Slowly I looked up at him, making eye contact, wondering what in the world he was doing in there and then realizing that he, as had the others, had come in response to my howls.

He could have said, *I told you,* at that moment. He had claimed that she was insane, and what was more insane than killing yourself on your wedding night?

But he said nothing.

I noticed that he was holding a rolled up parchment. When he saw that I was staring at it, he extended it to me. I took it, not understanding.

"It was lying amongst her clothes," he said. "It's a letter. I'm assuming it's to you."

"To me?" I took it, not understanding. "Did you read it?"

He shrugged. "I can't read."

"Right. Right."

And then he bowed. He actually bowed.

"I'll leave you to it, highness."

Highness. Oh my gods…

He strode out and I was alone.

I unrolled the parchment and read it:

Dear Moron:

Of course I have not forgiven you. Of course I still despise you. Every year, every day, every minute that you were gone, all I could imagine was how I would have my revenge on you. And then you walked back into my life and presented the ideal means through which to do it.

I have hated being queen. The only thing that ever gave me joy was my son, and when he left, I had nothing to live for except hoping, praying that he would return. When you informed me that he never would, that took the last thing from me that required me to keep existing. The only thing that remained was exacting my vengeance on you. And now I have.

You are now king. You must rule in my stead.

I know what your instinct will be. You will want to flee. Again. Turn your back on Isteria and leave others to sort things out.

If you do that, Isteria will fall. The knights and lords will battle each other to see who will rule. And while they are busy doing that, our enemies will seize upon the power vacuum and come sweeping into Isteria, determined to conquer us. Hundreds and hundreds of people will die. Innocent villagers. Men will be slaughtered. Women will be raped. The lucky sons will be executed; the less lucky, enslaved.

So by all means, go. Go and live with the subsequent calamity being on your head.

Or stay and rule in my stead, you stupid son of a bitch.

Farwell, Savior. Go fuck yourself.

Yours in hate,

Entipy

CHAPTER 19

The End

I SAT AND STARED AT THE note for what seemed an infinite amount of time.

Then, slowly, I rose from the bed. I was still clad in a sheet and I very slowly, very deliberately dressed myself. I did not put on any clothes that seemed appropriate to royalty. Instead I dressed myself in the outfit that I was wearing when I had first arrived.

My thoughts flew to the tapestry that my father, Odclay, had shown me so long ago. The one of me seated on a throne, a ruler.

I walked out of the room and made my way through the corridor. Never had I moved so slowly. I felt as if I had aged a hundred years while reading Entipy's last words.

My gods, how much had she loathed me, to have been willing to give up her life in order to inflict the throne upon me?

You knew it was too easy. This was all your fault. If you had been honest with her, if you had told her the real reason you had abandoned her, none of this would have happened.

My inner voice was right, of course. Just as I had been responsible for the deaths of everyone whom I had ever loved, it had happened once more. Whatever my motives had been, the outcome had nevertheless been horrific.

Soon I found myself in the main throne room. It was the middle of the night, and the only illumination in the room was coming from the torches that lined it.

I stood there and stared at the throne.

I was the king of Isteria. The next day, Entipy would be buried and I would be crowned. Someone had told me that, I now belatedly realized. When I had been in my disconnected state, sitting on the bed and oblivious to the world around me, someone had sat down next to me and told me what was going to happen. Perhaps it had been the Arch Mage, perhaps someone else. I had no recollection. How odd to be so absent from the world that you have discussions that you then remember only long after the fact.

I assumed that everyone was steering clear of me for the moment because I had been reduced to unmanly hysterics by what I had witnessed. I couldn't blame them. Since in theory I was the next king, it must have been quite disconcerting to see me react in so womanish a fashion.

But now what?

Now what?

I could leave. That would not be an issue. I knew ways to sneak out of the castle. Guards were there to prevent people from coming in, not getting out.

I could leave and be quit of the place. And yes, hundreds of people would die if I did so, but what of that? I'd been responsible for the deaths of thousands. What were a few hundred more?

Let it burn. Let the state of Isteria burn.

Slowly I became aware that something was watching me. I turned and saw the tapestry, that damned tapestry of the savior of Isteria on the phoenix. The one that everyone assumed was me.

If I could go back in time to one moment in my life, it would be to when I had stopped Tacit from taking the phoenix and going off to finish his quest. In that one moment, I had thrown the entirety of my life out of whack. Tacit should have ruled at Entipy's side and they would have lived happily ever after.

Instead I had destroyed her life.

And could now destroy hundreds more.

Just by doing nothing.

As I always had done.

I stared at that tapestry, and then I walked over to the nearest torch and removed it from its holder. I went to the tapestry and shoved the torch onto the lower right corner of it. It smoldered for long moments, black smoke rising from it, and then it caught. I moved to the middle of the tapestry and ignited that, and then the far end. It took several minutes to accomplish it but soon the entire damned thing was blazing.

I watched it.

I loved it.

The phoenix had ignited, and this time the damned thing would not come back from the flame. This time I was going to be rid of it.

"Fire!" someone shouted.

I glanced over and saw two knights in their night clothes, their eyes wide. The smell of the smoke had doubtless caused them to come looking for the source, and when they saw it was their beloved tapestry that had ignited, they were horrified.

Others were showing up now, ranging from servants to other knights and ladies in waiting and whoever the hell else resided in the place. Despite the lateness of the hour, it did not surprise me that everyone was awake. News of the queen's actions must have spread and everyone had doubtless been gathered in their rooms discussing what it all meant.

They were starting to shout for someone to get buckets, to bring water in to extinguish it, and then above their shouts, I bellowed, *"No! Leave it!"*

The command of my voice froze everyone. It was as if they were afraid to move.

The tapestry fell off the wall and lay spread on the floor, continuing to burn. The floor and surrounding wall was entirely made of stone, so I was not the least concerned that it was going to threaten the rest of the room or even the palace.

I stood there and watched it. Having no idea what else to do, so did everyone else.

For quite some time the thing burned. The smoke rose and

flowed out of the windows. In its haze, I watched imaginary images of everyone I had ever known. All their faces danced in front of me as if trying to provide me entertainment. I stood and watched them, and every single one of them mocked me.

Then, slowly, I turned and walked toward the throne. Without hesitation, I stepped up to it, turned to face everyone, and sat.

Slowly the knights approached me. Mace Morningstar was in the lead.

Very calmly, I said, "What is the current status of our neighbors?"

The knights glanced at each other and then Morningstar spoke up.

"We are currently at an uneasy peace with the Middlelands and the Lower Lumbar region. But my understanding is that Echelon has formed an alliance with the dreaded Warlord Shank of the Outer Lawless Regions. Once word reaches them that the queen is dead, they will likely launch an exploratory assault to test your strength and resolve."

For a long moment, there was nothing but silence.

And then I smiled.

"Bring them on," I said.

About the Author

PETER DAVID IS THE AUTHOR OF more than one hundred books, almost all of them published. He has written such fantasies as *Howling Mad* and *Knight Life* as well as an assortment of bestselling *Star Trek®* novels including *Imzadi* and the popular New Frontier series (which he co-created with John Ordover). He also co-created the TV series *Space Cases* with Bill Mumy, and has written for *Babylon 5* and *Crusade*. His comic-book career spans more than a decade and includes an award-winning run on *The Incredible Hulk*. *Sir Apropos of Nothing* is his longest single work, mostly due to the use of the word "the." He lives in New York with his wife, Kathleen, and his four daughters, Shana, Gwen, Ariel and Caroline.

WELCOME TO CAMELOT!

You thought you knew about King Arthur and his knights? Guess again!

Learn here, for the first time, the down-and-dirty royal secrets that plagued Camelot as told by someone who was actually there, and adapted by acclaimed *New York Times* bestseller Peter David. Full of sensationalism, startling secrets and astounding revelations, *The Camelot Papers* is to the realm of Arthur what the *Pentagon Papers* is to the military: something that all those concerned would rather you didn't see. What are you waiting for?